RE...
WI...

BY
KATHERINE GARBERA

AND

ONE MONTH WITH
THE MAGNATE
BY
MICHELLE CELMER

MILLS
& BOON

"A toast to knowing what you want, and getting it."

"A toast," Becca said.

Cam looked at her like she was the very thing he wanted. That made her feel warm all over and she knew no matter how hard she tried to keep this tame, it wasn't going to work. She wanted Cam. He was everything she liked in a man. She remembered the way they'd fit together when they'd made love, so perfectly, and she wanted him again.

"I have a confession to make," Cam said.

"And that is?" she asked.

"I'm going to kiss you before you get in the car tonight," he said.

She shivered and everything feminine in her came to attention.

"I was planning to let you."

Dear Reader,

I hope you have been enjoying meeting all the Stern brothers! Cam is up last and to be honest he was a hard nut to crack. So of course I had to find a little something unexpected to throw his way. And Cam handled it as I expected he would—with the same determination that he faces everything.

Becca is the perfect foil for Cam. Where Cam relies on family and the bonds of community he's created for his support, Becca is a lone wolf. She doesn't know how to ask for outside help and pretty much expects to be left on her own no matter what happens in her life.

I hope you enjoy this story!

Happy reading,

Katherine

REUNITED... WITH CHILD

BY
KATHERINE GARBERA

Published in Great Britain 2012
by Mills & Boon, an imprint of Harlequin (UK) Limited,
Eton House, 18-24 Paradise Road, Richmond, Surrey TW9 1SR

© Katherine Garbera 2011

ISBN: 978 0 263 89125 6

51-0212

Harlequin (UK) policy is to use papers that are natural, renewable and
recyclable products and made from wood grown in sustainable forests. The
logging and manufacturing processes conform to the legal environmental
regulations of the country of origin.

Printed and bound in Spain
by Blackprint CPI, Barcelona

Katherine Garbera is the *USA TODAY* bestselling author of more than forty books. She's always believed in happy endings and lives in Southern California with her husband, children and their pampered pet, Godiva. Visit Katherine on the web at www.katherinegarbera. com, or catch up with her on Facebook and Twitter.

This book is dedicated to my sweet husband, Rob,
for showing me that happy endings happen
all the time in the real world.

Acknowledgements

A special thank you to my editor, Charles,
for all his insightful editing on this book.

One

What had she been thinking when she'd accepted this invitation?

Becca Tuntenstall really didn't have time to go to a charity function in the middle of the workweek. But considering her former boss had invited her, she felt that it was just the second chance she needed. She'd walked away from everything and everyone in this world almost two years ago, and now she was ready to get back to it.

She checked her lipstick one more time in the ladies'-room mirror at the glitteringly decorated Manhattan Kiwi Klub. She'd designed this interior and really thought it captured the sparkle of the city with a sophistication that wasn't really found in society anymore.

She left the bathroom and walked into the ballroom. Her former boss, Russell Holloway, stood facing her. He smiled when he saw her and waved her over. She fixed a smile on her own face and headed his way like the confident, brash woman she'd been two years ago.

"Becca?"

She stopped in her tracks as she heard the one voice she'd thought she'd never hear again.

"Cam?" she said, not having to feign surprise at all.

She stared at him for what seemed like a frozen moment in time, and a million memories rushed through her mind. She remembered how hard it had been to just walk away from this man. "What are you doing here?"

"Russell invited me."

"Uh...okay. But don't you live in Miami?"

"I do. But I do travel from time to time," he said wryly.

She flushed, realizing she sounded like an idiot. "I'm sorry. You are just the last person I expected to see tonight."

"Or ever?" he asked.

"Definitely," she said. He looked good, damn him. Cam was tall, at least six foot five, with thick, dark brown hair and eyes that were so blue she couldn't look away from him. He had a strong, stubborn-looking jaw and a clean-shaven face. He wore his tux with an ease that most men simply couldn't carry off. He looked very comfortable and so devastatingly handsome that she had a hard time thinking straight. But then Cam Stern was the son of a socialite and a pro golfer. He'd been born with a silver spoon in his mouth and had only seen his wealth grow since he'd become an adult. In fact, she doubted there was anything that Cam couldn't buy. She knew that well enough from her experience with him.

"Well, I've got to go," she said, fully intending to walk away from him and never speak to him again.

"That's not going to work, Becca," he said.

"Why not? I believe your last words to me two years ago were that if I didn't want to be your mistress we had nothing left to discuss," she reminded him. She'd long gotten over her anger at the way he'd thrown her confession of love back in her face. Hell, no, she hadn't. She still wanted to see him writhe. She still wanted him to feel the intense pain she'd felt when he'd said those words to her.

"I owe you an apology," he said. "I have no excuse for being so cold. I was…your confession was unexpected and I wasn't in a position to make a decision to put a woman on par with my business."

"I know that," she said. "Despite how bitter that sounded just now, I really have moved on. Let's start over."

"Over?"

"Yes, pretend you are just running into me again and I'll be more polite," she said.

He started laughing. "I have missed you, Becca."

She shook her head. "Is there no one else who makes you laugh?"

"Not like you," he said.

She smiled at him, but she wasn't about to let herself

fall for his good looks and easy charm again. Cam had done a lot more than break her heart. He'd left her shattered, and she'd had to rebuild her entire life and who she thought she'd be. "That's too bad."

"Yes, it is. What have you been up to?" he asked.

"I started my own business," she said.

"I have to confess I knew that. Russell has been singing your praises to me for a while now."

"He has? I wonder why," she said.

"Because Cam has a project that could do with your touch," Russell said, coming up to them. Russell was a New Zealand millionaire who, like Cam, had been born with more money than Midas. At forty-one, he was two years older than Cam, and he lived the life of an international playboy, jetting from one cosmopolitan city to the next, managing his chain of Kiwi Klubs.

She never turned down work, and she wouldn't if Cam had a legitimate offer for her. She rarely saw her clients, and she could probably manage a few days of face-to-face time with Cam.

"What project?"

"I had hoped to discuss business at another time," Cam said.

"Nonsense. What else would you two have to discuss?" Russell said.

"What else?" Becca asked. Her short, red-hot affair with Cam had also been super-secret. They'd met in her hotel room each night and had white-hot sex. She'd thought it was a whirlwind romance, but it had turned out that the reason Cam had been keeping her secret was that he hadn't wanted more than sex from her.

"What else indeed," Cam said. "I'm not sure if you have heard any of the radio ads for Luna Azul's tenth anniversary celebration or not."

"I have heard them. Very good idea to advertise a Memorial Day weekend trip to Miami to be surrounded by celebs and balmy tropical weather."

"Thanks," he said. "That was my idea. Anyway, we have recently purchased a shopping mall that we are going to open as Luna Azul Mercado. And I'm looking for a designer for the project."

"And I thought of you," Russell said.

She opened her clutch purse, took out a business card and handed it to Cam. "I'd love to hear more about your project."

He took her card and glanced at it for a long moment before putting it in his pocket. "Business out of the way, perhaps we can enjoy the evening now. Can I get you a drink?" Cam asked.

"Gin and tonic," she said.

When he walked away, she was tempted to sneak out the back, but she'd paid a lot of money for her seat at this charity dinner with the intention of meeting a lot of Russell's friends and maybe securing more work for herself.

Becca doubted she would enjoy one second of tonight. There were few situations that she could think of that would be less fun than sitting next to two men from whom she'd kept important secrets. Russell didn't know that she and Cam had been lovers, and Cam didn't know that their affair had resulted in a child.

Cam had been prepared to see Becca again but he'd forgotten how he'd always reacted to her. One brief touch of her hand in his and his entire body had tingled.

Becca's heart-shaped face was pretty—not classically beautiful, but he couldn't take his eyes from her. Her nose was small and delicate, and her thick black hair was worn up with a few tendrils framing her face. Her mouth was full...seductive with that full lower lip, and he remembered the taste of her.

The scent of her had overwhelmed him, and he'd wanted to stand still and just breathe her in. He'd wanted to wrap his arms around her, plant his mouth on hers and say to hell with the last two years.

But he knew that wasn't going to be easy. He'd hurt her when he'd thrown her out of his life. He would never admit this to another person, but Becca had scared him and he'd had to walk away before he'd done something foolish—such as fall for her.

He got their drinks and walked back across the room. She stood talking to a well-dressed woman and looked up as he approached. She had a new life, he thought, watching her. She didn't need a former lover back in it. But he wasn't a man who gave up easily and there was only one thing he wanted...Becca Tuntenstall.

"Your drink," he said, handing it to her.

"Thank you. Cam, do you know Dani McNeil?"

"I don't believe I do," he said, shaking hands with the other woman.

Her hands weren't as soft as Becca's, and he didn't have any reaction to touching her. As though he needed proof that Becca was different—he'd already figured that part out.

"Dani works for Russell's foundation. She is the one who coordinated this tonight."

"Well done," Cam said. "I've attended a lot of parties and this one certainly ranks among the best."

Dani flushed. "Thank you. I've got to go check with the kitchen. I want to make sure everything is perfect." She walked away.

"I'm not sure I know many people at this function."

"I do," Cam said.

"Would you mind introducing me to some of them? I'm trying to grow my business."

"I'm not clear on what it is," he said.

"Tuntenstall Designers. I've designed interiors for hotels and nightclubs. I just finished work on a new hotel in Maui."

"Sounds like you don't need to grow too much," he said.

"There are always more hours in the day to fill," she said. "I'm afraid of running out of work."

"Has that happened?" he asked, wanting to know more about what made her tick.

"Not yet. But it could and I don't want that to happen."

He smiled. "You remind me a lot of me when I started the club."

"At least you had a trust fund to fall back on," she said.

He nodded. "That's true. But it didn't make the work any easier. And I was very conscious of the fact that if I failed I'd be putting my future and my brothers in jeopardy."

She quirked one side of her mouth. "I guess I didn't think of it that way."

"Why would you?" he asked. He was very aware that he and his brothers had cultivated an image of carefree playboys who'd never had to worry about anything.

"I hate it when people make assumptions about me," she said.

"We all do it," he said. "So who do you want to meet?"

"I really don't know. I heard that Tristan Sabina was here and he is a co-owner of Seconds nightclubs…"

"You want me to introduce you to the competition?" he asked. He was joking. Seconds was more competition for Russell's Kiwi Klubs than for Luna Azul. They had several branches in international hotspots instead of one dedicated location like Luna Azul. Someday Cam thought it might be nice to have another club, but he liked what they were doing in Miami. It would have to be just the right situation to tempt him to leave.

"Would you mind?" she asked.

"Not at all. In fact I know Tristan fairly well," he said, taking Becca's arm in his. He took a sip of his dirty martini and savored the salty taste.

"Do you need another drink?" he asked her.

"I'm good," she said. "Thanks for doing this."

"What?"

"Introducing me to Tristan," she said, drawing to a stop. "You don't have to."

"I know. I want to," he said. He'd let something slip away with Becca, and, to be honest, he regretted it. He hadn't been ready for her love two years ago, and he didn't know if he was now. But with his brothers settling down and Becca coming back into his life, he at least wanted to give it a chance.

He waved over Tristan, who was accompanied by his wife, Sheri. Cam made short work of the introductions.

"Becca is an interior designer," Cam said.

"Enchanté, mademoiselle," Tristan said.

"It's a pleasure. I hope you don't mind but I asked Cam to introduce us so I could give you my card. I've done a lot of work for nightclubs and hotels."

"I don't mind at all," Tristan said. He took her card and pocketed it. "But I can't talk business tonight or Sheri will likely kill me." His French accent was very smooth and barely noticeable.

"I will," his wife said. "He's promised me a night out and I intend to hold him to it. We work together, so I hardly ever have a chance to just spend time with my husband that doesn't involve work or family."

"Then I'm sorry I brought it up."

"Not at all. So how did you start your own business? My boss can be a bear…I might want to do the same."

"You aren't quitting, Sheri, and leaving me alone at the office."

"Why not?" she asked her husband.

Tristan leaned down and whispered something in her ear that made her blush. Then she kissed him, and he put his arm around her. Cam wasn't sure what had been said, but he knew that it was intimate.

And he wanted that. He had been alone for a long time and had grown used to it, but there were times, especially now that his brothers were both engaged, that he wanted something more.

He glanced down at Becca and noticed that she was watching the married couple, as well. He'd ruined things with her once by not...by what? They'd had an affair. Affairs don't turn into love overnight. Cam Stern had always known he wasn't the kind of guy that women fell easily in love with. He was arrogant and difficult. He might know his way around a bedroom, and he knew he was the kind of lover who ensured his partner's pleasure, but a life together was about more than sex. He'd learned that the hard way.

The conversation at the dinner table was fun and lively, ranging from politics to economic trends to fashion. Becca wasn't sure she was going to fit in with the billionaires, scandalous heiresses and socialites, but she was managing to hold her own.

Seated around the table for eight were Russell and his supermodel date; Becca and Cam; then next to Cam, Geoff Devonshire—a member of the British royal family—and his new wife, Amelia Munroe-Devonshire; next to them were Russell's CFO, Marcus Willby, and his daughter Penny.

Despite the fact that she expected Cam to focus on

doing his own thing he didn't. He'd taken the seat right next to her at the table and introduced her to as many potential clients as he could. She wondered if he was trying to make up for breaking her heart all those years ago.

She was seated between Russell and Cam. The friendship between the two men was evident by the way they teased each other and joked around. She forgot about the fact that she intended to stay on her guard. To just get through this night as best she could. Until the topic turned to Luna Azul's Tenth Anniversary celebration over the upcoming Memorial Day weekend. "Did you invite Becca?" Russell asked.

"I didn't," Cam said, turning to Becca. "Would you like to come to the party as my guest?"

"You always have time to party," Amelia said with a smile.

Becca realized that she and Amelia lived in two totally different worlds. To a socialite, it was no big deal to jet down to a party in Miami. But to a working single mother, it was a huge affair. While she liked Amelia, Becca had a feeling she'd never be able to understand the way she lived.

"I own my own business so if I take too many days off, then I don't get paid," Becca said.

She wasn't going to let a table full of socialites pressure her into something she wasn't sure she wanted to do.

But Becca was curious. "Tell us more about the plans for the party."

Cam smiled. "Nate is working the celebrity angle

so we are going to have a room full of A-listers. Justin has smoothed over the tension we had in the local community and we will be combining the party with the groundbreaking for our new Mercado. That is the work I wanted to talk to you about," he said.

"We should probably discuss it later," she said, not wanting to talk business now.

"Definitely," he said.

"We can all give you some business advice, Becca," Russell said. "No sense letting you screw up the way I did early in my career."

"I can't imagine Russell making many mistakes," Amelia Munroe-Devonshire said. She was the guest speaker tonight. There was a time when she'd been more infamous than famous as the heiress to the Munroe hotel chain. But then she had married Geoff Devonshire last year and had been in the spotlight lately for her humanitarian work instead of her scandals.

"I have made more than my share, Amelia. I just managed to keep them out of the headlines."

"Touché! It's remarkably easier to stay out of the tabloids these days than it used to be. I can't believe it," she said.

Becca smiled at the heiress. She was funny and very fashionable but also down-to-earth—something Becca hadn't expected.

"That's because I keep a firm hand on the situation," Geoff said. Geoff was a minor member of the current royal family.

"I believe that," Cam added. "Both of you are of

course invited to the Tenth Anniversary Celebration in Miami."

"We are scheduled to be in Berne for a special award that Geoff's brother's mother is receiving," Amelia said.

"You must be proud of her," Becca said. Like most people she knew that Geoff and his two brothers had the same father but different mothers. The scandal that had rocked the world in the '70s when they'd been born had followed the men into adulthood and only last year when Malcolm Devonshire had died had it seemed to be put to rest.

"We are. Steven asked us to attend and we can't say no to family," Geoff said.

"No, you can't," Cam agreed. "That's why I now have a brother in New York while our business is based in Miami. Justin is up here helping his fiancée close up her apartment before she moves back to Miami."

Geoff laughed. "You do what you have to when it comes to family."

Family. It was something she seldom thought about except in relation to her eighteen-month-old son, Ty. Her father had left when she was two, and her mother had died of breast cancer when Becca was a junior in college. She'd been on her own for so long that it had never occurred to her that she'd taken something very precious from Ty until this moment.

Ty had uncles and a father who might want to know him. Might.

That was a big word to base her fears on. One thing

she knew for certain was that he'd never intended her to be the mother of his child.

She'd never intended it either.

The conversations turned to more private matters, and eventually Russell got up to introduce Amelia. Becca didn't know if she could sit at the table for another minute. She needed to get out of there.

She wanted to go back home to Garden City where there was comfort in the walls of the home she'd grown up in and in holding her sweet eighteen-month-old son.

As the lights went down and Amelia took the stage, Becca fumbled for her purse. It fell to the floor. Cam leaned in close, his big arm behind her.

"Are you okay?"

"Yes. I just need to step outside for a minute."

Cam reached down and picked up her handbag, handing it back to her. She pulled out her cell phone and saw that she'd missed a call from Jasper, her nanny. Finally some karma that might be good.

"I've got to go," she said, standing and weaving her way through the tables. She got to the lobby of the club and saw that it was crowded with patrons.

She made her way to a quiet alcove set off the main entrance. She sat down on a padded bench before calling Jasper back.

"It's Becca," she said as he answered the phone.

"Sorry to bother you," Jasper said. "Burt is sick so I had to take Ty to my house. I wanted to make sure you knew before you came home."

Burt was Jasper's twelve-year-old English bulldog.

"Not a problem. Thanks for letting me know. I might stop by and get Ty tonight."

"I figured you'd want to. I can even meet you at your house if you call when you are about fifteen minutes away."

"I will do that," she said, hanging up the phone.

She stood up and turned to leave the alcove but found that Cam was standing there.

"Everything okay?" he asked.

She nodded. "No emergencies."

"That's good. Amelia's done talking and they've opened up the dance floor."

"And?"

"I'd like to dance with you, Becca. We've never done that and it's been too long since I held you in my arms."

Two

Becca found herself pressed close to Cam on the dance floor a short while later. He smelled good, like expensive aftershave, and she had to really struggle to keep from resting her head on his chest. But she wanted to. It had been so long since she had anyone hold her, and she'd spent the last two years feeling very alone. She didn't need a man…she got on very well without one. But there was something about dancing with Cam to the slow bluesy song "Love Is a Losing Game" that Amy Winehouse had made popular a few years ago.…

"You're a good dancer," she said.

"My mother insisted on lessons. She might not have been too involved in her sons' lives, but she did make sure we were raised proper gentlemen."

"What does a proper gentleman do?"

"He knows how to talk to a woman, how to romance her."

"Romance? Is that what you are doing to me?" she asked. She hadn't gotten a chance to know the real Cam Stern when they'd had their affair, and though she'd thought she loved him, she knew that had been based on sex and quiet moments in the dark of night. She'd never danced with him or really even seen him outside of that hotel bedroom.

"I am," he said, pulling her close and spinning them around. Though the dance floor was crowded, she felt like they were the only two people in the room. His eyes were intense as he looked down at her. She felt as if they could bore all the way through to her soul and the secret she kept from him.

She should go. She should walk out of his arms and leave. She needed to remember that no matter how romantic the night felt, Cam wasn't the kind of man who was interested in settling down or starting a family. And she came with a ready-made one.

He kept his arms around her, and she told herself she was Cinderella and this was for only one night. Even Cindy had gotten one night with her Prince. She knew that Cam wasn't some white knight who could rescue her. She'd seen the chinks in his armor. But when he held her close like this, it was easy to forget about that all that. It was so easy for her to just pretend that for once she was going to have her cake and eat it, too.

"What are you thinking?" she asked, as she glanced up and found him staring at her.

"That you are the most beautiful woman in the room," he said.

She flushed and shook her head. "I'm not."

"In my eyes you are," he said. He leaned down, and the warmth of his breath brushed her cheek as he spoke directly into her ear. "You are the most exquisite woman I've ever seen. You have haunted my dreams."

"Then why did you wait so long to get back in touch with me?" she asked.

"I didn't think you'd be able to forgive me. And I wasn't sure if I had fantasized about you so much that I made you into someone you weren't. But none of that matters now."

But it did. He was talking to her as if nothing had happened except a bad breakup. But she knew there was so much more between them, and she had no idea how to tell him.

He wasn't the evil ogre she'd made him out to be. She'd known that even back then, but she had pride. Some said too much pride was a bad thing, but Becca didn't really know how to define "too much." She had only understood that Cam wasn't the kind of man who'd take the news of her pregnancy well.

She twisted and started to walk away from him.

He caught up with her and grabbed her arm as she reached the edge of the dance floor. "Where are you going?"

"I can't do this, Cam. I am trying to pretend this is all just a nice night out, but every time I look in your face I see the past. And I'm just not ready to deal with that tonight."

"I'm not asking you to," he said. "I think we should forget about what happened between us—"

"I can't. It's way too complicated to go into now, but trust me when I say I could never pretend we didn't meet."

"That's a good thing," he said.

She shook her head and pulled away from him. "No, it's not. There are things about me that you don't know."

"Tell me about them," he said.

"Not here. Come to my house tomorrow morning."

"I can't wait until tomorrow," he said.

She smiled up at him as he leaned in close. The hardness of his body was a remembered thrill. "We already did lust. Remember?"

"Yes," he said. "I know you remember, too. It's there in your eyes when I hold you. You still want me."

She did still want him, but she liked to think she was older and wiser. Please, God, let her be wiser. She couldn't fall for him again. Wouldn't let herself be that weak where he was concerned. Cam Stern wasn't the kind of guy she could have a one-night stand with and walk away from.

But that was what she wanted. She wanted to pretend they were strangers with no baggage or no commitments. That they could have one night of passion with no consequences. But it was too late for that. She was emotionally entangled with him, even though he wasn't with her.

She went up on her tiptoes and rubbed her lips over his and then slowly opened her mouth and kissed him.

She held on to his shoulders and felt his mouth move against hers. He parted her lips with his own, and his tongue snaked over her teeth into her mouth.

His thrusts were light and teasing, making her crave so much more of him. She opened her mouth wider, held on to his shoulders and let everything drop away. She didn't think about the past or her secrets. She didn't think about the glittering people at this charity ball. She didn't think of anything except Cam Stern and his mouth.

That oh-so-talented mouth that was moving over hers and making her forget everything except the way he tasted and the way he felt.

His lips were firm but also tender against hers. His hands smoothed their way down her spine. One sprawled in the middle of her back and the other dipped lower to her hips, drawing her closer to him.

"Let's get out of here," Cam said. "We need to go someplace private."

Confused for the first time in a very long time, Becca really didn't know what to do. So she followed Cam out of the ballroom and onto the street as he hailed a cab.

Cam wasn't ready to let the night end. Seeing Becca again wasn't at all what he had thought it would be.

The April sky was clear, the night air a little cool but not cold when they left the club. Cam had said his goodbyes to Russell earlier and Russell had offered the car, but Cam had turned him down. He liked to do things his own way. He wanted to be in control.

Cam hailed a cab for them and asked to be taken to

his hotel, the Affinia Manhattan, which was a suite-only hotel. Though he'd only been in town for a few days, Cam liked to have room to be comfortable. At six-five, he was a big man, and he didn't like to be in a room crammed with a bed and a dresser.

"I thought you said you only wanted someplace private," Becca said, arching one eyebrow. "Why do we need to go to your hotel?"

"I don't know any other quiet place we can talk." He wanted her to himself. That was one thing he'd done right during their affair. They had spent all of their time together in her hotel room. Having sex and lying in each other's arms. Despite the fact that they were both working hard during the day, the nights had been filled with only each other.

She tipped her head to the side. She studied him, and he wondered what she was searching for. When he looked at her, he saw the same beautiful, sexy woman he'd known two years ago. But she had changed. There was something mysterious about the woman sitting next to him now.

"Okay, we can go to your hotel, but we are getting a drink in the lobby bar."

"Fair enough. I want to take my time and really apologize for the way things ended."

"Apology accepted," she said.

She was a graceful and charming woman, and as she sat next to him during the cab ride, he surreptitiously studied her. Her heart-shaped face was framed by her hair, and her eyes were dark and mysterious in this light.

He wouldn't have thought to look into his romantic past to find a woman to move forward with, but it made sense to him now that Becca was here.

He stretched his arm out behind her and toyed with the soft tendrils of hair at the base of her neck. "Thank you. But I know you like me so I have that in my favor."

"How do you know this?" she asked.

"The way you smile at me," he admitted. "And the way you kissed me."

"That wasn't about you," she said.

"It wasn't?"

"No. It was a gift to myself. A chance for me to taste the forbidden fruit of the past and then move on."

"Why are you in this car with me now?"

"I wanted to hear what you had to say," she said. "I really don't know much about you."

"Or I about you," he said.

"I think men like it that way," she said.

"Men? I hope I'm a little different than every other man out there," he said. "I think I want to know everything about you."

She shook her head. "I doubt that. As long as I have secrets then I will be mysterious and just a little more attractive to you."

"You couldn't be anything less than you are right now, Becca. I want you."

She shook her head again. "I know you do, but we aren't going down that path."

"I can't think of anything except you in my arms," he said, watching her blush.

"Why are you here? You said Justin is helping his fiancée move."

He laughed. "Fine. I will stop talking about your sexy little body for a few a minutes, but I can't stop thinking about you naked in my arms."

"Cam."

"Okay." He knew he was pushing her, but he only had this night before he had to return to Miami. And apologizing for the way things had ended between them wasn't enough to repair the damage he'd done. He wanted her back. He hadn't realized how much until he'd danced with her. Kissed her.

"I'm here visiting Justin and to attend this charity ball tonight. The African Children's Fund was one of my mother's pet charities," Cam said as the car started moving.

"Well, that's nice." She would have liked to think that she'd made a clean break with everything Cam Stern, but she still read about him in magazines, and late at night when she was feeling very alone, she sometimes went on the internet and read about him. She should have realized he'd be here tonight, but honestly, she'd been busy with work, and having an eighteen-month-old kept her on her toes.

"What have you been up to?" she asked.

"I think I mentioned we are celebrating Luna Azul's tenth anniversary. Even if you can't take me on as a client, I would like you to come to Miami. My invitation earlier was genuine."

"Um..."

"Think about it, Becca."

"I'll do that," she said, but she knew the answer had to be no.

"Ten years is a long time," she said.

"Yes, it is. Are you interested in redesigning the new marketplace?"

"Sounds like that will be a fun project. You can email me the details on that."

"Are you really going to make small talk and pretend that a casual business acquaintance is all that we have between us?"

"Yup," she said. "That's all we have."

"I remember," he said. "But I never meant for those weeks to be the only ones we spent together."

"I know you wanted me to be your mistress...I'm sorry I asked for more."

He said nothing and the silence grew between them.

"You travelled a lot for business back then and I expected you to be back in Miami frequently."

"I stopped working for Russell so I wasn't making as many trips to Miami as I used to."

She bit back a sad smile. To Cam she was just someone to have sex with. She'd seen that pretty early on, and while she enjoyed the white-hot passion that flowed so strongly between them, once she'd discovered she was pregnant, she knew she couldn't be with him.

She had someone else to think of...Ty. Her little gift from Cam.

But talking to him made her realize why she'd liked him so much. The truth was, from the first moment they'd met she'd liked him. He was honest and fair and so damned handsome that she couldn't stop staring at him.

Blue was such a nondescript word for the color of his eyes. They were deep blue, the kind of color that she'd seen in only one other place—the azure waters of Fiji. His jaw was strong and well-defined, but it was his mouth that captured her. Those strong lips that felt so soft and so right against her own.

"You're staring at me," he said wryly.

"I forgot how good-looking you are."

That startled a laugh out of him. "Why did you start your own business? Do you like it?"

"I do," she admitted. "More than I expected to. And being my own boss means I can control my workload. You know Russell is a complete workaholic, so if I'd continued at Kiwi I would probably be in the office tonight."

"Very true," Cam said, stretching his arm along the back of the seat. His fingers brushed her shoulder and she glanced up at him to see if he was trying to distract her. But he didn't seem to notice the accidental touch.

Cam watched her carefully, and she hoped that he took her story at face value and let the topic drop. She knew that right now she had the opportunity to tell him about Ty, but she couldn't find the words.

He tipped his head to the side, and she realized that this evening wasn't going the way she wanted it to. She should be home with Ty.

She thought about how scared she'd been the first night she'd brought him home from the hospital. She had always been focused on her career, so she hadn't had any girlfriends to come and stay with her. And every time little Ty had cried, she'd cried with him.

It had been the longest night of her life, and she'd missed her own mom so keenly it had hurt. But then morning had come, and she and Ty had found their own way.

"What are you thinking about?" he asked.

"Nothing," she said. Seeing Cam again gave her a chance to let him know that he had a son. But she had no idea how he felt about family. She knew he didn't believe in love and had two years ago wanted nothing more from a woman than sex.

"Have you ever thought about having a family? Not just your brothers. I mean a family of your own."

This was it. If he said, *Yes, I'd love to have kids,* then she would say, *Oh, that's funny, you have a son.*

"No."

"Why not?" she asked. Already she had an inkling she wasn't going to like the answer. Cam was too much of a workaholic businessman to want a family. He had only had time for the affair with her because it hadn't interfered with his job. And she knew that.

"I had a paternity suit brought against me right as Luna Azul started taking off. The suit was false but we had to go to court and I think that made me realize that having a child was something I wanted to take very seriously. I didn't want to have a child with just any woman."

Becca's stomach dropped, and she felt like she was going to be sick. She wrapped an arm around her own waist and knew there was no way she could just tell

Cam that Ty was his son. In fact, she just wanted to get out of this car and return to her safe little home as quickly as possible.

Three

Cam had a hard time looking at Becca and not touching her. There was something about her that called to him, and he knew part of it at least was the false feeling that they were still intimates. It didn't matter that it had been over two years since he'd last seen her. He wanted her, and it felt to him that no time had passed.

"I'm glad we met again tonight," he said. He rubbed his finger over her cheek. Her skin was so soft that he could touch it for hours.

The cab pulled to a stop in front of his hotel, and he paid the driver before following Becca out of the cab. The doorman held the door open as they approached.

"I have to call for a car now or I'll never get one later," she said. "I'll meet you in the bar. Go ahead and order me a Baileys."

"I'll take care of the car. You go get a seat and I'll be right there."

"I'd rather—"

He put his finger over her lips. They were full, and he was dying to kiss her again. Touching her mouth, he found it soft and even more tempting than he'd expected.

"I said I'll take care of it."

She playfully nipped at his fingertip and then turned and walked away.

He watched her. She'd surprised him, and he reminded himself that a lot had changed with Becca in the last two years.

And he was dying to know more.

But if he was going to build trust with Becca, he needed to respect the fact that she didn't want to be rushed into his bed. So he called for a car, asking for it to arrive in an hour.

He joined her in a quiet area of the bar where she'd found two large armchairs and a small table.

"I ordered you a Baileys, too."

"Thanks. Your car will be here in an hour," he said.

"Great. So what did you want to talk to me about?" she asked.

"Us. Are you going to give us another chance to get to know one another?" he asked.

As she nibbled on her lower lip, he wanted to groan out loud but didn't. He wanted her mouth, and promised himself that before he put her in a car back to Long

Island, he was going to taste her and prove to himself that she couldn't taste as good as he remembered.

"I'm thinking about it," she said at last. Their drinks arrived, and she held hers with both hands. "It's hard for me to just rush into anything with you."

"If we are going to get to know each other, we should talk," he said. "Tell me something about you that I don't already know."

She paused, her eyes darkening.

"I don't like surprises," she said.

"What kind?" he asked.

"Any of them. I like my life to go according to plan. I can adjust and change my plan but I don't want to have to do it too often."

"Me, too," he said. "Though to be honest, usually I just bully my way through a situation until I get the results I want."

"Hence me having a drink with you tonight," she said.

He just smiled and lifted his glass toward her. He took a sip and sat back in his chair.

"Tell me more about why you are in Manhattan," she said.

"Justin and I are exploring the idea of expanding Luna Azul someday. We are discussing eventually opening clubs in other parts of the country. Manhattan is the first location we are contemplating."

"That's a big step," she said.

"It is. And to be honest, I love our Miami locals. But we are ready for it. And now that you and I have reconnected I will have another reason to come up here."

"Cam—"

He shook his head when she tried to speak. "I want to get to know you better, Becca."

"I don't know if that is a good idea. I'm more complicated than you probably have time for," she said. Her eyes had narrowed, and she tipped her head to the side, studying him.

"I know that. That's why… Am I wrong here to think that there is something between us?"

"No. We've always had that attraction that is impossible to resist, but I want more than that. And you don't."

"I'm willing to try it."

"Try what? I had a hard time getting over you, Cam. I don't think I want to take a chance on letting you break my heart again."

"I can't make promises," he said. "But I do know that I want more than a secret affair. Will you at least agree to come to Miami for the Tenth Anniversary party and spend the weekend with me?"

"As your lover?" she asked.

"I hope so. Definitely as my friend. I want to get to know you better. I feel like we have something unfinished between us."

Becca didn't panic. But she wanted to. Cam had no real idea of what was unfinished between them. She knew that he was talking about sexual attraction or maybe the kind of thing that made her tick. And she knew she wasn't going to share too much with Cam until she could trust him.

"I think that isn't going to be as easy as you might think," she said.

"I know it's not. But anything and anyone worth having is worth working to get to know."

She wasn't sure if he'd mellowed or if it was simply that he was keeping the passion that had flared between them the first time under wraps. But talking was making her realize that Cam was a decent man. A man she wanted to know better and maybe a man that she wanted her son to know.

"I agree." She had to find out more about his past. Had to understand the best way to tell him they had a son. "So tell me what kind of woman you would choose to have a child with," she said.

It was the one thing she wanted to know. Telling him about Ty was only the first step—making sure that he treated her son well once he knew that Ty was his was the important part.

"That's a big jump in conversation."

"I know, but I want to know the kind of man you are."

He leaned back in his chair and took another sip of his drink. "I've never really thought about it. My dad was everything to me when I was growing up, and my mother was more concerned with her social position than her children."

"I'm sorry."

He shrugged. "It is what it is. No changing the type of woman she was. But I want to make a better choice

KATHERINE GARBERA   39

than my dad did. I want a woman who will want to be a mother to our children. Who will make them a priority," he said.

His words made her feel better that he was Ty's father. But she still didn't know if he was just paying lip service to the type of man he thought he should be. And to be fair, he probably didn't know either. She'd had similar uncertainty about becoming a parent. She'd never expected to be a mom and had thought she'd have a nanny who took care of the kid all the time. But once Ty was in her arms, she'd realized she didn't want to miss a moment of his life.

She nodded. "I want that, too. I mean in a dad. I don't want a man who is on his BlackBerry with the office while he is at home and supposed to be spending time with the family."

"Good. Something we have in common," he said. "We both think family should come first. That is partly why I wasn't ready to settle down with you two years ago, Becca."

"Life is complicated sometimes," she said.

"Very."

He leaned forward and took her hand in his. "I really do want this to be a fresh start for us."

She was afraid to believe him. She knew that they'd never be able to make a fresh start unless she came clean first about Ty. But tonight she didn't want to ruin the feeling between them. That excitement and hope that came from getting to know someone the first time—for her it was building on the fantasies she'd spun around Cam since she'd had Ty.

She wasn't going to lie; she'd wanted him to come back into her life. She just never thought that he would. And now here he was.

"Why are you staring at me?" he asked.

"I just realized that I like you."

That made him chuckle. "What's not to like?"

"You are autocratic and bossy," she said.

"I think you like that, too. You need a man who doesn't let you ride roughshod all over him."

"Did I do that before?"

"No, but I think I was the exception. You are very used to getting your way," he said.

"I am. I have had to be. Since I was twenty I've been on my own and that means I have to make good choices."

"Have you always made them?" he asked.

She shook her head. "No, but I try not to have regrets. I mean I can't change any decision I made to get where I am today."

That was one thing she'd learned growing up. Her mother had said that everyone makes mistakes. A wise person learns from them and moves on. A fool lingers over them and spends all their time wishing they'd done something else.

He lifted his glass. "A toast to knowing what you want, and getting it."

"A toast," she said.

He looked at her as if she was the very thing he wanted. That made her feel warm all over, and she knew no matter how hard she tried to keep this tame, it wasn't going to work. She wanted Cam. He was everything she liked in a man. She loved his height; he was taller than she was, with big shoulders and firm muscles. She remembered the way they'd fit together when they'd made love, so perfectly, and she wanted him again.

It had been a long time since she'd slept with a man—since Cam to be exact—and she felt overdue. But a one-night stand wasn't the answer.

"I have a confession to make," Cam said.

She didn't want him to tell her anything else. She just wanted this hour to pass and for her to get into the car and drive away. And this time she hoped that they'd stay apart because the more time she spent with Cam, the more she realized that she missed having a man in her life. Missed having this man in her life.

"And that is?" she asked.

"I'm going to kiss you before you get in the car tonight," he said.

She shivered, and everything feminine in her came to attention. She wanted to feel his big strong arms around her again. Wanted him to hold her and make her feel like she wasn't alone in the world.

"I was planning to let you," she said because she didn't want him to get the upper hand. And because it was the truth—other than the one big lie, she was going to be honest with Cam.

"I thought you wanted to start slow," he said.

"I do, but denying there is lust between us is silly. I want you and I suspect you are very aware of it."

"I am. But I don't want you to feel pressured," he said.

And that made her heart melt. That one comment

made her realize that Cam was a man that she wanted not only in her bed but also in her life.

The driver of Becca's car sent Cam a text when he was outside the hotel.

"Your car is here," Cam told Becca.

"So soon? I really enjoyed talking to you tonight. I'm glad you insisted we get together."

She sounded so casual, as if they were old friends and not old lovers. He knew that was the only way to be unless they wanted to rehash every moment that they'd been apart.

"Me, too," he said. He had enjoyed talking with her. She was intelligent and well-spoken and not afraid to laugh at herself. "I'm going to insist we have breakfast together as well, and then we can discuss business. If you can't help with the Mercado, I think that the Manhattan club will be right up your alley."

"It might be," she said, getting to her feet. "If we have breakfast it will have to be at my place. I hate the morning drive to the city."

He laughed. "Very well. I will come to your place. Give me your address."

She gave it to him as he led the way through the lobby. But instead of taking her out the front door, he pulled her down a hallway to a small intimate alcove.

"I don't want to say good night in front of other people." He put his hands on her waist and drew her into the curve of his body. She fit next to him like a puzzle piece that had found its mate.

"Why not?" she asked, tipping her head back to look up at him.

"I told you I'm going to kiss you, and some things should never be done in public."

He pulled her closer. "That was one thing we did right the first time, kept this private."

She stared up at him. Her eyes were wide and pretty, but he thought he also saw some trepidation in them.

"I agree there. I don't like everyone to know my business," she said.

He stroked his finger over her cheek and then traced her bottom lip with it. She opened her mouth and the tip of her tongue brushed his finger. Everything tightened in his body, and he leaned down, rubbing his lips back and forth against hers before gently mingling his tongue with hers.

She tasted just as good as he remembered, her mouth hot and moist. The Baileys they'd drunk flavored the kiss, but it was the taste of Becca that was addictive.

She moaned deep in her throat, and he tilted his head to deepen the kiss. He was starving for her and was only just realizing it. Letting her go had been a mistake.

He reached down her back and spanned her small waist with his hands, lifting her off her feet towards him. The small mounds of her breasts rested against his chest.

She pulled her mouth away. "I think this is getting out of control."

She had a point, but he didn't want to let her go. Not yet. He lowered his head again, and she lifted hers to meet him. Her tongue slipped into his mouth, rubbing seductively against his, and he hardened.

Letting her go was going to be difficult. But he had made her a promise that they'd go slower this time. And he'd keep it, even if it killed him.

Slowly he let her slide down his body until she was standing on her own again. He pulled back and lifted his head.

"Definitely out of control, but I like it."

She rubbed her fingers over her mouth. "I do, too. But I don't want to make a mistake."

"What kind of mistake?" he asked.

She shook her head. "Nothing. So how about nine-thirty for breakfast tomorrow?"

"Sure. But I'm not letting you change the subject," he said.

She bit her lower lip. "I just want to make sure we both know what we are doing."

"I do," he assured her. He took her hand in his and led her back out into the lobby. It was odd to think of the passionate embrace they'd shared happening so close to the real world and strangers.

"You sound confident but there are things you don't know, Cam," she said.

"Then tell me about them," he invited. "I want to know everything this time, Becca. No halfway for us."

"I'm not ready to talk about all my secrets," she said.

"I'm not going anywhere, so when you are ready we

will talk. There are things that take time to find their way out," he said.

"Do you have secrets?" she asked, then shook her head wryly. "Of course you do. You are a complex man."

"Am I? I think I'm a simple man with simple needs."

"And what are they?" she asked as they approached the front door of the hotel.

"Right now, they involve you in my arms. But that's not happening tonight."

"So what are you going to do?"

"I think I'll go to my room and pour myself a drink."

"Drinking is never the solution," she said.

"I know that, but it will take the edge off my wanting you."

"Does that really work?" she asked.

"I have no idea, but I'm going to give it a try," he said.

She turned and then leaned up and kissed him really quickly. Just a brief touch that sent sparks through his already aroused body.

"Thank you."

"For?"

"Stopping and not pressuring me. It would have been very easy for you to change my mind," she admitted.

He knew that, but he wasn't going to say it out loud. "I want more than one night with you, Becca."

She tipped her head to the side to study him. "I hope so. I'm not that temporary woman I was back then."

"I can see that. I hope you will learn that I'm a different man, too. I'm ready to settle down with the right woman," he admitted.

"I'm not sure I'm that person," she said.

"No pressure. I just wanted to let you know that I've changed, as well."

"I could tell right away. No BlackBerry in your hand during dinner," she said.

"With you by my side I'm not focused on work as much as pleasure."

She flushed. "You are very good about pleasure."

"Thank you." He kissed her hard and deep. "See you in the morning."

She nodded and walked to the car. He watched until the car drove away and then turned and headed back upstairs. He needed to know more about Becca but he had to be careful. He didn't want to be the man to hurt her...again.

Four

Becca woke early, as she always had since becoming a mom. She fed Ty his breakfast and then set him in his playpen while she checked her email. Last night she'd managed maybe two hours of sleep. Her dreams had been plagued with visions of Cam. The dreams were an odd mix of passionate embraces and tearful explanations. And today she felt very apprehensive about inviting him to her house for breakfast.

But it was too late. Cam and she had too much between them for her to just let him walk out of her life this time. And she couldn't move forward until he knew about Ty. It was going to be hard…how did you tell a man that he'd fathered a child with you nearly two years earlier?

She hoped he'd be accepting and understand why

she hadn't contacted him earlier, but she wasn't too confident of that.

The paternity suit he'd mentioned yesterday bothered her. She wished she had more time to do some research on it. But when she'd done a cursory search of the internet, she'd found nothing.

She glanced over at Ty and thought about Cam. What would he think of his son? She should just tell him, she thought, now, before things went any further between them. But she was afraid.

And she hated to give up control of a situation. Right now she made every decision in Ty's life. She chose the nanny and the food and when he went to bed. Once Cam knew about his son, everything would change.

Her life wasn't easy, but it was hers. And the choices she made about Ty's upbringing were hers and hers alone to make. She knew that when there were two parents, things could be difficult. Yet it was a dynamic she'd never experienced since just her mom had raised her.

Growing up alone with just one parent hadn't been easy, but it was what she was used to. So once she'd realized she was pregnant and made the decision to go it alone, she'd settled into it very easily. She'd felt she already had the best example of how a mom handled being a single parent.

The doorbell rang and she glanced at the clock. It was nine. It was a little early for Cam, but she wasn't expecting anyone else. She picked up the baby monitor, leaving Ty playing happily in his playpen, and headed for the door. A quick glance out the window confirmed that it was Cam.

She opened the door. He wore a pair of chinos and a golf shirt. He smelled of aftershave and looked well put-together. She felt frumpy in her slim-fitting yoga pants and T-shirt—so not ready to face the world or Cam Stern yet.

"You're early."

"Good morning to you, too," he said with a smile. "I brought bagels and coffee so I hope I will be forgiven."

She shook her head. Cam threw her off balance. Even without trying, he was doing it to her this morning. She needed that thirty minutes to get her mind wrapped around how to tell him about Ty. "No, you're not. I wanted to change out of messy clothes before you got here."

"You look lovely," he said.

"I don't feel it. I should make you wait on the front step but that coffee smells really good."

"Then I will come in and sit in the other room while you get changed." He seemed so reasonable that she started to feel a bit like a grump.

"Sorry I'm being so grouchy, but I am not a morning person. You can come in and wait for me on the back patio while I get changed," she said. She opened the door and turned to lead the way through the house.

"I'll want a tour later."

"If you're lucky," she said. She led him to the back screened-in porch where she had a glider in one corner and a small round table with four chairs. In the winter months she had glass windows installed to make the room usable year-round.

"I will take care of breakfast. I brought everything we'd need."

She thought she was handling the surprise of him very well when one word from the baby monitor shattered her composure.

"Mama?"

"Mama?" Cam asked.

"I...I have a son. Sit down and I'll be right back."

She left the patio and a perplexed Cam and went to get Ty from his playpen. She bent down and scooped him and kissed his little head. She hugged him close and closed her eyes, pretending that the next few minutes weren't going to completely change their world. But there was no denying it.

As they returned to the back porch, Ty became talkative. "Hi, man," Ty said, from her shoulder.

"Cam, this is Ty."

Cam looked at Ty and then back at her. And then back at Ty again. She saw in his face...he knew there was something familiar about Ty.

"Hi, Ty."

Cam turned to face them both and held out his hand. Ty reached for it and tugged on his finger and then squirmed to get down. He could walk and crawl and really liked being independent.

She bent over to set him down, and he immediately toddled over to Cam. He held on to Cam's leg and looked up at him.

Cam ruffled her son's hair. "I don't know if it is

because the last baby I was this close to was Nate, but he reminds me a little of my brother."

Becca felt as if her heart was going to beat right out of her chest. This would be the perfect moment to tell him why. "Well, it's funny you should say that—"

But his phone started ringing, and he pulled the BlackBerry out of his pocket. He glanced at the screen and then back at her.

"I have to take this. Do you mind?"

She shook her head and walked over to scoop up her son. She felt odd. She'd almost told him the most important bit of news he could hope to get and then business—work—had interrupted. Maybe that was a sign, she thought.

"I'll go get changed and be back in a minute," she said, walking away.

She had to remind herself that when she'd considered calling Cam and telling him that they were going to have a child, she'd decided not to because he just didn't seem like the type of man to want a family.

Their relationship had just been something to get them through the hot Miami nights. She knew that she was partially to blame for that. On some level, it had been exactly what she'd needed from him during that time. He hadn't been ready for anything else, and she knew that because she'd bared her soul to him and he'd told her to hit the road.

There were moments when she still wasn't sure she believed she was a mom. She still didn't believe that her life had taken this unexpected turn and she was where she was today.

But she did want a new start. A part of her did want a partner to share the rest of her life with. And she and Cam did have sexual chemistry in their favor. One thing that Becca had figured out about herself over the last two years was that she missed sex and having a man in her life.

She entered her bedroom and set Ty on the floor while she quickly changed into some nice caramel-colored trousers and a light blue sweater. She put her hair up in a chignon after she washed her face and applied her makeup. Looking in the mirror, she thought she seemed normal enough, but inside she was a mess.

She sat down in the large padded armchair in the corner of her room. It had been her mother's, and sitting there often made Becca feel closer to her.

"What am I going to do?" she asked out loud.

"Mama?"

She glanced over at Ty, who was walking slowly toward her, then decided crawling would be faster and dropped to all fours. "Yes, baby?"

"Where man go?"

She bent over and picked him up, holding him on her lap. "He's still out there making us breakfast."

Becca tried to talk in full sentences to Ty even though she wasn't sure he always understood things. She kissed his soft forehead and felt such joy, love and comfort just from holding him. She didn't want to do anything to jeopardize that.

Her own mother had kept her father's identity from Becca until Becca was eleven. But her father hadn't been a very successful man, and it hadn't been easy for Becca to locate him. In fact, she'd searched more than once for him but never found a trace.

And that had left an emptiness inside of her. Something no amount of soul-searching or club-joining could fill.

There had been other kids of divorced parents at her school, but she'd been the only one who hadn't known her father. Heck, she never even knew his real name.

She didn't want that for Ty. Not when she had an opportunity to give him a father—his real father. She'd have to do it, she thought.

She stood up and walked out the door with a purpose. Cam Stern was going to learn the truth about Ty today, and then she'd deal with the consequences because she wanted her son to have everything that she'd never had.

She wanted him to go to good schools and have new bikes and nice friends. But she also wanted him to have a father. To have a man who'd play catch with him and talk to him. And teach him to drive to someday. And she wasn't going to find a better man than the one who had unknowingly sired him.

Cam was still on the phone when she came out of the bedroom but looked up at her when he saw them. He smiled and then wrapped up his conversation. And despite her determination to tell Cam the truth, her determination to ensure that Ty had a relationship with his father, she faltered. Because she knew that Cam would never again look at her the way he did right now once she told him the truth.

* * *

Cam finished up his call. There was no way that Ty wasn't his child. He looked just like Nate and had the same cowlick that Cam himself had. But how was that possible? He wasn't a man who left things like that to chance.

Becca came back into the room holding the baby, and Cam waited to see how she would proceed. He was angry that she'd kept his son from him, but he wanted to hear what she had to say.

"I'm so glad our paths were brought back together. I felt like we had unfinished business after the way things ended," Becca said. "In fact I have something important to talk to you about."

"That sounds very cryptic."

"I hope that once I tell you...there's no easy way for me to say what I have to, Cam. I want you to know that the last thing I ever wanted to do was to hurt you."

"I repeat—that sounds very cryptic," he said. He glanced again at the boy.

"Oh, man, there is no easy way to say this."

"Just do it," he said.

"Yes. Um...sit down," she said.

As soon as he sat down, she popped up and paced away from him.

She shoved her fingers into her hair and pulled. "You're his father, Cam. I got pregnant when we were together."

"What?" he asked.

"You are Ty's father," she said. There—it was out in

the open, and now they could discuss it like two mature adults.

"I don't believe it."

"What's not to believe?"

"We used condoms every time."

"You know they aren't one-hundred-percent reliable, right?"

"Of course I do. But this has never happened to me before, so don't be snarky," Cam said, getting to his feet. He was the determined businessman she'd first met two years ago. A man used to getting answers. A man used to getting his way.

"I wasn't trying to be sarcastic. I just have been struggling to tell you about Ty and it never occurred to me that you'd doubt he was yours."

"That's where you made your mistake. I've had another woman accuse me of being the father of her child."

Becca put her hands up in the air. "I'm not going to argue with you about this."

"Of course you aren't," he said. "I'm not sure I can believe that I have son, but I see the resemblance and I suspected…"

"You do have one. I'm sorry I didn't tell you about him sooner but I never had any idea that you would care."

He turned back toward her, and she'd never seen anyone look angrier than he did. She took a step away from him, but he didn't walk toward her.

"How would you know that?" he asked.

"We weren't in a relationship, Cam. Don't you

remember—my boss didn't even know we'd slept together." She'd been so overwhelmed by Cam that she'd hardly been able to think of what to do. Two years ago...she'd been twenty-five, and no matter how adult and mature she'd thought she was, well, she wasn't. And Cam had made her feel...just feel. She'd had one other lover before him and it had been little more than a rushed coupling in a college dorm room. But Cam was a real man and he'd swept her away.

"Did you tell Russell?"

Becca felt horrified at the thought of her boss knowing she'd slept with one of his friends. She had kept that knowledge very close.

"No. Of course not. I didn't tell anyone. I don't think that Russell even knows I have a son. I told him I was leaving to start my own company. And he was my boss, not my confidant."

Each question was tearing at her confidence. She briefly wondered if she should have just kept quiet after all, then dismissed the thought.

"I got really sick a month after I left Miami and at first I figured it was just the malaise of a broken heart. I didn't realize I was pregnant until a few weeks after I got back home."

Cam ran his fingers through his hair. He was still sorting out the logistics of how things happened. Answering his questions brought back all those feelings she'd had when she'd learned she was pregnant.

"I almost called you. I didn't have any numbers for you but Russell's secretary had your office number. Do you remember her? Lani?"

"Yes, I remember her," Cam said.

"Then you will probably also recall that you were dating her cousin about that time," Becca said. "And I wasn't about to call you up and give you the news that you didn't want. At that point I wouldn't have been able to handle another rejection. It had seemed to me you had moved on."

"I guess it would. I still deserved to know I had a son."

"I know. I'm so sorry that I didn't tell you but I was in a pretty vulnerable state and you didn't seem like a viable option for someone to lean on," she said.

She crossed her arms around her waist and took a deep breath. "To be fair, back then we weren't anything but lovers. We didn't know about each other's lives or really even care. We just met up each night and had hot sex."

He looked over at her, his large blue eyes unreadable. He seemed so distant and so cold and she really didn't know what he wanted from her. She had no idea what she should say to smooth over this moment.

"That is a fair assessment of who we were."

"Yes, it is."

"Why did you decide to tell me now?" he asked.

She bit her lower lip and fought to find the right thing to say. "When I saw you last night, I realized I owe you the truth."

She was in an indefensible position. She knew what she'd done was wrong and there was no way to spin this. No way to turn it into anything other than the painful truth.

"Now I'm not sure what I believe. But I'm going to take your word that Ty is my son because I can't figure out why you'd make that up. Unless you thought you could get money from me?"

"Why would I need money from you?" she asked. Granted, she wasn't a millionaire like Cam, but she owned her own home and her business was doing very well.

"Everyone always needs more money," he said.

"I'm seeing a side of you I don't particularly like," she said.

"I could say the same. What kind of woman waits until her son is almost two years old to tell the father about him?" he asked.

"I just explained that to you," she said.

"I'm not buying it, Becca," he said. "I'm not buying into any of your act anymore."

"Stop talking to me like that," she said. "You are angry and you have a right to be, but you are just saying mean things right now."

"You're damned right I am. And I have a lot more that I'm trying to hold back. Nothing about this morning has done anything but make me doubt every word you've ever said."

"That's fine with me, Cam. Why don't you leave and we'll never have to see each other again?" she said. She marched over to the door and opened it.

But Cam shook his head. "I'm not leaving yet."

"Oh, I think you are," she said. "I don't care if we ever see you again."

"Sit down, Becca. We're about to come to an understanding and I'm not leaving here without my son."

Cam had never expected to hear anything like the news Becca had just delivered. He let anger roil through him because if he had a chance to think, he was going to be hurt and upset. Two emotions he wasn't about to let her know she'd caused.

"The first thing we will do tomorrow is to find a doctor who can do a paternity test."

"Why? I just told you that Ty was your son."

"I want an official document saying he is and then we will modify the birth certificate so that my name is on there," he said. Now that he was pushing aside the anger, there were a lot of housekeeping items that had to be tended to if they were going to sort out an arrangement for Ty that would ensure his welfare.

"Okay, I can see why you'd want that," she said.

"Good," he said, but he didn't care if she agreed or not. He had rights, and since she'd hidden his son from him since his birth, Cam intended to make up for lost time.

"Next up we will see my attorney and he will draw up papers for us to have joint custody. There will also be an agreement that states that none of my holdings or fortune will fall to you."

"Fine," she said. "This isn't about me, Cam."

He nodded. "That just leaves the matter of Ty moving down to Miami. I can't live in New York and I want my son with me."

"Wait a minute. I'm not ready to move," she said.

"Too bad. You and Ty are going to move down this week and you will live with me at my house. He needs his mother nearby to make this adjustment easier."

"What will I do there? My business is here."

"You will design the Mercado interiors for me."

"Are we going to get married?"

"Hell, no. I'm not about to repeat my father's mistake and marry a woman who puts her own needs first."

"That's not fair. I put Ty's needs first," she said.

"I will give you that," he said. "I have to make a few calls. Pack whatever you need for the next few days and we will leave on my private jet to Miami."

"I can't move that quickly."

"You don't have a choice," he said. "Either you do this or I take Ty and you never see him again."

She was shaking, and tears glittered in her eyes, but she still wore that determined, stubborn look. He knew that he was making her mad, but he didn't give a damn. He'd never felt as betrayed as he did at this moment.

"I will do the paternity test and I will agree to joint custody, but Ty will continue to live with me in New York. You can see him on the weekends if you'd like. But you aren't taking over his life or dictating to me about mine. If you'd been a different kind of man over two years ago, you wouldn't be so shocked now that you have a son."

"I'm not arguing with you about any of this. I know what I want and I will get it. You are welcome to hire an attorney and have him deal with mine. But my son is coming with me now."

"Fine, I will do that. I think it's time you left," she said.

"I'm not leaving without you and Ty. I can't trust you not to sneak off," he said.

"Of course you can. I wouldn't have told you about your son if I didn't mean for you to have a chance to get to know him."

"As noble as that intention is, Becca, it is too little, too late."

She just shook her head. "That's fine. I don't want to move, Cam."

"Too late," he said. "My life is in Miami and Ty's will be, too."

"I'm not giving up my son."

"Then go get packing. My secretary will arrange for movers to come and get your stuff."

"I will need to be here."

"That's your choice but you must know Ty will be staying with me."

"Dammit, Cam."

"Yes, dammit, Becca. How could you not tell me we had a son?"

"You told me I was mistress material and nothing else," she said. "Do you remember that?"

He did, but that didn't change the fact that she'd hidden Ty from him.

"I am not leaving until the movers have been called and I have a chance to talk to them. I will go to Miami with you but I'm not going to allow you to put me and Ty second in your life. If you want to be a father to him, then he deserves the best."

"What do you mean?"

"You can't be a workaholic and a good father. I understand you want to punish me but I won't let you punish your son."

Her words made him realize she was different than his mother had been when it came to her son. "I will be happy to put Ty first. Go pack up what you need. I will call a mover and get someone out here."

He stopped as it finally hit him. "Oh, my God, I have a son."

"Yes, you do," Becca said.

He ignored her and went over to Ty, who was playing happily with his toys. He stared at the boy, and Ty smiled up at him. Then Cam reached down and rubbed his finger over that soft cheek of his.

"My son," he said softly.

He stood there looking at the boy, and the anger that had been riding him since Becca made her announcement started to ease. He could never be mad at Ty or do anything that would jeopardize his son's happiness.

He looked over at Becca. "Why did you name him Ty?"

"It was my mother's father's name. I never knew him, so it seems silly to say he was my grandfather. His name is actually Tyler Cameron Tuntenstall."

"You gave him my name?" Cam asked.

"Yes. I...I knew someday he'd ask about you and I wanted him to have a connection. I know you think this is all some kind of conspiracy against you, but I made the only choice I could for my son. It was hard for me because I didn't want to follow in my mother's footsteps. I had promised myself that my children would have both a mother and a father."

Later maybe he'd be able to appreciate those words, but right now he couldn't. "I didn't think it was a conspiracy. I'm beginning to think it was pure selfishness on your part."

Cam turned and walked out the door without looking back. He knew she wasn't going anywhere in the time it would take him to line up a mover. Right now he needed some space. She'd knocked him for a loop, and he had no idea how he was going to recover. He only knew that his heart hurt.

Less than eight hours later Becca was seated on Cam's private jet and waiting for takeoff. Ty was seated next to her, his favorite stuffed animal—a yellow dog— and his blanket tucked close to him. He hadn't seemed too traumatized by today's events, and she had the feeling that he'd settle in to living in Miami more easily than she would.

Cam had arranged for a mover to get the stuff necessary for her and Ty to live in Miami. The rest of her belongings would be staying in the house. She had no idea what kind of strings he'd pulled, but the men had actually been at her house today and she'd told them what had to be boxed and moved. Her nanny, Jasper, would oversee the movers from here and in less than a week her belongings would be in Cam's house in Miami.

He sat across the aisle and hadn't said more than

two words to her since they'd gotten on the plane. The gentle lover of last night was clearly gone, and she had no idea how to reach him again. But she did know if she was going to move to Miami with her son, she wanted at least a shot at some kind of real relationship with Cam.

She wanted that picture-perfect family she'd always fantasized about. She knew she should try to break the ice but talking to him about Ty wasn't the way. Cam had demonstrated he was too volatile where their son was concerned.

Once they were in the air and could get up and move around, she took off Ty's seatbelt, but he was sleepy and nodding off in his car seat.

"There's a bed in the back," Cam said. "I can lay him down."

"Um…let me see the bed. We'll probably have to pile up some pillows around him. I don't want him to fall off."

Cam nodded. She reached over to unlatch the car seat and Cam was waiting right there. "I want to carry him."

"Of course," she said. Cam had been like this all day. He was genuinely trying to get to know his son, and she had been very careful to let him.

Cam lifted him, and his blanket fell to the ground. Becca picked it up and then followed them to the bed at the back of the jet. It was luxuriously appointed and very comfortable-looking. He laid Ty in the center of the bed, and they worked to put some pillows around him so he wouldn't roll off the bed.

"I am amazed that I have a son," Cam said.

"I am, too. He's such a precious little gift. I…my life changed the moment he came into it."

"I bet it did," Cam said.

He moved to leave the bed area, and she followed him. The jet pitched as they hit a pocket of turbulence, and Becca fell forward into Cam. He wrapped one arm around her as he fought to find his balance and keep them both on their feet. When the plane steadied, she looked up at him and he was staring down at her.

"Thank you."

"No problem," he said, but he didn't let her go. "I can't believe we are in this situation, Becca."

"What situation?" she asked. "Being parents?"

He shrugged. "That, but also moving in together. I still want you."

"I think we need to figure out how to be parents before we do anything else," she said.

"I would agree except for a pressing problem," he said.

"And that is?"

"I can't look at you without wanting to kiss you and make love to you. I want to strip you naked and take out all my frustrations over your actions on your lovely body."

"Sexual revenge?" she asked. His words thrilled her, sent molten heat pooling between her legs and made her nipples hard. She'd be lying if she said she didn't want Cam. That he wasn't the only man she thought of night and day.

"Yes," he said.

She shook her head. "Would you forgive me if I gave in?"

"I don't know. I think so."

She didn't know if she could do what he was asking. Being in his arms was one thing; knowing he wanted her just as some sort of way of getting back at her...well that wasn't exactly what she was into.

"Think about this," he said, lowering his head. His mouth took hers slowly and gently. She felt the warmth of his breath over her lips and then the first foray of his tongue rubbing over hers. His hand tightened on her waist and the other one went up to the back of her neck.

His fingers tunneled through her hair, and he held her head firmly in his grip as they continued to kiss. She wanted to think that this wasn't making her agree with his idea, but it was. It reminded her of how long it had been since she'd had a lover. And she wanted him; she wanted release.

She put her hands on his shoulders and slid them down his arms. He was strong and muscled, and she liked the way he felt under her touch. She continued touching him, finding his belt with her fingers and caressing her way along the edge of his waist to the center of his pants and the belt buckle. She tiptoed her fingers lower until she felt the hard ridge of his erection. She rubbed him through his pants, up and down until his hips canted toward hers.

He lifted his head and stared down at her. His eyes narrowed, and the flush of desire burnished his cheeks.

"Let me know what you decide," he said and walked back to his seat.

Becca stood there aching, wanting, and realized that Cam was still angry at her. She slowly walked to her seat and sat down, taking a magazine out of her bag. She flipped through it but didn't see the pictures or articles on the pages. She only saw herself and Cam, and she knew that if they were going to have a chance at a future together, one of them was going to have to bend. Was it going to be her? She wanted so badly for Ty to have everything she never had, and that included the family of her dreams. One with Cam.

Five

They arrived at Cam's house safely in the early evening. The drive was quick. The estate sat back from the road at the end of the palm-tree-lined drive. The yard was lusciously landscaped with blooming trees and perfectly mowed emerald-green lawns. The building itself was something out of a design magazine, and made Becca feel a bit like she had when she'd met Amelia. Out of place. She liked it, but it didn't look like somewhere she would live.

As she went in, she glanced around the high-ceilinged arched entryway and let out a low whistle between her teeth.

"Nice digs."

"Thanks," he said. She'd put Ty down, and he was

crawling toward the living-room area. "I will show you both to your rooms."

The little boy toddled over and tugged on his pant leg as he had earlier, and this time, Cam bent down and picked him up.

"Hello, there," he said to Ty.

"Hi," Ty said before putting his thumb in this mouth. He shook his head; Nate used to do the same thing when he was little. Cam's memory of that time was a little fuzzy, but this boy reminded him very strongly of his brother.

"How am I going to convince your mommy to just do what I want her to?" he asked Ty.

"Coffee," Ty said.

Cam lifted one eyebrow at the boy. Did he even understand what was being said? Cam suspected he did to a certain extent, but having a conversation with an eighteen-month-old wasn't going to give him any answers to Becca.

The boy held on to his shoulders as Cam turned to face Becca. There was something sweet about holding a baby—his son.

"I'll take him."

She held her arms out, but Ty didn't make any move to go to her. "Ty."

The boy took his thumb out of his mouth. "I like the man."

"I'm glad," she said, taking him from Cam and putting her son on a blanket where she'd laid out a couple of toys. She took Cam's hand and led the way to the hallway where they could still see Ty but he couldn't see them. "I...I wanted to talk to you."

"What about?"

"I..."

"Stop hesitating. You are a woman who knows her mind," he said.

"You have shaken me. I didn't expect to see you or tell you about Ty. Not like that. And then you kissed me and got me all hot and bothered but you want to make it about revenge and I'm not sure that's healthy for me."

"I think it would be excellent for me," he said. "But I am willing to talk to you about this. I'm still so angry, Becca."

"I get that. But we need—"

She glanced over at her son. And he saw the biggest change in Becca compared to the woman she was over two years ago. She had someone else to worry about when she made decisions.

"Is it because of the paternity suit that you're so bitter?" she asked.

"Not at all. I'm mad at you and you alone, Becca," he said. "You owe me an apology after the secret you kept from me. But if you choose to beg forgiveness in my bed, I won't complain."

She nodded. It was a moment of truth for them both. The chances of them changing each other's minds and actually getting to the point where they could trust each other were slim. He wasn't going to deny it.

"Don't judge me too harshly. I never knew my father. He left before I was born," she said.

"I'm sorry. My dad was the greatest influence on my

life. My mother wasn't very maternal, but my dad…I think you missed something really important there, Becca."

"I know I did. And I don't want Ty to grow up the same way," she admitted.

"I'm not making any promises," Cam said. "But you and I had something electric and I think it's time we explored it more fully."

His phone rang.

"Stern."

"Cam, it's Nate. I'm glad you are back because we have an emergency at the club. Some of the local leaders are raising a stink about the Mercado again. Can you get down here and handle it? I'm supposed to be upstairs with Jen practicing a waltz for our first dance for the wedding."

Jen was Nate's fiancée. Cam's little brother had fallen in love with the dance instructor at Luna Azul, and they were planning a wedding in less than a week's time. Love had hit Nate hard and Cam had a little bit of trouble believing it. But his brother had never been happier and Cam wished him the best.

"I'm on it. You go do your dancing thing. I'll be there in less than thirty minutes."

"Thanks, bro, you're the best. I want to hear all about the trip."

"I'll be happy to tell you about it later. Bye, Nate."

He turned to Becca. "I'm needed at the club. We can continue this discussion later."

"It's fine."

"Good," he said. "Becca, I know I said I'd put Ty first...not be a workaholic, but this is an emergency."

"I get that, Cam, but you said that family was important and we've just gotten to your house."

"In the future, I will be here more often. This is an emergency."

"Okay, but I'm not going to let you do it too often," she said, relenting.

He tipped his head to the side. He was still angry she hadn't told him about Ty, but he could see that she wasn't going to be resentful toward him about his work. "Thank you."

She just nodded. He pulled her into his arms.

She flushed and felt the stirring of desire deep inside her. She put her hands on his shoulders, then wrapped her arms around his neck. She lifted herself toward him. He rubbed his hands down her back, cupping her butt and bringing her closer to him.

She felt his erection nudging at the bottom of her stomach and looked up at him. It was a powerful feeling to know that she could make Cam react.

She leaned up to kiss him, but he controlled the embrace. His mouth moved over hers, and no matter how hard she tried to deepen the connection he wouldn't let her.

"Kiss me," Cam said.

She shook her head. "I want you to kiss me. I want to know that there is still a spark of something that's not motivated by your need for vengeance."

"Not yet," he said, rubbing his lips lightly over hers. "I want to make sure you really want me—and not just to get me to forgive you. You do want me, don't you, Becca?"

"I do," she said. "My entire body is vibrating waiting for your kiss. I hate to admit this but I've thought of you and our time together often in the last two years."

"Why do you hate to admit it?" he asked, stroking his thumb back and forth over the base of her neck.

"I think it makes me seem weak and gives you an advantage over me," she admitted.

He cupped her face with his big hands and leaned forward to kiss her so tenderly that she almost melted on the spot. Her knees weakened and her heart beat even harder in her chest.

"I will take any advantage I can get," he said.

He angled his head to the left and kissed her again. This time it was more passionate. He thrust his tongue deeply into her mouth. She shifted in his arms, holding on to his shoulders as he ravaged her mouth.

She wanted more from him. His tongue couldn't touch her deeply enough. She was aching for his weight to be more solidly against her. For his erection to be pressed against the apex of her thighs where she was so empty and needy. Her dreams of Cam had fed her libido for the entire time she'd been pregnant, when her hormones had been out of whack and she'd needed a man.

Now Cam was here and this was everything she remembered. The feel of him pressed up against her made her desire him even more. She wanted to touch his flesh, not feel him through his clothing. He shifted around until the wall was pressed against her back and he was pressed against her front. She lifted one leg and wrapped it around his hips.

He moaned and thrust his hips toward her. He rubbed himself along her pleasure spot until she thought she'd go insane from longing. She tunneled her fingers into his hair and held him to her as his mouth continued to taste hers.

He pulled back, breathing heavily. "I have to go," Cam said. His skin was flushed with desire, and she knew that leaving was the last thought on his mind.

She nodded and turned around to go get Ty. When she brought him back, Cam gave Ty a kiss on the head. His hands brushed Becca's and their eyes met. She said nothing as he walked down the hall and out the door.

Ty was the one man she could trust in her life. It was something she'd do well to remember; otherwise she was going to end up letting Cam Stern break her heart again.

Cam drove through the rush-hour traffic in Miami. He'd taken his new Tesla sports car and wanted to let the car run full out but knew better. He was the responsible Stern, the one who kept his own wants and desires well-hidden from the world, and he sure as hell wasn't going to let Becca change that.

He realized this wasn't the kind of car a family man should have. Hell. He was a dad. He'd had no way of planning for this. It was the one eventuality he *hadn't* planned for. He knew he could do it—he'd raised his brothers and given them a secure platform to launch from when their parents had died.

He'd do it for Ty. He knew he could be a good dad. But he had no idea what to do with Becca. She was the fly in the ointment of his plans for the future.

There was no discounting the sexual attraction between them, and he wished he could honestly say that he only wanted her in his bed…but he knew that he wanted her in his life. He really liked her as a mom. He knew that there were women who loved their children and would put them first. But this was the first time he'd actually encountered one. Then again, Becca had always been different. When their affair had ended, he'd felt her absence in his life. He'd wanted to somehow reconnect with her but…had been afraid of an emotional commitment. That had come back to bite him in the ass—now he had a son and a woman he wasn't sure what to do with in his life.

He pulled into the parking lot at Luna Azul and got out of the car. He walked toward the building and felt that sense of home he so often experience here. This was the place he'd poured all of his dreams and desires into. And the club had taken off. It was more than he and his brothers had ever expected it to be.

Luna Azul was in the heart of Little Havana right off Calle Ocho. It had been a cigar factory in its heyday but had closed and fallen into disrepair when Cam had found it and purchased it for a very good price. He'd decided to make it the premiere club in Miami and had done just that, transforming the former cigar factory's entryway with a Chihuly glass sculpture installation of the night sky showing two moons—a blue moon. And then decking out the rest of the club all in dark Latin tones. Upstairs there was a rooftop club that echoed the streets of Havana back in their pre-Castro glory days.

Now he knew he had to find something else to pour his energy into and Justin had suggested a club in Manhattan. Nate liked the idea because the A-listers there were more accessible than other areas of the country, but Nate had said he'd make it work wherever they wanted to open their new club. He had to think through he details, and he would need to start putting together a team to bring the project to life. They'd all agreed that another Luna Azul wasn't exactly what they wanted. They needed to make that club unique from the one in Miami.

Opening a club was time-consuming, which was why he'd always been into short-term affairs. He'd had to raise his brothers and he hadn't had for another emotional commitment.

"You look very serious, bro," Nate said, coming up behind him and patting him on the shoulder. "Don't worry. I calmed down the local leaders over the latest Mercado drama. We have a meeting set for tomorrow."

Cam turned and gave his brother a quick hug. "I'm glad. I'm thinking about the new club idea."

"Good," Nate said. His brother looked like he'd stepped off the pages of *GQ* magazine, which was why he was the public face of the company, the one who always showed up in the tabloid gossip columns. "What are your thoughts?"

His ideas were rough, but they were starting to take form. He needed something different. The club scene in

New York was just as competitive as in Miami, maybe even more so, and they'd need to be different to stand out.

"That we need something to reflect whatever community we are a part of up there. I was hoping to do something in Spanish Harlem."

"Really? Tell me more."

They'd played a key role in revitalizing the stylized Little Havana area here in Miami, and he was pretty sure they could do the same thing in New York. They just had to have the right idea.

"I know. I was thinking a retro-styled club that captures the glory of the old days. It might fit the city better than a Luna II-type deal."

Nate rubbed the back of his neck. "I like the idea, but it's really different from what we've done before. That will mean a new design team and everything. I think we should stick to doing what we do best and that's a Little Havana-style club."

"I have the perfect designer in mind for this new project. In fact, she's going to do the interiors on all the redesigns of the shops in the Mercado."

"Of course you know the perfect person. Cam, when are you going to realize that life isn't perfect? You always have every angle covered," Nate said.

Cam tried to always appear to his younger brothers as if he had it all together. It was easy enough when things were going well as they had been for the last few years. But when the company had initially struggled or when their parents had died and Cam had had to find the strength inside himself to step up and keep his brothers focused and happy, it had been hard.

"I try, but Nate, I know that life isn't perfect. We grew up in the same house, didn't we?"

"Yes. And I came out of it with my own baggage and lately I'm beginning to see that for you it's a desire to make everything picture-perfect. No faults allowed."

Was that true? "I don't think I'm that difficult."

"Listen, man, I love you. You're my big brother and you always have my back, but you are one demanding son of a bitch and I think that you should accept that nothing is going to ever be as perfect in the real world as you want it to be."

Cam tucked that nugget away for later contemplation. He wasn't going to change overnight or probably at all. He was too set in his ways.

"So who's the designer?" Nate asked.

"Becca Tuntenstall. She used to work for Russell Holloway."

"Are you sure she's the right choice? We don't want our club to look like Russell's." Nate scratched the back of his head. "It's hardly my area of expertise. I just want to make sure I'm asking the right questions now that Justin is out of state."

Justin was their corporate attorney and handled most of the legal problems that cropped up. Recently, he'd negotiated a deal with the local community leaders to launch the Luna Azul Mercado, an upscale shopping center to complement the nightclub. It was fair to all parties involved, and Justin had wrangled himself a fiancée out the deal.

Cam didn't know what was going on with his brothers up and getting engaged.

He smiled at his little brother. Nate had always been the charmer—the one who skated through life with a smile. Now he was stepping up, and Cam was proud of him.

"She's done some work for other chains, as well. She's the best designer for the job," Cam said. He'd already decided to give the assignment to Becca if she proved worthy. He couldn't uproot her life and not provide some work for her. Besides, he wanted her completely under his control. He was going to make her regret not coming to him when she'd first found out she was pregnant.

Nate's expression changed. "Is she more than a designer to you?"

Cam hesitated. He wasn't the type of person to talk about the women he was involved with, even to his brothers. Plus, she was the mother of his child... something that he had absolutely no idea how to tell his brothers. He wanted everything with Becca and Ty figured out and wrapped up before he said anything to either of them.

"Yes, she is."

"Wow. You haven't been seriously involved with a woman since Myra."

Myra had been a mistake, and he'd been too young and too eager to have it all with her. Myra was the woman who'd brought the paternity suit against him. Did he just have bad taste in women or what? Myra had wanted him to pay for another man's mistake, and Becca didn't think he was worthy of his own son.

"She's not really like Myra."

"I didn't mean to imply that she was. How about if you bring Becca to our rehearsal dinner Friday night? A nice casual affair, and I think it would be nice to meet this gal."

But Cam wasn't sure that he was ready for that. "I'll let you know."

"Why not?" Nate asked. "If you are serious about her, I want to meet her and get to know her."

Cam rubbed his hand over the back of his neck and tried to find the right words to say to his brother. "We had an affair a few years ago and it ended abruptly, so this time I'm trying to get to know her more slowly. Listen, there is more going on than a normal relationship."

"Hanging out with the family doesn't seem slow enough to you?" Nate asked.

"I don't know, Nate," Cam said. He stopped and took a deep breath. "Um...I have a son and Becca's the mom. I just found out about it and moved her down here, but I have no idea what we are going to do next."

Now it was Nate's turn to pause. His eyes widened.

"I have a nephew?"

"Yes."

"How dare she keep him from us?" Nate said.

Cam smiled. Nate was always there for him and Justin. They had always been close, and family was more important to them than anything else. "I said the same thing. I have her in my house with my son and I have to figure out what to do next."

"Um, I vote for suing the hell out of her and then cutting her off from the boy."

"She's not like that," Cam said. "Ty needs her. She quit a high-powered job so she could work from home and raise him."

"Damn. I liked it better when I could envision her as the evil bitch queen."

Cam laughed for the first time since Becca had told him he had a son. "Thanks, Nate. I need that."

"I do what I can," Nate said and then pulled him close in a bear hug. "I'm here for you whatever you decide."

None of the Stern men was really built for long-term happiness in relationships. He was very glad to see his brothers settled with new fiancées, but at the same time a part of him feared that it wouldn't last. And he wanted more happiness for them than their father had found in his marriage to their mother.

Cam had been watching after his brothers for so long that it was hard to realize he finally didn't have to really worry over them any longer. He was at a point in his life where he had everything set in motion. Now he could relax.

"How about brunch on Sunday at my place?" Cam said. "I think that will give me the time I need to get used to Becca being there and figure out where we are going next." Then he could control everything if he had them to his house. He was the kind of person who didn't like to be surprised by any eventuality.

He and Nate walked into the club, and, as always when he crossed the threshold into Luna Azul, he paused to appreciate everything he'd worked and sacrificed for to create. Jen was waiting for Nate and came over to them. Cam left them and made his way to the bar on the main floor. He needed to check on the situation with the Mercado and then meet with the head chef and make sure that everything was going well in the back of the house.

He told himself he walked away so quickly because there was work to be done, but he knew that it was really because he wanted what Nate and Jen had. Sure, he already had a son; now he needed to see what kind of arrangement he'd have with Becca. It couldn't be anything as pure as what Nate and Jen had, right? He didn't like himself for thinking that way, but he still felt so empty over the time Becca had stolen from him and his son.

Becca got out of bed in the middle of the night and walked out onto the porch. It was April, and the smell of jasmine was heavy in the air. She walked away from the house carrying with her the small listening unit to the baby monitor. She found a bench nestled next to the pool and sat down.

She knew that, for her, fear came calling in the middle of the night. It was the time when she felt most alone and most afraid of the decisions she'd made in her life. At this moment she felt she shouldn't be here in this house. Coming to Miami had been part cowardice—because she hadn't wanted to stand up to Cam—and part fantasy—because she'd hoped and prayed for some white knight to come and rescue her.

She didn't know if that made her a masochist because Cam was the man who'd left her high and dry. And while he wanted to play up the fact that he didn't know about Ty, in her mind it came down to the fact that he hadn't loved her.

She was here because…she glanced up at the moon and had no real idea why she was here. She felt lost in a way that she hadn't felt since her mother died. Even Ty's presence in her life, as unexpected as it had been, hadn't shaken her the way Cam had. And she had no earthly idea what to do next.

"Trouble sleeping?" The voice was deep and steady. Cam. Of course he'd be out here when she was.

"Yes. I keep trying to figure out what to do next," she said. No use lying to him or pretending a bravado she didn't feel. Tomorrow morning she might be stronger, but tonight she was lonely and confused and needed a pair of strong arms around her to tell her she wasn't alone.

"With what?"

"With you," she said.

"I already told you what I want. I want you. I'm not sure what to do with you once I have you but I know I'm not going to let you walk right back out the door."

"How about if we try to build a realationship together?" she asked. "Something slow where we get to know each other beyond the sex?"

"That won't work."

She couldn't really see his features since he was hidden by the shadows. He stood just out of the light provided by the landscape fixtures.

"Why not?" she asked. She shook her head and leaned forward to put her head in her hands. "I just need time to breathe."

She didn't hear him move, but a moment later his big hand was on her shoulder rubbing in a circle. "I can give you that."

She turned her head to the side and looked up at him. He didn't have on a shirt, just a pair of low-slung pj bottoms. It was hard for her to see him but she remembered that muscled chest with the light smattering of hair. She reached out and touched him. "I've dreamed so many times that you came back to me."

"You did?"

"Yes. It was so hard doing this alone and I wanted to tell you." She started crying, surprising herself with how much emotion she'd bottled up since Ty's birth. "You have no idea...it was only the echo of your words that you wanted a mistress and nothing more that kept my silence."

He stroked his hand over her head and then bent down and lifted her up. He sat down on the bench with her or his lap. "You still should have told me, but I understand why you were hesitant to. I'm truly sorry."

"I am, too," she said, looking him straight in the eyes. She had no place to put her arm but around his naked shoulder, and she did just that.

"I want to start over. But not from a place of anger," she said.

"I can try," he admitted. "But I'm not making any promises. What do you suggest?"

"It's obvious we both want to be parents to Ty. I suggest we try to work and live together for his sake."

"And sex?" he asked.

"I'd like to see it develop naturally," she said. "Not because of some arrangement. Or out of spite."

She held her breath. Hoping that Cam was the man she'd glimpsed earlier tonight while they'd played with Ty and made him supper. Hoping he could see that with all this anger between them, they were never going to be able to move on.

"Okay," he said. "But if you hide anything from me again all bets are off. Ty will be my son alone and you will have no rights to him. I'll make sure of that."

"I'm not hiding anything else from you," she said.

"I'm not kidding," Cam said.

"Neither am I," she promised. She wanted that family of her dreams too much to do anything to compromise it. And if Cam was offering her a second chance, she was going to jump on it with both feet.

He held her in his arms, and they both said little. His hands moved over her as she sat there just listening to the sound of his breathing. She knew that the answers she'd come here seeking were still just out of her reach. But she felt closer to her dreams of a real family and a man who she could trust than she'd ever been before.

When he tipped her head back and lowered his mouth to hers, she knew she should push away and go back inside. She knew that sex with this man wasn't safe for her. But she also knew that she'd been alone too long with only her dreams to keep her company—and that every one of them had been of him.

Six

Becca might need some breathing room, but all Cam needed tonight was Becca. He'd heard her leave her room. He'd put her in the room next to his so he could come and visit her at night once she became his lover again. And he'd had no doubt that she would become his lover. He was determined to have it all this time.

Becca's lie about their son had given him a nice safe place from which to approach this entire relationship. He didn't trust her, and that meant he was safe from falling in love with her. And love was something the Stern men weren't particularly good at. But making love to a beautiful woman—well, that was something else entirely.

And Becca was the only lover he'd never been able to forget. He skimmed his hands down her back and around her hips. He flexed his fingers and squeezed her before moving his mouth from hers.

He nibbled his way to her ear and traced the shell of it with his tongue. "Did you want me on the plane?"

"Yes," she said, her voice light and breathy. "Very much."

"Good," he said, rewarding her with a nibbling kiss at the base of her neck that sent shivers through her body. She shifted on his lap, arousing him even further.

"Have you thought about finishing what we started?" he asked.

She nodded. "But I have to ask you about your reputation as a playboy, Cam. Are you clean?"

That surprised a laugh out of him. "Yes, I am. I give blood regularly. Do you want to see my blood-donor card?"

She flushed. "No. I'm sorry if that made you uncomfortable."

"You had every right to ask," he said. "But tell me, Becca. I want to hear from your lips how much you want me," he said. He brought one hand down low between her legs, stroking her buttocks, and then he lifted her up so she straddled him on the bench.

The fabric of her nightdress fell away from her chest and he had a quick glance of her cleavage. He reached up, cupping her right breast. He rubbed his palm over the globe until he felt her pert nipple blossoming against his hand.

He leaned down and licked her shirt where her nipple was pressed, and she shivered again, her hips moving against his erection.

"Tell me," he said.

"I thought of nothing but that moment and wished you'd taken the kiss so much further," she said. "I want your mouth on my breasts and your hands all over me as I move against you."

Her words enflamed him, and he felt his erection strain against the fabric of his pajama pants. He pulled her night dress up and off her body and stared down at her breasts.

She put her hands on his chest and leaned toward him to kiss him. Her nipples rubbed against his chest, and he felt her rotate her shoulders so that they brushed through his chest hair. He put his hands on her butt and lifted his hips. His erection brushed between her thighs. She moaned and rode him a little harder, her hips moving back and forth without the motion of his hands.

She reached down between them and tried to free him from his pants. He lifted his hips off the bench and reached down to do it himself. Immediately he felt her wet hot core rubbing over his length. He groaned and closed his eyes, hoping to give himself a little breathing room, but he was ready to come. He wanted to be inside the velvet glove of her body. He wanted to hear her breath catch and then make her call his name again and again while he filled her.

"Are you on the pill?" he asked, barely able to get the words out. His voice sounded guttural and deep to his own ears.

"Yes. I am not trusting condoms anymore."

"Thank goodness," he said. He shifted her on his lap

and maneuvered his hips so the tip of his erection was poised at the entrance of her body.

She quivered, and he felt her melt as she started to push down on him. To try to take him. But he wanted to be the one to take her. He held her still with his hands on her hips and pushed up into her one slow inch at a time. She bit her lip and moaned deep in her throat. Her nails dug into his shoulders, and he felt her tightening around him, but he kept his entrance slow and steady. He wanted it to last forever because he knew once he was buried hilt deep, he was going to give in to the tingling in his spine that called for him to thrust into her until he came.

"Cam…."

"Yes," he said between clenched teeth.

"I need you," she said.

"I'm giving you what you need," he said.

"It's not enough," she said, her words like an electric spark in his nerve endings. "I need all of you filling me up."

He groaned her name and stopped torturing them both with his slow entry. Using his hands on her hips, he moved her up and down with a speed that drove them both toward orgasm with no chance to breathe or think. There was only the feel of her nipples rubbing over his chest. The taste of her tongue buried deep in his mouth and the feel of him wrapped so tightly in her sweet center that he thought he'd never want to leave her.

"Cam…I'm coming," she said.

Her words triggered his orgasm, and he pumped once more before he emptied his seed inside of her. She was breathing heavily, and he was covered in sweat as she collapsed against him. He wrapped his arms around her and rubbed his hands up and down her back. He tried to pretend that this was just a little game of getting his own way, but somehow in the midst of seducing Becca, he had been seduced himself.

Cam carried Becca back up to the house and tucked her into her own bed before he left. He wanted to stay and sleep in her arms, but he knew better than to give in to that desire. He walked across the hall to Ty's bedroom and stood over his sleeping son.

He felt as if he'd taken a punch to the chest when he realized that the little boy sleeping there was his. Not just his son, his and Becca's. She meant more to him than he'd ever admit out loud, and tonight had proven it. With any other woman he'd have kept his cool and seduced her on his own terms, but she'd made him lose it.

He leaned down and brushed Ty's hair off his forehead. He needed to make sure that Ty's future was secure. Cam's parents had died in a plane accident so their loss had been unexpected. Luckily, he and his brothers had been in their twenties. But if something happened to him or to Becca, where would Ty be?

He didn't want to take a chance on Ty being left with nothing or no one. His brothers would step in, but they needed to have wills and guardianship issues worked out. He left Ty's room and walked back to his own, hesitating in front of Becca's door.

He wished...hell, he wasn't some wussy guy who

wished for things, he made them happen. So why the hell was it so hard to get Becca to do what he needed her to do? Why was he standing out here instead of holding her in his arms?

Because Becca made him weak. He would never have forgiven a business associate who'd lied to him. And he knew whether he said the words out loud or not, he'd forgiven Becca. He didn't know if it was because of the sex—that would make it easier for him to explain to himself, but he suspected it was because of her tears and the fear she'd expressed so easily tonight. She didn't have all the answers to this parenting thing, and she was feeling her way the same way he was.

He didn't go into her room. That would send a message to her that she had him. Instead, he went down the hall to his office and sat behind his big oak desk.

Worn with age, the executive leather chair had been his father's. Cam had vivid memories of playing under this desk while his father had talked on the phone to his sports manager.

He sent an email to Justin initiating two things. The first was joint custody for Ty. The second was a will that would name his brothers as the guardians for Ty if anything happened to him. He didn't want to leave Becca on her own with no one again. And he knew that she'd never agree to sharing custody with his brothers, but he wasn't about to ask. Some things were just too important to leave to chance.

Feeling better about Ty's future, he got up to go back to bed when he got a text message from Justin.

You have a son?!?!

    Cam quickly typed in his response.

It's after midnight. Why aren't you sleeping?

Selena and I are working. Now tell me I read that email right you have a son?

Yes. 18 months old. Ty Cameron Tuntenstall. Can you do everything I asked?

First thing tomorrow. What about the mother?

She is living with me. I don't know where it will lead.

We need to talk.

Tomorrow or Friday night before Nate's rehearsal dinner party.

Selena's home so I'm going to let this drop until tomorrow. But I want to know what the hell is going on. We'll talk later.

    Cam walked over to the bar and poured himself two fingers of Johnnie Walker, slinging it back in one gulp. He had made mistakes in business and some of them had been costly, but they'd never made him doubt himself the way this thing with Becca and Ty did.

He didn't know if it was simply because he'd never intended to have a family of his own. Or because, having been presented with Ty, now he was starting to rethink himself and his entire life.

His brothers had settled down, and he wasn't sure that he ever would. But now that he had Ty, he sort of wanted to. Becca was an added complication. One he thought he'd have a better handle on if he had her back in his bed.

But sex hadn't made things any easier to figure out. That ticked him off. He poured another glass of Johnnie Walker and sipped it this time, taking the glass with him back to his bedroom. He walked in and didn't bother to turn on any lights. He went into the bathroom and washed up from earlier when he'd had sex with Becca and then padded naked back to his bed.

The moonlight streamed in through the one window blind he'd left open, and he stared at it. His dad had always said that with the moon to guide life's journey, nothing bad could befall them. But Cam knew his dad hadn't counted on a journey like this one.

He walked back across the room, pulled back the sheets and slid into bed.

Becca rolled over into his arms.

"What are you doing here?" he asked her, pushing himself back a few inches.

"I didn't want to sleep alone tonight. I'll do anything as long as you let me stay."

He couldn't push her away. Not when she'd given him the one thing he'd desperately wanted but had been prepared to deny himself. He pulled her into his arms and held her close as they both drifted off to sleep.

The next morning, Becca woke up to an empty bed and quickly climbed out and went back to her room. She was embarrassed that she'd been so needy last night but was determined to make today a much better day.

She showered and got dressed and realized she hadn't heard a peep out of Ty.

She raced across the hall to his room, but the crib was empty. She hurried downstairs and found the housekeeper, Mrs. Pritchard, in the kitchen.

"Have you seen Ty this morning?" Becca asked.

"I have. Mr. Stern took him with him to the golf course. He should be back in about twenty minutes. Breakfast is going to be served on the terrace shortly."

"Thank you, Mrs. Pritchard."

"No problem. Mr. Stern left word you weren't to be disturbed."

"I appreciate that. Yesterday was a long day. Moving is tough work," she said.

"So I hear. I've lived in the same house since I was born. My parents gave it to me when I got married."

"Really?" Becca asked.

"Yes, dear. They wanted to buy an RV and drive around the country."

"Did they do it?" Becca asked.

"They sure did. They are still out there on the road. My dad says he doesn't think he'll get to see everything before his time runs out."

Becca was touched by the sweet sentiment and

realized how much she'd missed by not having a father. This reinforced her belief that Ty and Cam needed to have a relationship. She took a mug of coffee to the terrace and sat there to wait for them.

Ten minutes later Cam walked out onto the terrace carrying Ty. Cam was wearing golf slacks and a polo shirt. Ty had on a pair of khaki pants and a matching shirt. "Good morning, Becca."

"Mama!" Ty said and squirmed to be released.

Cam set him down, and he toddled over to her. She scooped him up and hugged him close, peppering him with kisses and saying all the silly nonsense she said to him each morning.

"Thanks for letting me sleep in," she said to Cam.

"You're welcome. I figured you needed it."

"I did. Today we need to figure out what I'm going to be working on for you."

"Yes, we do. I think if you come to my office at the club later we can go over it. Ty is going to need a nanny," Cam said.

"Why? I usually keep him with me. I work at home," she said. "If you don't have the space, I can make a corner of my room into a home office. I just need room for my drafting table and computers."

"You can have a home office here, but at times you will be needed in meetings that Ty won't be able to attend with you."

"Good point," she said. "I'll figure something out."

"I took care of it already. Justin's fiancée has a cousin who is going part-time to college and she will be happy to nanny for us when we need her to."

"Us?" she asked.

"We are his parents," Cam said.

It was the first time he'd mentioned being a part of Ty's life long-term. She'd known that moving them here wasn't a temporary thing, but to be honest, she'd thought he'd reacted without thinking through what a life together would entail. And for the first time she saw him as a partner in raising Ty.

"Yes, we are. I want to meet with her before I agree. I don't want just anyone watching our son."

"She's not just anyone. I've arranged to speak to her this afternoon."

"We can do it together," Becca said. She realized, as much as she liked the fact that Cam was stepping up as a dad, she also resented his intrusion into Ty's life. She was used to being the only one who made the decisions for him.

"If you insist," he said.

Mrs. Pritchard brought out the breakfast trays and set them on the table. Ty munched happily on dry cereal on Becca's lap while she picked at a fruit salad.

"Friday night is Nate's wedding rehearsal and then dinner. I am going to bring Ty to breakfast that day to meet my brothers and I'd like you both to come with me to the dinner."

Becca nodded. "I don't have any plans."

"Good, because the wedding is on Saturday and again you are both invited to come with me."

"I'm not sure that's a good idea. Your brother might not want us there."

"Nate does. Family is important to the Stern men

and little Ty is the next generation, so he needs to be included."

Becca hadn't realized how much she'd deprived Ty of. She hadn't just kept him from a father but also from uncles. And in a family as close as the Sterns she knew that Nate and Justin wouldn't look too favorably on her actions.

"Do they know that I just told you?" she asked. Then put her fork down. "Of course they do. What did they say?"

"That I needed to watch my back and they'd support me in whatever course of action I decided to take."

She shook her head. "Course of action?"

Cam leaned back in his chair and looked her straight in the eye. "If I decided to pursue sole custody and take Ty from you."

She wrapped her arms around her son. "Would you do that?"

"No. Ty needs you too much for me to do that. But we had bad experiences with our mother...well, I've already told you about her. It makes them distrust you as much as I do."

"I've already said I was sorry."

"I know. You asked me what they thought of the situation," he said.

"I did, didn't I? I'm just not used to having any family. I didn't think about the fact that you have brothers."

"And I'm getting sisters-in-law, too. Our family is growing a lot, Becca."

"Our family?"

"I meant the Sterns," he said. Cam's phone rang, and he left the terrace to take the call.

She felt left out of something that she hadn't realized she'd wanted to be a part of until this moment. She sat there with Ty on her lap reflecting on how desperately she wanted Cam to be in her family.

Then again, she was going to be thrown into the Stern clan full force this weekend, and she knew she'd better be prepared to deal with hostility and a lot of personal questions. She thought about it for a long minute. Was Cam worth that? Was the chance to make her dream family into a real one worth being grilled by his brothers?

She'd have to wait and see.

Seven

Becca arrived at Luna Azul exactly at noon on Friday. She was still glowing after Cam had sent her a beautiful bouquet of flowers yesterday to celebrate the acceptance of her final design for her hotel project in Maui. She'd finished the job and her clients were very happy.

Cam was the first man she was romantically involved with to send her flowers. It was silly to let her heart melt over it, but it had meant the world to her.

Little gestures like this made it easier every day to overlook the autocratic way he had dictated her move to Miami.

The Florida sun was shining down on her; it was a beautiful April day. Just the kind of day that made her want to skip work and head to the beach or, if she'd been a different type of woman, plan some romantic surprise for Cam. But she had been avoiding any additional intimacy since the night they'd made love.

She stepped inside the club and paused under the blue night-sky Chihuly installation, remembering the last time she'd been here. She shivered a little and reminded herself not to lose her head around Cam the way she had the first time.

"Becca, welcome back to Luna Azul."

His deep, rich voice wrapped around her senses like a warm breeze on a cold day. She turned toward him and forgot to breathe. Though she'd just seen him this morning when they got Ty dressed, it might as well have been a lifetime ago. He had that kind of effect on her.

Cam's light brown hair was thick and disheveled, his features strong. He had that stubborn jaw and those big blue eyes that he shared with her sweet baby boy. He was tall and looked a bit leaner since she'd reunited with him in New York.

"Thank you, Cam." She smiled at him. She wasn't going to let him know how deeply he affected her. But it was too late—he already knew.

He walked over and leaned in to hug her, but she quickly and awkwardly held her hand out for him to shake instead. She didn't think she could handle a hug from him right now. She was trying desperately to be confident and calm and not let her emotions shine through.

But what she really wanted was to run into his arms. To wrap herself in him and just rest her head on his chest. And that wasn't going to happen. She couldn't let what she felt for Cam make her weak. She had to be strong for herself and for Ty.

She didn't want to get too used to having his arms around her, too used to his embrace. It was why she'd spent the last two days in her office buried in work. She didn't want to admit that she wanted him.

"This was a mistake," she said out loud.

He arched one eyebrow at her. "Already. We've hardly said hello."

"Trust me on this. I've got to go," she turned on her heel, prepared to beat a hasty retreat, but he stopped her.

His big warm hand rested on her shoulder, and his body pressed against her back. She melted. That was the only word for what was happening inside her body. Every part of her was enervated and quivered when he lowered his head and spoke directly in her ear.

"Don't go. We are starting over, remember? I'm not going to let you back out on this now. We made a deal."

She turned to face him and realized her error. His face was so close to hers that she was staring into those big blue eyes. His minty breath was washing over her lips, and it was all she could do not to lean over and kiss him.

She stepped back and stumbled. "I can't pretend that we are just doing business together and that you are just another client."

"I'm not asking you to," he said. "I think we made a good start the other night at rebuilding our relation-ship."

"I do, too. And thank you again for the flowers," she said, finding her equilibrium as her panic eased. "You didn't have to do that."

"Yes, I did."

She was touched. And realized that Cam might be seriously trying to make things work between them. She was, too. And she had to remember that. But all she could think about was his broad shoulders and that the last time they'd been this close, he'd kissed her socks off.

"Come upstairs to my office and we can talk."

She shook her head. "I don't think that is a good idea. You were going to show me the marketplace."

"Seriously?"

"Yes. I can't trust myself alone with you," she said.

He gave her a wicked smile. "Perfect."

"Ha. I came down here to work. I don't want to lose perspective and wake up two days later naked with you."

"I do."

"Cam. I can't do that this time."

"I know we're parents and both busy professionals. But you have been distant the last few days."

"I am worried about facing your family," she said, swallowing hard.

He arched one eyebrow at her again. He was the only person she knew who did that. It was arrogant and right now felt a bit condescending. "There is nothing to worry about. You and I are doing what we can to figure out how to be the best parents to Ty."

He was so wrong, but for this moment she wanted to

believe him. He held his hand out to her and she took it. He led her up the stairs past the rooftop club to a large office tucked behind some rehearsal halls. His name was on a brass plate on the wall. Once they were inside, he closed the door.

"Where is Ty?"

"I left him with his nanny," she said. In the end, she'd needed Jasmine, Selena's cousin. She'd liked the woman, too. She was young and used to being around kids.

"I guess you are wanting to say thank-you to me for finding her?" Cam asked.

"I guess so," she said.

"I think you owe me something for finding the nanny and averting a problem before it arose."

"Like what?"

"A kiss."

"A kiss? I thought we said none of that stuff," she said. "Unless I'm in the mood."

"This is just a thank-you between lovers," he said.

She licked her lips. She wanted to feel his mouth on hers and his tongue thrusting deep in her mouth. She knew the way he kissed. Loved the way his mouth moved over hers and she wanted to experience that again.

"Don't say things like that," she said.

"Why not?" he asked. "Before you say anything else, I want my kiss."

He walked over to her and pulled her into his arms. She knew she should put up some resistance, but she felt safe. As if the past wouldn't hurt them and as if all of her secret dreams were going to come true.

Becca stopped thinking as Cam's mouth moved over hers. He was everything she wanted.

He lifted her onto his desk and raised his head. "That would be a nice kiss if I'd helped you out with something small, but this is a nanny, Becca. I'm giving you the freedom to make your business bigger. I think I need more than just that little kiss."

He was in a good mood, she realized. He was teasing her and playing with her in a way that she knew would make it easier for them to actually build a bond together.

She wanted to argue, but the truth was she also really wanted this. She relaxed and let the material of her skirt slide a little higher on her thighs.

"Come here," she said.

He gave her a wicked grin before taking his first step toward her. He put his hands on her knees and slowly caressed his way up her thighs until the skirt was bunched at her waist. She glanced down and felt a shiver of delight go through her at the sight of his big, tanned hands on her slim, white thighs.

His thumbs stroked both of her legs toward the very center of her, and she felt herself moisten. She shifted on the desk, bringing her hips forward, trying to tease him into touching her where she needed it most. But he kept his touch light and thumbs teasingly close to her feminine mound.

She reached out and loosened his tie.

"No, leave it. I want to be dressed while you are almost naked," he said.

"I'm not almost naked." She squirmed. It did turn her on to have his hands on her while he was fully dressed.

"You will be. Unbutton your blouse," he said.

She reached for the buttons and undid them slowly. His hands moved in circles on the insides of her thighs, and each time she undid a button his thumb brushed over her hot, moist core. By the time all of the buttons were undone and her shirt hung open on her shoulders, she was hungry for more of him.

"Beautiful," he said.

She glanced down at her own body. Her breasts were encased in a pretty, cream-colored lace-and-satin bra. The demi cups revealed the full white globes of her breasts.

Cam moved one of his hands from her waist and tugged at the right cup of her bra until her nipple popped out. She watched his finger move around her areola as his other hand moved in the same circle on her intimate flesh.

"Cam…"

He slipped one finger under the crotch of her panties and his finger rubbed along her lips. He traced the flesh with his large, blunt finger. And surprised a moan out of her when he pinched her nipple.

The two sensations were too much. She felt everything in her starting to tighten. Her skin was flushed, her heart beating stronger and she needed his mouth on her.

She reached for his shoulders and drew him closer to her. He leaned down until his lips brushed over hers. She opened her mouth and felt the hot exhalation of his breath in hers. Then the tip of his tongue touched hers just as the tip of his finger found her opening. He slipped it inside and then back out.

His other hand kept circling her nipple, and she felt the delicate scrape of his fingernail over her as he rubbed his finger up and down.

She moaned and shifted her legs farther apart. "I need more."

He shook his head, his lips rubbing over hers. "This is all you get right now. I want to keep you right here on the edge of desire."

"Why?" she asked, shifting around, trying to make his finger on her intimate flesh touch her harder. She was so close to coming. It would take the barest brush of his fingertip to send her over the edge.

He moved his mouth along her cheek until he reached her ear. "Because I've been like this since I left your house."

He took her hand and brought it to the front of his pants. He was hard, so she stroked her fingers up and down him and then found the tip of his erection through his trousers.

She circled that tip with her fingers until she found the tab to his zipper and slowly lowered it. She reached in to the opening slit of his boxers and pulled him through it. His flesh was hot and hard in her hand, and he moaned her name as she gripped him.

He continued to cup her between her legs, rubbing

along the spot she needed him to, but he wouldn't bring her any closer to a climax. His mouth moved along the side of her neck. She felt the teasing edge of his teeth along that sensitive spot where her neck and shoulder met, and then he bit her so gently that goose bumps spread down her arm and chest, tightening both of her nipples.

He moved lower, teasing her with his mouth. With his tongue he traced the edge where the fabric cups of her bra met her flesh, and the first touch of his tongue on her nipple made moisture pool between her legs.

"Like that?" he asked. His voice was low and husky and arousing. It made her feel very powerful and sexy to be able to elicit a reaction from him.

"Yessss."

He caressed the very tip of her nipple with his tongue circling her flesh until she felt him suck it into his mouth. He suckled her as his fingers moved between her legs. Her grip on his manhood tightened as he drove her closer to a climax. She stroked him up and down as his fingers moved faster between her legs, and then everything convulsed inside of her and she threw her head back and cried out his name.

He still sucked strongly on her nipple as everything inside of her clenched and then released. She let go of him and brought her hands to his head, tunneling her fingers through his thick, chestnut hair and holding him to her.

He lightened his touch but didn't let her go. He turned his head on her breast, and she cradled him to her. It was nice but it wasn't enough. She wanted Cam inside of her.

"What are you thinking?" he asked.

"That I never want you to let go of me," she answered honestly, hugging him as closely as she could.

Cam had put off his pleasure as long as he could. He wanted to have a bond that couldn't be broken.

He pushed her blouse off her shoulders and leaned forward to undo the clasp of her bra. It loosened, and she shrugged it off, tossing it aside.

She couldn't be more beautiful. He ran his hands down her shoulders to her chest and cupped her breasts in both of his hands. She leaned back on her elbows and looked up at him.

It was the most sensual thing he'd seen in his life, and he knew the image of her like this—on his desk—was going to stay in his mind for a long time.

He played with her breasts until she reached for his erection, drawing him closer. "No more games, Cam," she said. "Come inside of me and make me yours."

He reached for her hips and lifted her with one arm while he pulled her panties down her legs and tossed them on the floor.

He glanced down at her almost bare body. She looked so sexy lying on his desk like a feast waiting for him.

She rubbed her finger over the moisture at the tip of his erection, then brought her finger to her lips and licked it. Her eyes closed as she sucked his essence from her finger, and he knew he couldn't wait another second to get inside.

He pushed her thighs farther apart and came forward, poised to enter her. The sensation of flesh on flesh gave him pause.

He looked down at her face. She lifted herself toward him, her mound rubbing against him. He groaned her name. Her breasts jiggled as she moved and he leaned down to take the tip of her nipple into his mouth. He suckled her, searching for something that could only be found with her.

She shifted her thighs, and he moved closer as she wrapped her legs around his waist. He nudged her opening and teased her by slipping just the tip of his erection in and out of her body.

She moaned his name, and he pulled back, looking down at her feminine secrets, which were exposed to him. He traced his finger over the smoothly shaven area.

She reached for his hips and tugged him forward. He entered her slowly at first and then plunged all the way to the hilt. She felt so good, and he told her so, whispering dark sex words in her ear as he pulled slowly out of her body.

Her skin was smooth and smelled of peaches. He just couldn't get enough. He kissed her neck, then licked the skin at the base of her neck.

He was addicted to the taste of her. The feel of her. She went to his head and consumed him. All he could think of was staying inside her body forever. He had it right a couple years ago when he'd taken her to his bed and kept her there for a matter of weeks.

He felt her tighten around him, and he wanted to

get deeper inside. Needed to take her as deeply as he could. He put his arms under her thighs and lifted her legs high, resting her heels on his shoulders.

She leaned back on his desk. Her pert breasts with their berry-hard nipples were tantalizing. He reached down and palmed her as he thrust even deeper into her body.

And it still wasn't enough.

He felt everything in his body driving toward climax. Tingles started to move down his spine as she reached up for his shoulders and pulled him closer to her.

She lifted her neck and shoulders and found his mouth with hers. She sucked hard on his tongue, and he responded by thrusting into her harder until her hips were lifting toward him.

She held him tightly to her, and she cried out his name as she came. He tried to hold on, not wanting to come so quickly, but everything inside of him clenched and he spilled himself at that instant.

He kept thrusting into her and felt her tighten around him again as she continued to come. Then he stopped and fell into her arms. She held him close. For the first time since she'd come back into his life, he felt a moment's peace.

This—she was what had been missing in his life up to this point. And having her again made him acknowledge that it had been a mistake to ever let her go. Becca was his.

"You're mine now," he said.

"Am I?" she asked.

"Yes."

He leaned over her on the desk, keeping their bodies connected. He kissed her softly and tenderly, letting the emotion of this moment overwhelm him. She was more than just sex to him, and he had no words to tell her but hoped that one small kiss would convey what he was feeling.

She wrapped her arms around him and toyed with the hair at the back of his neck. He could rest in her arms for a lifetime.

A lifetime.

She went to his head faster than anything else ever had. He'd always been disciplined, so alcohol and women had never been a distraction for him.

But Becca was.

Looking down at her at this moment, he realized he didn't want to spend another day without her by his side. He wanted to give her things she couldn't give herself.

There was something very rewarding in doing that, and he wasn't about to let her slip away. Or was he? It wasn't just Becca whom he was getting involved with. There was his son to think about.

The son she'd hidden from him.

He glanced down at her. She had her eyes closed sleepily. He knew she wanted to stay in his arms—and he wanted her there. But too much. At some point she'd become too important to him, and that was dangerous. He needed distance.

He pulled back. He wasn't ready for this type of feeling or commitment.

He pulled out of her body and handed her some tissues from the box on the corner of his desk. He couldn't think of anything to say as he turned and walked to his private washroom.

Then he looked at himself in the mirror and knew that no matter how much he wanted to pretend that nothing had changed between him and Becca, it had.

He had no idea how he was going to go back to being the man he'd been before. The man who had a barrier between himself and everyone except his brothers. Damn, she'd shown him that he was vulnerable. Something he'd never wanted to admit or acknowledge before.

But now he wasn't sure he wanted to go back to his old life. And he'd never been the kind of man who didn't know what he wanted. He wasn't going to let Becca slip away, so he had to figure out how to keep her in his arms *and* keep the space between them that he needed for his life to stay on track.

Becca was everything that he needed to make his life the complete package. But he didn't want to lose his head and forfeit everything he'd already worked hard for.

Eight

Becca hopped off Cam's desk as soon as he closed the bathroom door behind him. She found her panties and bra and quickly put them back on. Making love had seemed the right thing to do, but after he'd walked away she felt small and vulnerable.

More vulnerable than she'd expected to. The last time they'd had sex she'd just felt fulfilled. But she knew this time the stakes were much higher. She wanted Cam to be more than her lover. She wanted the little pretend family they had to be real.

She put her blouse on and buttoned it swiftly. She put her shoes back on and stood there for a few more minutes, wondering what she should do. She wanted to leave but that didn't feel right.

It was clear that making love had affected Cam as

deeply as it had her. The thing she didn't know was *how* it had affected him. For her it had felt like the confirmation of everything she'd been longing for. For him...well, she had the feeling that he wanted to pull back and put some distance between them.

She was tempted to leave right now. She heard the toilet flush and realized he was going to be back out in a minute. Was she staying or going?

She started for the door but stopped as she heard him behind her.

"Where are you going?" he asked.

"I wasn't sure you wanted me to stay," she said. What she really wanted—no, needed—was a hug. She needed his arms around her so she wouldn't feel so alone and so damned fragile. But the look on his face said there wasn't going to be any cuddling. Not now.

"I'm not sure either," he said. "I thought that having you would ease the tension between us, but I may have created more problems."

She swallowed hard. "I don't know. I wanted to be your lover and spend every night with you. You were right—living together and not sleeping together is weird."

"Me, too, but we are still strangers. Sexually compatible strangers, but maybe we need to cool it for now."

She nodded. "Um... I need to go home and have a shower before the rehearsal dinner."

"Why?"

"Because I can still smell you on my skin and I need to be thinking with my mind and not my hormones if I'm going to meet your brothers."

"I like the thought of my scent on you," he admitted. "And I want to talk about the Mercado before you go home. If you stay on that side of the desk I think we can conduct business and then you can go home. I will pick you up at seven."

She nodded. He talked about what he wanted for the Mercado, and she took copious notes. When he was finished, he walked around his desk. He turned to the credenza along one wall and picked up a portfolio. "This contains the design specs for our new project. Take it with you and look it over."

She took the leather binder from him, and when their hands brushed against each other, she shivered. She still wanted him. During their affair two years ago they'd spend an entire afternoon making love. And to be honest, now that her body had had him again, it craved more. She craved more.

Why was Cam the one man in the world who could make her feel like a sex-crazed teenager? It had been that way from the beginning, and she shouldn't have been surprised that two years later nothing had changed.

"Why are you staring at my hands?" he asked.

"I was remembering the way they felt on my body," she said.

He cursed low under his breath and put his hands on her waist, drawing her closer. "I was thinking the same thing. This starting over is hard."

"Yes, it is. I wonder if we are making a mistake," she said, tipping her head back so she could look up at him.

She wanted to see a sign in him that everything was going to be okay but his dark blue eyes were unreadable. There was no sign. And she felt foolish for even looking. Since her junior year in college she'd been on her own. Why should now be any different?

She was the one who took care of herself and made sure that she had what she needed. Cam wasn't going to be her hero or her white knight. That wasn't the kind of guy he was.

He was a modern man who expected the woman he was involved with to be her own savior. And it didn't matter one bit that all she wanted was to cuddle close to him and rest in his arms. That she wanted some kind of comfort from him and the assurance—no matter how false it was—that everything would be okay.

"No," he said. "This wasn't a mistake. I won't let it be." He kissed her tenderly on the forehead. "I'm sorry I'm rushing you out the door, but Justin just got back to town and I have a meeting with him and Nate in twenty minutes. You have made me forget about work."

"Oh, okay."

"I had no intention of seducing you this afternoon. But I'm glad I did."

"Are you sure?"

"No. But I don't regret it and I think if we ignored this side of our relationship we'd be starting over on a lie and I don't want that."

She flushed and nodded and walked away without saying another word.

* * *

He felt as if he was missing something important but had no idea what it was and could only watch her leave.

Calling her back to him would be the right thing to do, but he needed some space. Some distance to figure out who he was and what he should do next.

He had never encountered anyone who shook him up the way she did. He wanted to pick her up in his arms and lock the door and make love until they didn't have the strength left to lick their lips. But that wasn't going to happen.

He also wanted to make sure she knew that she was more to him than a lover. He had to keep reminding himself that he was moving on to another stage in his life. But he didn't want to put the white-hot lovemaking with Becca behind him.

He realized that the two of them were always going to be incendiary, and nothing was going to change that. He just had to figure out how to manage that part of the relationship.

Added to that was the fact that they were parents. Ty was important to him and Becca was important to Ty. So they were tied together in way that he hadn't anticipated. A way he'd never been attached to someone before.

He sank back in his chair and tried to concentrate on business. It had never been hard for him until now. He knew where his focus needed to be, but Becca challenged that. He wasn't going to be an absentee father to Ty. Not that he wanted to be but, honestly, he knew more about babes than babies and he was struggling to find his way with his son.

There was a knock on his door and he beckoned the person to enter. It was Justin and his fiancée, Selena. Cam got up and walked over to his brother, embracing him.

"Glad to have you back home," Cam said.

"Good to be here," Justin said.

Cam leaned over and gave Selena a kiss on the cheek. "Have a seat, you two, and I'll tell you about our problems."

"With the Mercado?" Selena asked.

Selena was a beautiful Latina with olive-colored skin and thick ebony hair. She was petite and curvy. And she had eyes only for Justin. Something that always made Cam feel good. He liked seeing his brothers with women who clearly adored them. He wasn't sure if it was because his mother had been so cold or not, but he had never thought any of them would find a woman they could be that comfortable with.

At moments, he thought that he might find that with Becca. But he doubted it. He'd have to relax his guard around her and she'd have to do the same and they were both wary of each other to do that.

"Yes, with the Mercado. We need to close down the businesses while we are doing construction," Cam said.

"I thought we'd already agreed that you would keep them open," Selena said.

Selena had been the big-gun New York City attorney

that the Mercado merchants had hired to repre-
sent them.

"We did. But there are safety concerns."

"What concerns?" Justin asked.

"We can repair the sidewalks and redo the facades
while the businesses are open. Some of the repairs can
wait until we have a new design in place but there are
concerns about the cracked sidewalks and the parking
lot is a mess. It's not safe to have people in and out of
the shops while we have that machinery there," Cam
said. He knew that the business owners were concerned
about their bottom lines but safety was important, too.
They were flirting with a lawsuit if someone got injured
during the construction phase.

"I'm sure they don't want anyone to get hurt," Selena
said.

"Tomas is stubborn, Selena. Your grandfather argues
with me about everything. Even if he knows that I'm
not trying to hurt his business, he still has to make me
negotiate everything."

Justin started laughing. "I will see what I can do. He
is always looking for a little more."

"Yes, that's it exactly. Now that business is out of the
way…we need to talk about Nate's bachelor party."

"I think that's my cue to exit," Selena said. "I'm
going to my *abuelita's* house, Justin. Meet me there
later?"

"Yes. I think we'll be done in an hour or so."

"Perfect," Selena said. "Bye, Cam."

Selena left and Cam was alone with his brother.

"Becca is going to be at the party tonight...I want you to be...well, nice."

"Geez, Cam, I'll try."

"Good. That's all I ask. Nate is stoked about the wedding," Cam said, changing the subject.

"I know. He keeps texting me about what Jen did or said. It's funny, I never saw him as a family guy, but then I never expected him to quit playing pro baseball, either."

"Life has a way of making you change," Cam said. Realizing that life was doing that to him right now. He had to change or lose Becca and Ty.

"Yes, it does. I think I'll walk over and talk to Tomas, then meet up with Selena. Do you need me for anything here?"

"Nah, I'm good."

Justin left, and Cam went back to work on some details for the tenth-anniversary celebration.

When she got back to Cam's house, Becca walked into her room and tossed the portfolio on the bed. There was a note from Jasmine saying that she and Ty were down at the pool. She kicked off her shoes and fell back on the bed. Staring at the ceiling, she searched for answers. Just once she'd like something in her life to go easily.

She wished her mom were here so she'd have someone to talk to. Becca knew that if her mom were alive, she'd have some good advice about what she should do. Her mom had always been a big proponent of truth and consequences. And Becca knew if she'd sent Cam a letter or told him about Ty when she'd first gotten pregnant, she wouldn't be in this predicament now.

She rolled over on her stomach and stared at the luxury room. The scent of Cam lingered on her skin, and the feel of him seemed to be imbedded in her senses.

She got off the bed and went to the bathroom, showering off Cam and what had happened between them. Tonight when they had dinner, she'd see how he treated her around his brothers. She was keen to know if they were really a couple in his eyes or if she was still just his secret lover.

She emerged from the bathroom determined to take control. Since Cam had forced her to move down here, she had to let the situation dictate what she did and how she acted, but now she had be the one in charge.

She took the portfolio that Cam had given her and opened it. Work had always been her solace, and it was now. The design specs were right up her alley, and as she read over them, her mind was filled with visions of how to bring the Stern brothers' desires for the Mercado to life.

She started sketching and drawing and making notes, and when Jasmine and Ty came back from the pool almost two hours later, she had the beginnings of a spec design for Cam.

She stopped working and held her son in her arms. After a while, she sent the nanny home and went to bathe him. She wanted them both to look their best when they met Cam's brothers. She was so nervous, she could hardly think straight.

She smiled, but her heart wasn't in it. This thing with Cam was a black cloud hanging over her. It would continue to be until she knew what it was he intended for the two of them. Would they just continue to live together and raise their son and make love? Or was there going to be something more? Already she felt her emotions building, and she knew she was very close to falling in love with him again.

She looked at herself in the mirror and saw how lost she looked.

"Ah, Becca, don't look so sad. You have a wonderful son and a good life. If Cam is half the man you believe him to be somehow this will work out," she said to herself.

She'd been alone too long, and she wanted what every mother wanted...to have the father of her child in her life and to create a family.

She didn't know if the desire was keen for her because she'd never had that nuclear family growing up, but she knew that it was important to her and she wanted it.

After getting Ty dressed, she cuddled him close to her so that she could find some solace in holding him. And waited for Cam.

Cam showed up promptly at seven to pick them up. Earlier this week, he'd bought a new SUV for them to drive Ty around in. Yet another sign that he was warming up to being a father. Cam got out of the car and took Ty.

"You both look nice. The rehearsal went well and I

think you are going to find my brothers on their best behavior."

"Why?"

"I told them that we were trying to do right by Ty and I don't want them to make you feel uncomfortable," Cam said as he buckled Ty into his car seat.

"Thank you, Cam."

"It was the least I could do. I did drag you down here and install you in my home. It wouldn't be fair of me not to look out for you."

Her heart melted. This was what she'd been waiting for. For the first time since she'd made that decision to let Cam manipulate her into coming here, it felt like the right one.

She leaned over and kissed him hard on the lips. "Every time I think I have you figured out, you do something unexpected."

"Good," he said. He opened her door for her and she got into the car. She watched him walk around the front and climb behind the wheel.

"I never thought Nate would settle down with one woman," Cam said.

"From what I've read, he always did seem to be the ultimate playboy."

"Part of that was for the club. He has always used his celebrity to keep patrons packing our dance floors."

"It's obviously worked," she said.

"Yes, it has. When I first had the idea for the club I never imagined that Justin and Nate would find the work as fulfilling as I did. I really just wanted their help financing the business and an excuse for us all to have to stay close."

"And instead you created the hottest nightclub in Miami and your brothers are your best friends."

Cam tipped his head to the side to stare at her as he braked for a traffic light. "They are. I hadn't realized it until you said that. Who are your friends, Becca?"

She shrugged. "I have some casual acquaintances at the Mommy-and-Me program in Garden City, but I'm really not the type of person who shares much with others."

"I can vouch for that. You are a very hard woman to figure out," he said.

She really wasn't, but she was glad he thought so. She hoped it added to her mystery to have him not too sure of her.

He pulled to a stop at Luna Azul a few minutes later.

"What are we doing here?"

"The rehearsal dinner is at the rooftop club. It's where Nate and Jen met."

"Great. Can we bring Ty?"

"Definitely. Someday this is going to be his club and he should start getting used to the place now."

Cam opened her door before getting Ty out of the car seat. As they approached the club, Cam held Ty in one arm and had his other around Becca. She caught a glimpse of them in the reflection of the glass door as they approached, and they looked like a real family. The one she'd always wanted for herself.

* * *

The nightclub wasn't really suited to kids, but there was a family atmosphere to the rooftop club tonight in addition to Nate's A-list celebrity friends like Hutch Damien, the rapper turned actor, and several New York Yankees players both past and present. Jen had brought her family. And Justin's fiancée, Selena, had brought her grandparents and several cousins.

Nate waved Becca, Cam and Ty over as soon as he saw them. At the same time, Selena's cousin Jasmine came up to them and took Ty away to meet some of the other kids. "You two enjoy yourselves. I will watch little Ty."

"Are you sure?" Becca asked.

"He'll be fine," Cam assured her.

Cam grabbed two mojitos off the tray of a passing waiter and handed one to Becca. "Just be yourself."

"I don't know how to be anyone else," she said.

Damn, if that wasn't true. It gave him an insight into why she was so special to him. But he didn't have time to analyze it.

"Hey, big bro," Nate said, hugging Cam. "I'm so glad you are finally here."

"I am, too. Nate, this is Becca Tuntenstall. Becca, my youngest brother, Nate."

"It's so nice to meet you," Becca said, holding out her hand. "Congratulations on your upcoming marriage. I'm looking forward to meeting Jen."

Nate took her hand and shook it. "I want to know about my nephew."

"Ask me anything," she said. "I love to talk about Ty."

Cam stepped back and watched as Becca did that for about fifteen minutes. It was clear to him and to Nate as well that Becca loved her son.

"Let me go get him so you two can meet," she said.

Becca walked away before Nate or Cam could say anything, and they just watched her go.

"I like her," Nate said.

"Good. I do, too."

"Yeah, I kinda figured that out by the way you keep watching her."

Nate laughed.

"So are you ready to settle down with Jen, little bro? Is the whole domestic routine treating you well so far?"

Jen stood off to the side, talking to her sister and nephew. She was animated during their conversation. She held her nephew's hands and danced to the music with him.

"More than I thought. I mean, I like a good party but I don't have to do a club crawl every night to feel like I'm alive. I get that from Jen."

Cam was relieved to hear that but also a little worried. Nate was the one who made sure that Luna Azul kept drawing the celebrity crowd and stayed in the paper.

"What about our publicity?"

"Don't worry. I've got you covered. I blog from here and already sent in some photos from earlier tonight. And when you guys leave I'll hit Luna for a few minutes before calling it a night."

"That's a bit of an odd schedule," Cam said.

"Yes, but it works for us. Jen likes spending the evening with me."

"That is a very good thing. I wonder what Dad would make of this," Cam said.

"He would probably go running for the hills. As much as he loved us, I don't think this was his kind of gig," Nate said.

Cam looked around the rooftop and wondered if Nate had a point. Perhaps domestic bliss hadn't been in the cards for their parents. But at least their father had loved being a dad. And that was important.

"Are you sure you are ready to tie the knot tomorrow?"

"Positive."

"Good. I'm happy for you," Cam said.

He glanced over to see Becca coming back with Ty. Just then, Cam thought that Ty was going to need some cousins.

He turned back to his brother. "Have you and Jen considered having kids?"

Nate nearly dropped his drink, which made Cam laugh. "I'll take that as a no."

"You just asked me about clubbing—you know a dad doesn't have time for that stuff. And Jen's a dancer, so she has to think good and hard about what she'd be giving up before we even entertain that idea."

"Okay, that's the stock answer you guys give everyone. I'm your big bro, so what's the real deal?"

Nate turned and looked over at his wife. "I've thought about it a lot, but the subject hasn't come up between us. And I don't know if I'm ready, Cam. The last thing

I want to do is have a child and not be the parent that Dad was."

His words resonated with Cam. Their dad had been a great father, and living up to the old man would be hard. But when Cam looked at Becca and Ty, he wanted to be a parent. He wanted to be the missing piece in their little family.

And that didn't fill him with panic the way it once would have. He thought that was a good indication that he was on the right the track with Becca. That she was the one.

"I guess you think about it," Nate said.

"I didn't before Becca came back into my life."

Cam rubbed the back of his neck.

"I bet."

Becca walked right up between them. "Ty, this is your uncle Nate. Nate, this is Ty."

Nate looked down at Cam's son, and Cam felt a moment of familial bonding that until now he never could have imagined. He was glad to see his brother and his son together. And when Nate held out his arms to Ty and Becca handed him over, Cam realized he'd made the right choice in going after joint custody and in naming his brothers as guardians in the will.

"He is so cute," Jen said as she came up to them.

"My brother sure is," Cam said with a wink.

"I meant your son. But I have to agree—my husband is a hottie."

She slipped her arm around Nate's waist and looked up at Cam. He was very happy that his little brother had found a woman who loved him. And that that love was clear for everyone to see.

"I am a hottie," Nate said. "I think the entire world knows that."

She laughed. "Gosh, I hadn't noticed."

Nate kissed her soundly on the lips and then smacked her butt. "Smarty. Everything is almost ready here. Go get ready for our dance."

Jen pinched Nate's butt. "I will but only because I'm the one who thought of the idea to get everyone in the party mood."

Cam laughed at the two of them as Jen walked away. There was something welcoming and refreshing about being in their presence. Nate handed Ty back to Becca.

"I don't pretend to understand what's between you and my brother," Nate said. "But I'm glad you and Ty are here."

"Me, too," Becca said.

"I have to agree," Cam said. "I'm very glad to have you both in my life."

Nine

Becca hadn't expected to enjoy herself as much as she did at the rehearsal dinner. But when the music started and as the mojitos kept flowing, she found herself on the dance floor with Cam.

"This is where it all started," he said.

"The dance floor? We met in Russell's conference room," she reminded him.

"No, that's the past, when we were too involved in ourselves to figure out what was really important. I knew when I danced with you in New York that something had changed. You weren't the woman I had known before," he said, spinning her around as one of Shakira's slow, sexy ballads played.

"I'm definitely not the same woman. It was hard

for me to be attracted to you and know I had a big secret."

"I bet. Did you think about running away?" he asked.

It was the first time they'd really talked about everything, and she was glad to finally have the chance. "For a minute. But I had Ty to think about. And once I talked to you that night I realized there was more to you than just a sexy guy I had an affair with. I'm not sure how to say this, but I think you were right to tell me I wasn't in love with you two years ago."

"You do? Why?"

"I didn't know you at all. If you had taken me up on my offer…we would have been married with a kid and both felt trapped and miserable," she said.

"Or would we have uncovered the truth about each other as we have these last few weeks?"

"I'd like to think we would have, but I don't believe in fairy tales anymore."

"Did you at one time?"

"Yes. When I was young. I spent a lot of time dreaming up where my dad was and making up excuses for why he never came to see me."

"Ah, Becca," he said, pulling her close in his arms. "I'm so sorry."

"It's not your fault," she said. "Life is like that sometimes. Then other times the man who you cursed for being a jerk shows up and turns out to be a hero."

"Me?"

"You."

He leaned down to kiss her. And saw his brother walk up right behind her on the dance floor.

"No need to ask who this is," Justin said. "Your son's mother, I presume."

"I am Ty's mother," Becca said, turning to confront Cam's other brother. "You must be Justin."

"I am. I'm also the family attorney. Did he mention that?"

"Back off, Jus."

"I'd be happy to if I could understand why she kept your son a secret for so long," he said.

"Cam had told me he wasn't ready for a family and I am a loner. I like to do things on my own. That's the only explanation you are going to get," she said.

"That's more than he deserves. I told you not to bring this up tonight," Cam said.

"I'm sorry, Cam. I don't like the feeling that she's trying to pull one over on us," Justin said.

"She's not."

"I'm not," Becca said at the same time. "I didn't trust your brother to be a good man."

"I didn't see it that way," Justin said.

"That's because you are used to seeing the worst in everyone," Selena said, coming up net to her fiancé. "I'm Selena Gonzalez, by the way. You must be Becca."

"I am. Nice to meet you," Becca said, holding her hand out to Selena.

"You, as well. Please excuse Justin. He just—"

"Doesn't want to see his brother treated poorly," Justin said.

"I'm not treating him poorly. That's why Ty and I are here," Becca said.

"I'm sorry for being so rude," Justin said, easing up a little after a moment's pause. "I don't trust people who keep secrets like that one."

Becca nodded. "I don't trust men."

Cam looked over at her. "Do you now?"

"Yes," she said.

"That's all that matters," Cam said. He pulled Becca back into his arms and danced her away from Justin.

After that, Cam held her close for the rest of the night until it was time to go home. He collected Ty from Jasmine, and when he left with his son and Becca, for the first time since his dad died, Cam felt like he had something of his own.

When they got home, he watched Becca tuck their son in and felt another surge of some emotion he refused to define. She turned to catch him staring at her.

"What?"

He waited until she was out of Ty's room, and then he pulled her into his arms and whispered hot needy words in her ear. Told her exactly what she made him feel and how happy he was that she'd come back into his life.

He carried her into her bedroom and placed her on the center of the bed. He reached up under her dress and pulled off her panties and then opened his own pants and slid inside her. He rested there for a minute and looked down at her.

He kissed her long and hard, the way he'd wanted to

since he'd pulled her into his arms. His tongue rubbed over hers as his hands swept over her body.

"Thank you for my son," he said.

"You're welcome," she said. "Now make love to me."

And he did. He made love to her, and then when they were done, he undressed them both and slowly built them to a fevered pitch again. He held her in his arms all night and didn't question the fact that he'd never had a relationship with a woman feel as right as the one he had with Becca.

He held her through the night, awake while she was sleeping, and watched her. She had changed his life, and he had no idea what he was going to do with her.

Marriage didn't seem to be the solution. Becca was used to being alone and he didn't want her to feel trapped. There was a reason beyond his callous behavior that she'd kept Ty to herself.

Though his brothers were getting married, he knew that the institution wasn't necessarily for him. He did know that he wanted Becca to stay in his life and in his home, and he wanted to figure out a way to make her presence here more permanent.

He drifted off to sleep without finding a solution, which later on would bother him. He was the kind of man who always had to solve a problem before he could sleep. But not with Becca.

It was odd to him, but he finally thought he was coming to trust her. And that scared him almost as much as the fact that he needed her.

* * *

Her cell phone rang a week later, and she glanced at the caller ID. It was Cam. "Hello."

"Hi, Becca. I have an emergency meeting with the community leaders at the Mercado. We are supposed to have one of the tenth-anniversary events there and I thought you might want to come and join me."

The week had been hectic. Nate's wedding was beautiful and had made Becca long for something more with Cam. She knew she should be content with what they had—it was more than she ever dreamed of. But a part of her—that little girl who'd waited for her own family to be complete, she suspected—wanted Cam as her husband.

She'd continued to work on designs for the Mercado and was slowly settling into a routine here in Miami. Cam had adjusted his schedule and had early dinners with her and Ty before he went to the club at night. He was making time for Ty, which was what she'd asked for, and she saw the signs that he could be a very good dad.

Though they hadn't really discussed it, she felt as if they'd found a new truce and were moving toward a committed relationship. There was a certain peace between them. Justin still didn't seem to trust her, but Nate and Jen had been friendly each time she'd seen the newlyweds.

"Okay. Why?" she asked.

"I want you to talk to the community leaders and get some of their input on the stores you will be designing."

"That sounds great. When should I come down there?" she asked. Work had been her solace and her guiding light, and she needed it to help her get back on task. She needed to focus and not let Cam throw her so off balance.

"Now would be perfect."

Of course it would be. "Um...I just gave Jasmine the afternoon off."

"That's okay. You can bring Ty with you."

"We will be right down there," she said.

"Good. I'm sorry about the last-minute notice."

"It's okay. Just let me get dressed—"

"Whoa, are you working naked?"

She laughed. "No. Why did you think that?"

"I'm a man," he said.

"And men think about sex all the time?" she asked.

"Exactly."

"So are you not thinking about it now that we've become lovers again?" she asked, kidding him. They had never had a teasing relationship before and she was interested to see another side of Cam.

"Hell, no. In fact, I'm thinking about you even more often than before. I can't for the life of me figure out why I let you go two years ago," he said.

"You were a fool," she said. She wished that he would have kept in touch or that she hadn't let her pride keep her from contacting him. Because the future—Cam's, Ty's and hers—would be a lot easier to navigate if she had.

"I was."

"I'm glad to hear you say that, but I was only kidding," she said.

"I wasn't. I don't know why I couldn't see you for the gem you are," he said.

Her heart melted a little bit. "I think it goes back to the guy thing where you just think about sex."

"Probably. Maybe fate stepped in to give us a second chance," he said.

"How do you figure?" she asked.

"It gave us Ty."

The more she got to know Cam, the more she really liked him. When the time came and she found the words to tell him that she had fallen for him again, she hoped he'd believe her and react like the man of her dreams.

Cam hung up the phone with Becca. He wanted to get something for her. But he'd already sent her flowers, and he really didn't have any other ideas.

He walked through the club and heard samba music playing in the rehearsal room. He paused and debated for a minute if he should interrupt Jen to talk to her. Finally he decided it was okay and opened the door. Jen danced around the rehearsal room. His new sister-in-law smiled at him as he entered the room.

"Are you here as my boss or brother-in-law?" she asked.

"Brother-in-law," he said. "I need some advice."

She hit a button and the music stopped. "What's up?"

"I need...what kind of gifts does a woman really like to get?"

"I think it depends on the woman," she said. "I like music and things related to dance. But I suspect that Becca might like something different. What does she like?"

Cam thought about it for a minute before he had his own idea. She liked art and drawing, and finding the right gift for her would be easy now that he knew what direction to go in.

"Thanks, Jen. That was exactly what I needed to know."

"I don't think I said anything worthwhile," she said.

"Yes, you did," Cam said. He hugged her and then turned to leave the rehearsal room.

"Why are you hugging my wife?" Nate said, coming into the room.

"Because she's brilliant." Cam walked over to Nate, who was scowling in the doorway.

"I know that. That's why I hug her," Nate said.

"I thought you hugged her for a different reason," Cam said.

"So did I," Jen said, laughing. "Did you come to help me learn my new dance?"

"No, I stopped by because I missed you. Why were you hugging my brother?"

"He needed some advice on a gift."

"What gift?"

"None of your business," Cam said. "Go hug your wife."

"I will. And I'm going to talk to her about letting just anyone hug her," Nate said.

"I'll leave you two to discuss that," Cam said, heading toward the door.

"Sounds good. I wanted some alone time with my wife," Nate said.

Cam walked out and couldn't help smiling. At this moment his brother was very happy. Nate's romantic past hadn't been so rosy. He'd been dumped by his fiancée when he'd been injured and had to leave pro baseball. And that had cemented in Cam's mind the fact that most women were only out for what they could get from their men.

Jen seemed different, and she made Nate happy, so Cam was hoping for the best. Was Becca cut from the same cloth? He thought so. She was sweet and sexy and seemed as honest as the day was long now that she'd opened up to him about Ty.

She'd changed over the past few weeks, or maybe he was just getting to know her. He had found that Becca was just the woman he needed. She was very good at creating a family bond. Each morning, they had breakfast by the pool and then every evening she cooked them an early dinner and they ate with Ty sitting at the table. She asked questions about his day and made a point to let Ty babble on in his baby talk so he had a chance to talk, as well. It was…something unexpected.

He wanted to find a gift for her that would let her know how important she was to him. When he thought of Becca and art, he thought of Chagall with his romantic abstract images. The perfect painting came to mind.

He called Val Martin, a friend of his from college who was now an art dealer. "How quickly can I get a framed lithograph of Chagall's *Les Trois Cierges?*"

"I might have one. Let me look through the catalog. Does it have to be that picture?"

"Yes," he said. He wanted Becca to have that picture. He wanted it hanging in her home.

The scene was colorful with a big green tree dominating the top of the painting. It had pretty white blooms on it and angels flew under its branches. A sleepy little town painted in a warm reddish brown could be seen in the distance. Three candles—from the title—were in the front left corner. But it was the couple on the right that had him convinced this was the right portrait for Becca. The man had dark hair and wore a brightly colored coat and held the woman tenderly in his arms. She wore a white flowing dress and her head was tucked on his shoulder.

"Do you want it framed?"

"Yes, that would be perfect. It's a gift, Val. So it's important that I get it as quickly as possible."

"I don't have one for sale in my shop but I do personally own a number of Chagall prints," Val said.

"I know. That's why I called you."

"I have a litho of *Les Trois Cierges* that is number 3 in the limited 450-print run, but it is one of my favorites."

"Would you be willing to sell it to me?" he asked. "I know that you have a ton of art work and can easily move another print or painting into its place. And who knows, maybe this will make room in your collection for another Chagall."

There was silence on the phone while Val thought it over. "Okay. I will sell it to you for $1,700. That's a bargain."

"Thank you, Val," he said. He would have paid double that to get the perfect gift for Becca. "How soon can I have it?"

"How soon do you need it?"

"I'd love to have it today," he said.

"If you want to come by my condo in Miami Beach, you can have it today."

"Thank you, Val. I'm on my way."

"Why is this so important to you, Cam? You've never been a big collector before."

He didn't want to share the details of his personal life with anyone, even an old college friend. "It's a gift for someone and I need it today."

"Someone? You mean a woman?" Val asked.

"Yes, a woman. And that's all I'm going to say on the matter. I will be at your place in forty minutes."

He pocketed his cell phone and went to deal with other details at the club. Little things that needed his attention—made him realize that this time he wanted every detail of his relationship with Becca to be perfect. He was realistic enough to know that they weren't going to have smooth sailing, but he wanted to make up for the way he'd let things end between them before.

The Chagall print would do that. In his mind he could see the image of the man holding the woman in his arms, and he hoped that Becca would never feel alone once she had it hanging on her wall. That Becca would know that he was always right there for her.

He left the club and got in his Tesla. He put the top down and drove out of Little Havana toward Miami Shores. He was a man who was very used to making things happen, and this was no different...Becca was no different. He was going to make her his completely. And if he made any missteps this time, he would make it up to her. It was important that Becca realize this time he was back in her life to stay.

He drove the hour or so to Val's house, handling business on his Bluetooth headset as he wove in and out of traffic. He arrived at her condo and parked, sitting outside for a few minutes while he finished up a call with Justin. Finally he got out of the car and went to Val's door. She had the painting all wrapped up and he handed her a check.

"Thank you," he said.

"You're welcome. I'm always happy to see a piece go to someone who will appreciate it."

He picked up the painting and put it in the trunk of his car. Val didn't ask too many questions, and Cam was glad. He wasn't ready to talk about Becca with anyone. What he felt for her was too private to be shared.

Ten

When Cam got back from picking up the picture, he walked the short distance between Luna Azul and the Mercado. Now that Justin and Selena had returned to Manhattan, he had to oversee more of the marketplace project than he had previously. But that sat well with him because he liked to keep busy.

He had to remind himself that just because Becca had come back into his life, he wasn't going to change the basics of who he was. Today had reinforced that. He had no idea if she was aware of how much she shook him up. But he was determined to control his reactions to her and to keep her in just one corner of his life.

He liked the fact that they were going to be able to work together, and he hoped her designs for the Mercado were acceptable to the shop owners. But he knew that, in his personal life, he had to ensure that she was...what?

Cam was interrupted in his thoughts by Selena's grandfather, lead shop owner in the Mercado project. "I'm glad you are here. The construction company is insisting on tearing down the sidewalk leading to my Cuban Grocery Store," Tomas Gonzalez said as he approached. "How are my customers going to get into the store if there is no sidewalk?"

He shook Tomas's hand. "We'll figure it out. Who is in charge?"

"Junior. And that boy never did have any sense. I'm tempted to call his father," Tomas said.

Cam bit back a laugh. Working on a project in a community where everyone knew everyone else, it was inevitable that emotions ran high. "I'll take care of it."

"Good. I knew you would do right by me," Tomas said. "We are family now."

"That's right, we are. Why don't you go back to the grocery store and I'll come and find you when I'm done talking to Junior."

Cam was given a hard hat by the work site foreman, and Junior Rodriquez met him halfway across the lot. "That old man is making me crazy. The sidewalk is cracked and a safety risk. I'm tempted to not let my men go in there to buy lunch."

"We need to figure out a solution that will fix the sidewalk and keep his store open to customers."

"He won't even talk about anything, Cam. He just wants his store left alone."

"That's why you and I are going to work this out. Can you do it tonight after the store closes?"

"It would mean overtime and I would go over budget," Junior said. "I pride myself on bringing jobs in on time and on budget."

Which was one of the things that Cam appreciated about Junior. He was a hard worker and he did the job right the first time. "Okay. I will pay your men in a separate contract to do the sidewalk tonight. You tell me the rates and we'll do it. Just the part in front of the store—the rest of it you can do tomorrow during the regular workday."

"Let me talk to my guys. I will get back to you in ten minutes or so," Junior said.

Cam left the other man and walked out of the construction area just as he saw Becca walking toward the shopping site, holding Ty on her hip. Seeing her with their son never failed to stir strong emotions in him.

He had already admitted to himself that he cared for her and he wasn't going to deny it now. There was something about Becca that made him want to be a better man. And he realized he wanted a relationship that was more real than his parents' had been. He didn't want to have his own independent life...he wanted to be a part of hers.

She and Ty both waved when she saw him. The boy made Cam smile with his sweetness. He'd never been aware of kids before Ty, but there was something about seeing his son that made him think of the future in a way that didn't involve shopping malls or night clubs. Not just plans for a bigger and more profitable

Luna Azul, but a personal future that didn't involve his club—a future that included something more than work. A future with Becca and Ty.

"Hello," he said, as they got closer. She wore a short pencil skirt that ended just below the knee, a big red belt and a button-down blouse. The belt drew his eyes to her tiny waist. Her hair was pulled back in a clip, and a layer of filmy bangs fell over her eyebrows. She had on a pair of large black sunglasses, which kept him from seeing her eyes.

"Hello. I didn't realize there was so much construction going on," she said. "I would have dressed a little differently."

"I'm glad you didn't. I like this outfit," he said.

"I thought you would but these heels are going to make navigating the parking lot pretty difficult."

He offered her his arm. She slipped her hand through the crook of his elbow, balancing Ty on her other hip.

"We have to tear down a lot of the older buildings because they aren't up to code. So I figured we'd get that out of the way while we were soliciting designers."

"That makes sense. Who did you want me to talk to?"

"Tomas," Cam said. "He owns the Cuban Grocery over there. Come on, I will introduce you."

He held her arm as they walked over the cracked sidewalk at the entrance of the grocery store.

"Some of these places are in a sad state of disrepair," Becca said.

"Yes, they are. But we got a good deal on the

marketplace, so we have the money to invest to make this a premier shopping venue."

"I can see that. What do you envision?"

"Did you have a chance to look at the portfolio?" he asked.

"Yes, I made some preliminary sketches based on a market I saw in Seville last year when I was in Spain."

Becca had always been a hard worker. Cam remembered that Russell said she was an asset to his team because she brought authenticity to the work she did. "Why did you stop working for Russell?"

She shrugged. "That's an odd question."

"No, I was thinking about how dedicated you are to your job and how starting your own business while starting a single-parent family was a double whammy. Why did you do it?"

She looked over at him. "I couldn't continue my busy schedule with Russell and be the kind of mom I wanted to be to Ty."

Cam tilted his head to study mother and child. She had said she was alone, but he realized as Ty continued to grow she'd always have her son by her side. He felt a pang knowing that they shared a bond he could never be a part of, but he knew he was building his own relationship with Ty.

"Russell would have let you work part-time."

She shook her head. "I couldn't do it. I didn't want him to know I was pregnant and put two and two together. And I had agreed to a certain work schedule with Russell and I know I wouldn't have been able to just do half the work I had done previously. It wouldn't have been fair."

"You wouldn't have been working to your own standards?"

"Yes. I would have ended up working all the time and never seeing Ty. And that didn't sit well with me. If I was going to have a child, I intended to be the best mother I could to him."

He hadn't thought he could respect her any more than he already did, but hearing her thoughts on working and parenting made him even more convinced of her basic integrity.

Becca was the embodiment of everything he'd ever imagined when he thought of the perfect woman. He leaned over to kiss her briefly on the lips.

"What was that for?"

"For being you," he said. He wasn't going to say more than that. Already Becca was making him reveal things about himself that he'd rather keep hidden. He would never have admitted even to himself that he felt safer working all the time. Until Becca and Ty had come into this life and his home, he hadn't realized what he'd been missing.

Becca put Ty down as she sat in the café area at the back of the Cuban Grocery store. Tomas sat across from her, and even Cam managed to get his tall frame into one of the tiny café-style chairs. The store was in disrepair and needed fixing up, but there was a warmth in the café that made her feel at home.

The Cuban grocery store didn't feel like any supermarket she'd shopped in during her life. It definitely made her want to come back here.

"What is your vision for this place, Tomas?" she asked. She'd found that once she talked to the people who were going to work in the clubs, hotels or buildings she designed, she had a better insight into what was needed from her.

"My vision?" he asked.

"Yes, tell me what you want your consumers to feel when they are here."

He rubbed his chin and then glanced around the store. "I guess I just want it to feel like home so that they can remember the old ways and not lose so much of who we are to American commercialism."

Becca was surprised to hear him say that so bluntly. "You know that Luna Azul also brings a lot of celebrities into the area. Is there a way that you can incorporate that consumer into your market?"

"I think that you and your brothers are looking to do something a little different here," Tomas said, looking at Cam. "But we also carry specialty food items that can't be found in other places, so I think that will appeal to some of the Luna Azul clientele," Tomas said.

"We are thinking about doing something different here. That's why I hope you will talk to Becca about the store you had in Cuba," Cam said.

"It wasn't my store but my papa's," Tomas said. For the next twenty minutes, Tomas talked about pre-revolution Cuba with a fondness that was infectious. Becca took notes as he spoke.

Ty was getting a little restless, which distracted her. She had to keep getting up to take things from him.

"I have to go check in with Junior outside. How about if I take Ty so you and Tomas can talk?" Cam suggested.

"Are you sure?" Becca asked. It would be a lot easier for her to take notes and concentrate on what Tomas was saying if she didn't have to worry about Ty doing something he shouldn't.

"Yes, I am," Cam said. He walked over to Ty. "Come on, buddy, let's go outside where you won't be getting scolded."

"Thank you, Cam."

"No problem," he said. She watched them walk away. Seeing Ty's little hand in Cam's, she felt a pang in her heart. She continued staring as Cam bent down and scooped Ty up when they reached the door leading outside.

"You and Cam have something between you," Tomas said.

"Business, but also our son," she said. She wasn't doing a good job of keeping her feelings for Cam hidden. She liked looking at him and being close to him.

"More than business, I think. Why do you try to hide your feelings?" Tomas asked.

She shrugged. She was used to being on her own, and a part of her was very afraid if she let Cam in and he left, then she'd feel even more lonely. "It's hard to own your own business and be involved with a potential client. I don't want to give the impression that Cam has brought me here for any reason other than my skills as a designer."

Tomas laughed. "You remind me of Selena, my granddaughter. She is the same way. Very much wants her business and personal lives to stay separate."

"Do they?" Becca asked. "I think I could use some advice from her."

Tomas shook his head. "Alas, they don't for her. At least not where Justin Stern was concerned. And I think it's the same way for you. No matter how many limits you put on Cam, he will always be more to you than a potential client."

"I agree. I just didn't want the world to know," she said, desperately trying to think of a way to turn the conversation back to business and not offend Tomas.

"What else do you want to know about Cuba?" he asked, changing the subject himself.

Tomas was at least seventy but wore his years well. He had thinning hair and a thick mustache, and he smiled easily, especially when he spoke of his family.

She thought about it for a minute. "Well, I want to know what your visual impressions were and why you remember those things. I think you mentioned you were a boy when you left. What is the one thing that lingers in your mind when you think of Cuba?"

Tomas leaned back in his chair and rubbed his chin. "I remember lots of flowers and old brick streets. There were some fountains and of course the shops had lots of outdoor seating. The open-air cafés where poets and revolutionaries sat around and argued about their worldviews. The coffee shops where my father would always buy me a cup of sweet coffee in the mornings and sometimes in the evenings as we'd walk back home from his store. I remember that the doors were always open and big paddle fans stirred the air."

When he spoke, she had an image in her head that matched a little of what she'd seen in Seville, and she knew what she was going to do. She started sketching as he talked, just a doodle really, but it captured what she needed for this moment.

"Will the redesigned store be more focused on groceries or the café?" she asked. That would make a huge difference in how the interior would be designed.

"The café," Tomas said. "When I was growing up I sat in the café part of my papa's store and listened to the old men tell stories while they sipped their coffee and smoked their big cigars. I want to ensure that the current generation and the future ones don't lose sight of where we came from. That the old stories stay important."

"Maybe you could have murals on the inside walls of the store, Tomas. Ones that captured the scenes you were just talking about. I think that would be a nice way to make your store feel different than the local chains. And to give parents and other visitors something to talk about."

"I love that idea. And I know the perfect local artist for the job," Tomas said. "Do you want me to give you his name?"

"That would be great," she said.

Becca knew exactly what he wanted. And she had a vision of how she could bring it all together. She liked working to bring the past and the future together. It was something she'd learned working for Russell. His Kiwi Klubs were successful because they took the best of the existing culture and melded it with the trendiest things happening in the world.

"Thank you for sharing your past with me, Tomas."

"You are very welcome. And good luck to you with your design. I hope that you create the one that captures everything the Mercado can be."

"Me, too," she admitted. She gathered up her papers and notes and walked out of the grocery store.

Cam was talking to a construction worker while holding Ty. They all had hard hats on, including Ty.

She blinked and then turned away, needing a moment to gather her emotions before she went over to them. Cam was exactly the kind of man she'd always hoped to find. He was sexy and dashing and charming. But more than that, he was a man who put family at the top of his priority list.

She'd had no idea he was that kind of man when they'd been involved two years ago. That was her own fault because she'd been embarrassed to be having an affair with one of Russell's friends. She'd tried to keep him a secret. So they hadn't really had a chance to know each other outside of the bedroom.

Her biggest regret was that she'd cheated both of them out of years they could have spent together with their son. And she could only hope that she hadn't cost them their future, as well.

Cam's cell phone rang as Becca came over to him. He handed Ty over to her and then glanced at the caller ID. "It's Nate, give me a minute."

She nodded, and he stepped aside to take the call. She seemed tired and a bit unsure as he walked away.

"Hey, Nate, what's up?"

"Not much. Jen and I are done early at the club and are having her nephew over for dinner. We wanted you and Becca and Ty to join us."

He glanced over at Becca. He wanted time alone with her yet he didn't. He needed time to figure out just how he was going to handle the intense emotional and physical rush he felt every time she was near him.

"Yeah, let me check with Becca and call you back."

"Yes. Definitely."

He hung up and walked over to Becca, who was making baby talk with Ty. They were so cute together. He stood there for a moment just watching the mother and child bond and feeling a little bit envious that his mother had never cuddled him close the way that Becca did with Ty.

"Is everything okay?" she asked when he approached her.

No, he thought. She had a way of finding empty pieces inside of him that he'd never been aware of.

"Yes, fine. Nate invited us over to dinner. What do you think?"

"I...I was hoping to talk to you alone tonight," she said.

"I want that, too," he said. "We will be alone when we get home. Nate will help you with your designs, too. You can get his insights into the Mercado, as well."

Becca looked up at him. She'd pushed her sunglasses

up on the top of her head, and he could see her pretty eyes. She was very serious. "I think I have enough insight. What's this really about?"

He rubbed the back of his neck. He hated not feeling sure of himself, and for some reason that was how she made him feel. "I want you to get to know my brothers better, and I want Ty to have a real relationship with his uncles."

She studied him for a long minute, and then she nodded. "Okay. Then I'd be happy to go to dinner at his house. I know how important family is to you," she said.

"You and Ty are important to me, too," he said. "I wish we hadn't lost so much time together."

He'd replayed their first relationship in his head a dozen times, and he didn't see any way for it to have gone differently. He had been a man driven to keep his eye on business back then. And she had been the same way. Just two workaholics scratching an itch, and he wished they would have been able to see into the future and this moment. Maybe things would be different now.

"You didn't want me to stay."

"I know," he said.

It was odd that they were having this conversation in the middle of a parking lot, yet somehow fitting. With Becca the most inconspicuous moments turned into the most monumental.

"You made me forget about everything except being together with you. That's not any way to live your life.

I would have lost myself, and I think that would have destroyed me and whatever we had between us."

Cam considered her for a long moment. He would have enjoyed having Becca lost in him. But she had a point that eventually it would have wrung them both out, and they would have broken up any way.

"You'll know when you're ready to meet someone who can be everything to you."

"Am I everything to you?" she asked. "Do you think I could be?"

"Yes, you are." And in that moment, Cam realized he was telling God's honest truth.

"I'm flattered," she said. "You are the first man that has made me feel this way, Cam."

"I'm glad to hear that," he said. He wanted to be the only man she thought of from this point forward.

She shook her head. "You confuse me sometimes. It's one thing to think of you as my lover but something else to think of you as Ty's father. The other night when we had that fever…you were really there for me, and I don't want to make that into something more than it was to you."

He reached over and hugged her with one arm. "It was nice for me. I don't think anyone other than my brothers has trusted me when they needed something. I mean outside of business."

She tipped her head back to look up at him. "I trust you."

"Let me call Nate back and then we can head over to his house."

"Okay," she said.

He stepped away to return the call but couldn't take his eyes off of Becca and Ty. No matter how unsettled he felt around her, he still wanted to spend all of his time with her.

"Hey, big bro," Nate said as he answered his phone.

"Hey, little bro," Cam said.

Nate laughed, and it was a good sound. Cam remembered how solemn Nate had been when he'd gotten injured and had been forced to give up baseball. Nate was a very different man today.

"So? Are you coming tonight?"

"Yes, what time?"

"An hour or thereabouts," Nate said.

"What can I bring?" Cam asked.

"Nothing. I got it covered. I'm a married man now," Nate said.

"Good. It's great to hear you so happy," Cam said.

"I think so, too. I can't believe how much I love my wife," Nate said.

Cam just chuckled. "That is good to know, but you should tell her."

"I will. In fact I have to go and find her and tell her right now."

Cam hung up the phone and walked back to Becca. "Is everything set?" she asked.

"Yes, it is. But I need ten more minutes on the site. I have to do some more negotiating with Tomas to get the sidewalk fixed in front of his grocery store, and he can be stubborn."

"Can he be?"

"Yes. Normally I make Justin do this kind of thing

but since he's still flying back and forth from New York..."

"You have to do it. Can I help? Tomas and I got along pretty well."

"Of course you did. You are a beautiful woman, something that Tomas can't resist," he said. Which was a good argument for using her to help get Tomas to agree to close one door of the store early. "Actually, if you don't mind just standing next to me and smiling at him I think it would help."

Becca laughed. "I'm arm candy?"

"Yes, you are, and very distracting arm candy, too," he said, bending down to kiss her. He didn't want to admit it to himself but having Becca by his side made him happier than he'd ever been in his life.

Eleven

Becca changed Ty into his cutest outfit and then sat on the bed. What the heck was she doing? She knew it was past time to tell Cam that she was tired of living in limbo and wanted to stay here with him forever.

Ty babbled his sweet baby talk at her and she looked down at him. The resemblance to Cam was striking.

"Hungee, mama."

"Hungry," she said, gently correcting him. She opened a package of baby carrots and handed him one to chew on. Then she finished getting his bag ready for their trip to Nate's house tonight.

When she was done, she smiled at Ty. "Are you ready to go?"

"Go," he said, nodding at her.

She slung his bag over her shoulder and then bent

over to pick him up. She'd dressed carefully for tonight, wearing a pretty sundress and leaving her hair to hang around her shoulders in soft waves. She'd applied her makeup with the precision and care of a runway model. She wanted to look good for Cam.

In the hallway she caught a glimpse of herself in the mirror. She looked the way she always did. Confident and average. Her son was cute as a button, though. In the mirror she didn't seem like the type of person that had always been alone and was afraid to spend the rest of her life that way. But did the mirror reflect her true self?

Cam had pulled the SUV up in the circular drive and waved when he saw them. He was on the phone, probably talking business. Was taking time out of his day for dinner with Nate going to mean he had to work later?

She hoped not. He'd promised her some time together alone. And she was going to insist that he keep that promise.

Yeah, right. That was never going to happen. She didn't have the kind of courage it would take to blurt out something like that. She'd told Cam she loved him before, and it had backfired...big time. She was going to just keep biding her time until she couldn't keep quiet any longer.

And it was torture. Because when Cam smiled at her, she hoped that he would always look at her that way. And realizing he might not hurt worse than anything she'd experienced since her mom died.

Once they'd strapped Ty into the car seat, Cam turned to her. "You okay?" he asked.

"Yes, why?"

"You looked sad just then," he said.

"I was just thinking about my mom."

He gave her a hug. "I'm sorry. Do you worry about leaving Ty alone?"

He had no idea how big a worry that was. "I...I really don't have any close friends."

"You have me," he said, gently stroking her cheek.

"We have to talk, Cam," she said.

"I know that we do, but that was Nate telling me not to be late."

"I guess family comes first," she said.

"Yes, it does," he replied.

"Oh."

"Becca?"

"Yes?"

"You and Ty are family, too." He closed Ty's door and rested his arms on the SUV, trapping her between his body and the vehicle.

He leaned in and kissed her firmly on the mouth, his chest rubbing over hers. She shivered with awareness as his mouth moved to her ear.

"I can't wait until we are alone later tonight," he said in his low, raspy voice.

"Me either," she admitted. He kissed her again before opening her door and helping her into the car.

She watched him walk around to the driver's side. The bond between them was growing much stronger, and she couldn't help but hope that this time Cam was going to be hers forever.

Being with Cam felt like home. It was a warm feeling, and she hadn't experienced anything this wonderful since she'd given birth to Ty.

Dinner was a lot of fun and kind of relaxing. They'd ended up playing Dance Dance Revolution. Which may not have been fair, considering that Jen was a professional dancer. But it had been a riot watching Nate, a former baseball player, trying to keep up with his wife and, surprisingly, with Cam. Jen shouldn't have been surprised that Cam knew how to move his body, but she was. She kept learning more about him, and sometimes it made her feel a little silly that she'd told him she loved him back before she'd had Ty when it was so clear now that she'd never known him.

Jen and Nate waved goodbye to Cam and Becca as they walked down the circle drive to their car. Ty was nestled on her shoulder, happily sleeping. He'd played hard with Riley, Jen's nephew, until Ty suddenly just sat down next to the couch and fell asleep.

She rubbed her hand over her little boy's sleeping head as Cam opened the back door for her to put him in his car seat. The last thing she wanted was to set him in the seat, but she knew safety came first.

She buckled him in and then turned to look at Cam. The resemblance between him and Nate was uncanny, but more than that the bond between the brothers was very strong. Family was such a huge part of who these men were.

And tonight had brought into sharp relief how selfish she'd been to keep Ty to herself for so long. But when Nate had held her little boy, she knew that he was happy to have Ty as his nephew, and that she would be forgiven.

A warm spring breeze stirred the air as Cam gave her a hug. "Thank you for a great night."

"It was pretty special for me, too. Riley was so good with Ty. I was worried about that."

"Me, too," Cam admitted. "I think I watched them like hawks for the first hour we were there before I finally relaxed."

"Cam, there is something I have to tell you."

"Good, because there is something I want to ask you. I hope we are on the same track," he said.

Becca wrapped her arms around his lean waist and rested her head over his heart for a really long minute. She wanted to stay right here in his arms for the rest of her life. Too bad that wasn't a possibility.

She inhaled deeply so that the masculine scent of him was imbedded in her senses and then stepped back. "I can't wait to hear what you have to say. I think that you and I are so much stronger this time."

"Me, too," he said. He closed Ty's door and opened hers. "We can talk more when we get home."

Home. She hadn't felt that way about anyplace but Garden City before, and now she was coming to realize that Ty and Cam were her home.

She sighed.

If everything worked out the way she secretly hoped, one day soon she'd be sharing major decisions with Cam about everything, not just Ty. And if it didn't—well, she'd continue moving along making choices. Some of them would be really good ones and others would be mistakes. And some of the mistakes, she thought, glancing back to make sure Ty was okay, would turn out to be the best choices she ever could have made.

"That was a big sigh," Cam said. "Are you worried because you didn't keep up with me during the game?"

"Not at all," she said. "I'm worried about where we are heading."

"Why?" he asked. "We're getting on well. Ty is adjusting. I think things are fine the way they are."

She shrugged, then realized he couldn't see her gesture, since he was driving. She had to respond but what would she say? "The more stuff we do together as a family...the more I wish we were a real one."

"We are a real one. You're Ty's mom and I'm his dad. Doesn't get more real than that," Cam said.

"That's not what I meant," she said. "I want us to be more than that. I think I told you I never knew my dad, but I created this image in my head of what would be the perfect family."

"What was it like?" he asked.

Like us, she thought, but didn't say that out loud. "It was a mom and dad who cared about each other and who loved me."

"I wanted that, too."

"Didn't you have it?" she asked.

"Not from my mom. She might have loved me, but I always felt that I was wanting in her eyes."

"I'm sorry, Cam."

"Don't be. Childhood isn't perfect for anyone. Haven't you found that out?"

She nodded. "But I want to do whatever I can to make sure that Ty's is."

He glanced over at her. "Me, too."

"I think you are a very good mother," he said, smiling over at her. He pulled into the garage at their home. He parked the car and got Ty out of the back. He was sleeping as usual, and Becca followed behind Cam as he took Ty inside and put him to bed.

She was glad he thought she was a good mom but realized she wanted him to think about her as a woman.

She went into the kitchen and took down two snifters from the shelf. She put in a couple of ice cubes and filled them with Baileys before heading back into the living room.

"I'm glad you got us drinks."

"No problem. I have something I want to talk to you about," she said.

"Okay. I wanted to speak to you, too."

She took a deep breath and a big sip of her drink. It burned because she'd swallowed too much, and she felt like an idiot when she started coughing.

Cam patted her on the back. "Are you okay?"

"Yes. I am okay. In fact, I'm better than okay. Cam, I…"

She put her glass down and then put her hand on his knee. "I love you and I want us to live together as man and wife."

* * *

Cam didn't know what to say. Love. Of course she'd have to say the one thing that he couldn't give her. She couldn't ask for diamonds or pearls or priceless works of art. She had to ask for something ephemeral.

"I'm flattered, Becca. I think this time you really do love me," he said.

"I do, too," she said. "I've known it for a while now."

"I'm so glad. I think we are making a very fine family with you and me and Ty. I was planning to ask you to make this move permanent and to live with me for the rest of our lives."

"I think it's a sign of how close we've become that we were on the same page," she said. Her smile was so bright that he almost didn't want to correct her. But he knew he wasn't going to marry her, and she needed to know that.

"Almost the same page, Becca. I'm not talking about marriage. It's not really for me. My dad was trapped in a loveless match with my mother, and I don't want to mess up what we have by making the same mistake as he did."

"What?"

"We both know you heard me. I'm not sure of us, Becca. Few people know this, but my parents married because my mom was pregnant with me. Having me and my brothers didn't make them any happier together. I don't want to repeat my dad's mistakes."

"I'm not sure what you want from me," she said.

"I want you to move into the master bedroom with me and I want us to raise Ty together."

She shook her head. "I don't think that will work for me."

"Why not?"

"I want more kids, Cam. I want Ty to have siblings. Plus your brothers are both married. I don't want to be the only live-in lover. I want to be your wife."

"I'm not going to get married to please you, Becca. I know myself well enough—"

"I don't think you do. I've never met a man more ready for marriage than you. You are just being stubborn because you are afraid to change your personal life."

"I am not."

"You are too. You are so foolish you can't even see that it's already been changed by me and Ty."

"I have already realized that. Why else do you think I offered…it doesn't matter," he said. "I take it your answer is no?"

She shook her head as tears started to roll down her face. "What was the question?"

"Live with me as we have been but move into my bedroom."

"How is this different from being your mistress?"

"We have a son," he said.

"Which is all the more reason I should be your wife, not your mistress. So I guess my answer *is* no."

"That's it, then. Nothing more to say."

He stood up and walked out of the house. She just watched him leave, knowing that she was out of words.

She couldn't talk him into loving her—not two years ago and certainly not now.

Becca watched Cam walk away and tried to keep from sobbing out loud. She tried to tell herself that it was for the best. That they would never have been able to work as a couple. But she couldn't help remembering the flowers he'd sent her. And the sweet way he'd taken Ty with him so she could work.

It was the warmth of her tears on her own cheeks that made her realize that she was crying. She hadn't meant to. She never thought she'd cry over Cam. She hadn't the first time they'd parted.

She wrapped both arms around her waist and sank down on the couch. It was amazing to her that she'd lost Cam in the same way she had before. She'd been searching for someone to be the missing link in her family. And she knew she'd found the right man in Cam. Was it because of Ty and the circumstances of his birth that Cam couldn't accept that they were meant to be together? She thought Cam had forgiven her for keeping the child a secret.

Perhaps it was something he'd never forgive. She tried to equate it with something that Cam had done to her, but could find nothing. Maybe he'd never really be able to forgive her.

She wished she could go back in time and let him know about Ty, but there was no use wishing for a chance to redo the past. That would never happen. She knew she had to move on. But she loved Cam. So walking away from him wasn't an option. Or was it?

She was always going to love him and she was going to be in his life as Ty's mom until she died.

If Cam had wanted to make her pay for keeping Ty a secret for eighteen months of his life, he couldn't have designed a better punishment than this. Having to see the man she loved and to know that she couldn't ever have him.

She got to her feet and went into Ty's bedroom. She stood over Ty's bed and remembered seeing Cam do the same thing when he'd realized that Ty was his son.

She tried to make excuses for Cam because she didn't want to spend the rest of her life without him. She hoped he was simply overwhelmed. She'd had nine months, give or take, to get used to the idea of being a mom. He'd had a couple weeks.

Even so, there was no doubt that he was already a great dad. It didn't matter that he was an executive and he had demands at work; Ty came first. She'd seen Cam keep his BlackBerry in his pocket for most of the evening and only checked it once during dinner.

But why couldn't he take the next step and be a great partner to her, too? She wanted to give them both the family they'd never had. To give Ty the parents she and Cam had lacked.

She couldn't believe it, but she still loved him. Even after he'd said hateful things to her, she really just wanted him back here with her. She wanted to feel his strong arms around her.

She was saddened that she wouldn't get to sleep next to him and wake up in the morning with him to Ty's soft calls. She wanted that for both of them, but it wasn't meant to be.

She leaned over the crib and kissed Ty on the top of his head and then retreated to her own bedroom, quietly undressing and changing into her nightgown. It was sleek and sexy, and she'd hoped to have a chance to wear it for Cam. It seemed now that would never happen.

She knew she had to stop thinking about him. And she needed to have a plan. She was going to have to be on her toes tomorrow.

She could stay. But that would make her feel like her soul was slowly dying if she had to spend day in and day out around the man she loved. The man who didn't love her back and was never going to.

She was so sad she started crying again and hugged the spare pillow to her chest as she fell onto the bed. She felt so alone and scared.

She had no one to ask advice from, and every decision she'd made...well, they didn't seem too smart at just this moment. And frankly, she was out of good ideas. She'd used her last one up when she'd decided to tell Cam she loved him.

She wanted to believe that tomorrow everything would be better, but she doubted that it would be. Cam wasn't going to suddenly fall in love with her. She was going to have to figure out a way to share custody with a man who was going to treat her like a stranger—worse than a stranger—every time they saw each other.

She rolled over, hugging the pillow to her stomach and stared at the clock. But no answers came to her. The last time she'd felt this lost and alone she'd called Cam. But she wasn't sure that he'd take her call.

Because it was midnight and because she felt like she had nothing else to lose, she picked up the phone and called him. He didn't answer. It went to his voice mail, and she hung up. She closed her eyes and wished her life were like the romantic tales she loved so much because then happiness and forgiveness would be waiting right around the corner for her and Cam. But she'd been alive long enough to know that dreams really didn't come true.

Twelve

He wanted to talk to both of his brothers, and though it was late, he knew they'd both be up if he called.

But he also knew that they had women in their lives now. And he didn't want to intrude. But this was big. He had a chance to change the course of his life. The way that Becca had changed her own life when Ty had been born.

A son that Becca had hidden from him. A love that she never did.

He called Nate as he pulled into his driveway.

"This better be a damned emergency," Nate said by way of greeting.

"I don't know what to do," Cam said.

"What? Where are you?"

"In your driveway," Cam said.

"Good, I'll be right down and we'll get Justin on the phone...is it Ty? Is he okay?"

"No, he's fine. I just don't know what to do about Becca," Cam said.

"Damn," Nate said. The front door opened, and Cam hung up his cell phone as he walked into the house. Nate hugged him close, and right away there was something comforting in having someone on his side.

"Okay, tell me everything from the beginning," Nate said.

"I will, but I want to call Justin, too. I'm going to need an attorney."

"This keeps getting better and better," Nate said, leading the way down the hall to his office.

Cam walked over to the wet bar and poured himself a scotch. He turned and held the bottle up toward Nate. "Yes, please. I'm going to tell Jen that I'll be a while. You can call Justin, okay?"

"Sure. Should I come back another time?" he asked.

"No, definitely not. I'll be less than a minute," Nate said.

He watched his brother run out of the room and poured himself two fingers of scotch, downing the drink, then quickly pouring himself another one. He poured a glass for Nate, too, and then walked over to the big walnut desk. He'd given the desk to Nate when he'd come back to Miami from playing baseball. Their father had given Cam one just like it when he'd graduated high school.

Cam hit the speaker button on the desk phone and dialed Justin's number.

The phone was picked up on the second ring. "Hello?"

Damn, it was Selena. "It's Cam. I'm sorry to call you so late. Can I speak to Justin?"

"Yes, just a minute," she said.

"What's the matter? Is Nate okay?" Justin said as soon as he came on the line.

Cam wondered if he shouldn't have waited until tomorrow to do this. But he'd known he needed to talk tonight, and this was a family matter.

Nate came back in the room wearing a dark navy robe. "Cam's got problems with Becca."

"What the hell?" Justin asked.

Nate sat down in one of the leather armchairs near the wall, and Cam stayed where he was, reclining against the desk. "Do you want the entire story?"

"No, I think I know what I need to know," Justin said, the bitterness in his voice coming loud and clear through the speaker. "The bottom line is, Ty is eighteen months old. What are you going to do? Are we suing for custody and taking the kid from her?"

Though part of Cam wanted to say yes, he knew he wouldn't be able to do that to Becca or Ty. And suddenly he had his own answer. He didn't need to be waking his brothers up in the middle of the night to try to figure out what to do next. He only doubted himself because he'd never had a good relationship except with these two and his dad.

"She's a good mom."

"I agree," Nate said. "But if you don't get along with her, you're going to have to take action."

The only action Cam wanted to take was to smash his fist through a wall. All because he couldn't admit to himself that he wanted to build a life with Becca. One that would include a cute little son named Ty. But now those dreams were dashed and he had to start over from scratch. Or did he? Because to be fair, he couldn't see a future with Ty without Becca.

Not without her.

"I don't know what to do. This is the first time in my adult life that I'm unsure what the next step is and I'm scared."

"Well, you're not alone and neither is Ty. We are going to figure it out and rally together. That's what the Stern brothers do best," Nate said.

Cam was grateful for his brothers, but he knew it wasn't going to be as easy to pick up the pieces as they made it seem.

"Do you think that Dad had it wrong when he said that Stern men weren't made for monogamy?" Cam asked.

"Yes," Nate said. "I was definitely made to be Jen's husband. I think Dad picked the wrong woman to tie his life to."

"Jus?" Cam asked.

"I agree with Nate. Dad was a great father but he didn't try to be the partner to Mom that I am to Selena. And that you are to Becca."

"How do you know?" Cam asked. "You didn't seem too fond of her."

"Selena pointed out that Becca was living with you and not angry at you at all. Do you know what kind of love she must have for you to do that?" Justin said.

"I do," Cam admitted. "I'm afraid to love her."

Nate started laughing.

"What?"

"You already love her. You just don't want her to know. You're not fooling anyone else."

"True that," Justin said. "You don't want to sue her, you want to live with her and Ty and are afraid to marry her. That tells me you don't need an attorney, you need to decide for yourself if you are going to keep hiding from life or grab it by the balls... My money's on you grabbing it."

"Mine, too," Nate said. "You have never been some-one to stand on the sidelines."

His brothers had a point, and Cam knew he had already made up his mind. "Good night, boys. Sorry for the late night."

"It's all right. That's what family is for," Nate said.

"Just don't make a habit of this," Justin said, before hanging up.

Cam left Nate's house ten minutes later and drove back to his home.

In the corner of his bedroom propped against the wall was the Chagall print that he'd bought for Becca. Looking at it made his heart ache. He wanted to be that man in the picture holding on to the woman. And he wanted that woman to be Becca.

He took his cell phone out of his pocket and saw he'd missed a call from her but she hadn't left a message.

What would she say to the man who'd broken her heart? He loved that woman. It didn't matter what had happened and that she'd lied to him, he needed to have her in his life.

Becca was up before dawn and had all of her stuff packed. She knew she couldn't just take Ty and disappear so she'd made a call to Jasmine and asked to stay at her house for a few days. Jasmine had been surprised but said yes. She also knew she'd have to talk to an attorney and hammer out some kind of legal agreement with Cam. She was more than willing to do whatever she had to do so that Ty was the winner in this. He shouldn't have to suffer because love had dealt her a losing hand.

Becca had no other choice but to leave. She had figured out at about two this morning that if she was ever going to be able to function again, she was going to have to stay away from Cam. Being around him would mean staying in love with him, and that wasn't healthy.

She wished it had turned out differently.

It didn't matter what she wished. Real life had intruded on her fairy tale, and it was time to just stop pretending that it hadn't.

She opened the room to her room. Sitting in the middle of the hallway was a large framed print. She closed the door behind her and walked closer to it.

It was a Chagall. She didn't know the name of the painting, but she immediately knew who had given it to her. She went into Cam's bedroom to see if he was there, but he was nowhere to be found. She sat down in front of the painting. It was a print, she realized on closer inspection.

A man held a woman in his arms as they floated near a house. There were three candles in the foreground illuminating the scene. But what really caught her attention was the way the man held the woman.

He was protecting her and, to Becca's eyes, loving her. He seemed like a man who would do anything necessary to protect the woman he loved. And not just against physical dangers but also against loneliness.

She hugged Ty close to her chest and blinked to keep from crying. She loved Cam—and his giving her a gift like this sure wasn't going to make her stop loving him.

In fact, it made her want to do whatever he asked. Anything just so she'd have some small contact with him during the rest of her life.

She put Ty down when he started squirming. She stayed where she was, keeping her eyes on the painting.

"Hi, dadada," Ty said.

Becca glanced over her shoulder at Cam, who was approaching from down the hall. She had to fight not to cry. He looked ragged and tired. He wore an oxford broadcloth shirt untucked over a pair of faded jeans. And though this was the most casual she'd ever seen him, he looked perfect to her.

"Did you hear what he called me?" Cam asked as he picked up his son and held him.

"Yes, we have been practicing it." After a brief pause,

she said, "I…I love this painting. Thank you so much. But why did you give it to me?" she asked as he set Ty down.

Ty toddled over to them and tugged on Cam's pant leg. Cam ruffled Ty's hair, but that wasn't enough for the boy, who held his arms up.

Cam picked Ty up again and then kissed him on the top of his head. Becca knew it wasn't going to take these two very long to bond with each other. She was glad. Every child should have a solid relationship with his father. And she wanted that for Ty and for Cam.

"I had purchased the Chagall for you before we had our argument. And in my mind it was already yours."

"Oh. So it doesn't meant you've changed your mind?"

"No, Becca, I haven't changed my mind."

She nodded, a tear trickling down her left cheek. "I love you so much, Cam, it hurts. But I can't keep begging you to stay in my life."

"I don't want to hurt you, Becca. I want to be that hero who makes all your dreams come true. So I'm asking you to give me a second chance. Can you do that?"

"What? Oh, my God. Yes. Yes, I can," Becca said, a huge smile spreading on her face. "So you *have* changed your mind?"

"I haven't. It's what I wanted all along but was afraid to reach out and take. My only real desire was to be part of the family you and I have been building. I need to make you mine. To have Ty is a sweet bonus. So I'm asking you to give me a another chance. Let's start over this time with the air cleared between us. I think we have a real shot at happiness."

Becca ran to his side and threw her arms around his neck. "Me, too. You won't regret this."

"I know I won't," he said. "I want you to marry me, Becca."

"When?" she asked.

He laughed. "Is that a yes?"

"Yes, it is. I love you, Cam."

"I love you, too, Becca. I know our lives are going to be better than either of us imagined."

"Me, too," she said, hugging him and Ty close. Cam lifted her off her feet and spun them all around. Then he kissed her hard and deep, and she knew he was back to stay.

Epilogue

The Saturday morning of Memorial Day weekend dawned bright and sunny. Cam woke Becca early with a kiss.

"Why are you waking me up at 5:00 a.m.?"

"I have a surprise for you today."

"Okay. Do I have to get out of bed to get it?" she asked, sliding her hand down her fiancé's body and pulling him closer.

"Yes," he said with a laugh and a fierce kiss. "We can't be late, so hurry it up, woman."

She smiled at him and got out of bed. An hour later, they were all dressed and in the SUV heading toward Luna Azul. "What are we going to do at the club this early?"

"Something special," Cam said. He looked sexy in

his Luna Azul celebration golf shirt and a pair of faded jeans. She wore a matching aqua-blue shirt, as did Ty.

"I hope we can get a picture today of all of us. We look like a family," she said.

Cam reached over and took her hand and brought it to her lips. "We are a family."

He pulled into the parking lot, which was already bustling with activity, and led the way upstairs to the rooftop club. There the staff had set up a long buffet table with a highchair at one end.

"Good morning," Nate said, entering the rooftop club a few minutes behind them with his new wife. They both wore pink Luna Azul shirts and Jen had paired hers with a long ballet-type skirt.

"Morning," Cam said, and the brothers moved off to talk.

"Hi, Jen."

"Becca. I can't believe Nate made us get up this early. We were out until two with Hutch," Jen said.

"Neither of you looks the worse for it," Becca said.

"I'll need a nap later," Jen said. "Maybe I'll borrow Ty and lie down with him."

Becca laughed as Jen reached over and tickled Ty under the chin. She had never thought that she'd think of Jen and Selena as...sisters.

"I need coffee, Justin," Selena said as they entered the rooftop club. She wore a slim-fitting black skirt and a purple Luna Azul shirt.

"Yes, darling, anything else?" Justin asked.

"A kiss," she said, which he gave her before walking over to his brothers.

"Ladies. Can you believe the hour?" Selena asked.

"No. But I am excited about the weekend," Becca said.

"Me, too," Selena agreed. "I never thought I'd say this, but those three have made something special here."

"Yes, they have," Jen agreed. "I got a second chance from them."

Cam called them over to the table and they all took their seats. And Becca realized that Cam had given her so much more than a son as they sat there. He had given her that secret childhood dream she'd harbored of a family of her own. Not just a nuclear one of mother, father and child, but an extended one that would some-day include cousins and aunts and uncles.

The staff poured mimosas for the adults. Ty happily held his sippy cup of juice in his pudgy little hands.

Cam stood up and everyone turned to face him. "I wanted to take a few minutes this morning to say thank you to all of you for your work on this celebration. I know that the hour is early but I wanted to start this celebration the way Nate, Justin and I started Luna Azul—just family.

"I'm so happy to be welcoming Jen, Selena and Becca into our ranks and to see the first seeds of the future of Luna Azul in Ty."

Becca smiled up at her fiancé and felt something close to true happiness and peace spread over her.

"To Luna Azul. May the next ten years be just as exciting and successful as the last," Cam said, lifting his glass.

"To Luna Azul," everyone said, raising their glasses and taking sips of their drinks.

Breakfast was a chatty affair and Becca enjoyed every second of it. Soon the festivities started and they were all pulled in different directions but Cam always stayed close by her and Ty. At almost midnight, Ty was sleeping in Becca's arms. Cam embraced them both, rocking them slowly back and forth to the music of the country music act performing at the Mercado stage.

"I love you, Becca," Cam said, leaning down to whisper in her ear.

"I love you, too," Becca said.

Becca had the feeling that she and Cam were going to be together long after Luna Azul celebrated its fiftieth anniversary, as would Jen and Nate and Selena and Justin.

* * * * *

She squared her shoulders and told Emilio, "You don't scare me."

He stepped closer. "Are you sure? For a second there, I could swear you looked nervous."

She resisted the urge to take a step back. But not from fear. She just didn't appreciate him violating her personal space. She didn't like the way it made her feel. Out of control. His presence still did something to her after all this time. He would never know how hard it had been to tell him no back then, to wait. So many times she had come this close to giving in. But he had been too much of a gentleman. A genuinely good guy. He had respected her.

Not anymore.

"I know you," she said. "You're harmless."

He moved even closer, so she had to crane her neck to look into his eyes. "Maybe I've changed."

Dear Reader,

I love all of my characters, and all of the stories I write. But every so often I start a story that from day one just feels…*special*. This is one of those stories.

In the first BLACK GOLD BILLIONAIRES book, Emilio was a bit of a mystery. Quiet, thoughtful and a little intense—he left an impression on me. It wasn't until I started to write his story that the complexity of his character became clear. On the outside he's confident and successful and take-your-breath-away sexy, but on the inside…well, suffice it to say, there's more to this man than meets the eye.

Then there's Isabelle. At first she seemed so broken down and vulnerable, I was afraid readers would want to give her a firm shake and shout, "Honey, grow a spine for God's sake!" But she had a few surprises for me, as well. By the end of the book I found myself envying her. Wanting to *be* her.

As much as I would love to take all the credit for creating these two, they honestly wrote themselves. And helping them to put their story into words was an exciting, humbling and heart-warming experience. I hope you enjoy them as much as I did.

Until next month…

Michelle

ONE MONTH WITH THE MAGNATE

BY
MICHELLE CELMER

All the characters in this book have no existence outside the imagination of
the author, and have no relation whatsoever to anyone bearing the same name
or names. They are not even distantly inspired by any individual known or
unknown to the author, and all the incidents are pure invention.

Published in Great Britain 2012
by Mills & Boon, an imprint of Harlequin (UK) Limited,
Eton House, 18-24 Paradise Road, Richmond, Surrey TW9 1SR

© Michelle Celmer 2011

ISBN: 978 0 263 89125 6

51-0212

Harlequin (UK) policy is to use papers that are natural, renewable and
recyclable products and made from wood grown in sustainable forests. The
logging and manufacturing processes conform to the legal environmental
regulations of the country of origin.

Printed and bound in Spain
by Blackprint CPI, Barcelona

Bestselling author **Michelle Celmer** lives in southeastern Michigan with her husband, their three children, two dogs and two cats. When she's not writing or busy being a mom, you can find her in the garden or curled up with a romance novel. And if you twist her arm really hard, you can usually persuade her into a day of power shopping.

Michelle loves to hear from readers. Visit her website, www.michellecelmer.com, or write her at PO Box 300, Clawson, MI 48017, USA.

To my editor Charles, who has been, and continues to be, an amazing source of support and encouragement. It has been a privilege, a joy and a lot of fun working with you.

One

This was, without a doubt, the lowest Isabelle Winthrop-Betts had ever sunk.

Not even the sting of her father's open palm across her cheek had caused the humiliation she was feeling now thanks to Emilio Suarez, a man she once loved with all her heart and had planned to marry.

Her father had made sure that never happened. And Isabelle couldn't blame Emilio for the bitterness in his eyes as he sat behind his desk in his corner office at Western Oil headquarters, like a king on a throne addressing a local peasant.

Thanks to her husband, Leonard, that was really all she was now. She had gone from being one of the richest women in Texas, to a pauper. Homeless, penniless, widowed and about to be thrown in prison for fraud. And all because she had been too naive and trusting. Because when her husband had put documents in front of her, instead of reading them, she had blindly signed. How could she question the man who had rescued her from hell? Who had probably saved her life?

And the son of a bitch had up and died before he could exonerate her.

Thanks, Lenny.

"You have a lot of nerve asking me for help," Emilio said in the deep, caramel-smooth voice that strummed every one of her frayed nerve endings, but the animosity in his tone curdled her blood. Not that he wasn't justified in his anger, not after the way she'd broken his heart, but she'd had no choice. She didn't expect him to understand that, she just hoped he would take pity on her.

His charcoal gray eyes bore through her, and she fought not to wither under their scrutiny. "Why come to me? Why not go to your rich friends?"

Because his brother, Alejandro, was prosecuting her case. Besides, she had no friends. Not anymore. They had all invested with Lenny. Some had lost millions.

"You're the only one who can help me," she said.

"Why would I want to? Maybe I want to see you rot in prison."

She swallowed the hurt his words caused, that he hated her that much.

Well, he would be happy to learn that according to her lawyer, Clifton Stone, nothing would prevent that now. The evidence against her was overwhelming and her best bet was a plea bargain. And while the idea of spending even another minute in jail terrified her, she was prepared to take full responsibility for her actions and accept any punishment they considered appropriate. Unfortunately, Lenny had gotten her mother involved in his scams, too. After suffering years of physical and emotional abuse from her husband, Adriana Winthrop deserved some happiness. Not to spend the rest of her life in prison. Not for something that was Isabelle's fault.

"I don't care what happens to me," Isabelle told him. "I want my mother's name cleared. She had no part in any of Leonard's scams."

"Leonard's and *your* scams," he corrected.

She swallowed hard and nodded.

One dark brow rose. "So, you're admitting your guilt?"

If blind trust was a crime, she was definitely guilty. "It's my fault that I'm in this mess."

"This is not a good time for me."

She'd seen coverage on the news about the accident at the refinery. The explosion and the injured men. She'd tried to visit him last week, but the front of the Western Oil headquarters building had been crawling with media. She would have waited another week or two, but she was running out of time. It had to be now. "I know it's a bad time and I'm sorry. This couldn't wait."

Arms folded across his chest, he sat back in his chair and studied her. In a suit, with his closely cropped hair combed back, he barely resembled the boy she'd known from her adolescence. The one she had fallen head over heels in love with the instant she'd laid eyes on him, when she was twelve and he was fifteen. Although, it had taken him until college to notice her.

His mother had been their housekeeper and in her father's eyes, Emilio would never be good enough for his precious daughter. That hadn't stopped her from seeing Emilio in secret, fully aware of the price she would pay if they were caught. But they had been lucky—until her father learned of their plans to elope.

Not only had he punished her severely, he'd fired Emilio's mother. He accused her of stealing from them, knowing that no one else would hire her.

She wished her father could see them now. Emilio sitting there like the master of the universe and her begging for his help. He would be rolling in his grave.

See Daddy, he was good enough for me after all. Probably even better than I deserved.

Emilio never would have hurt her, never would have sacrificed her reputation out of greed. He was honest and trustworthy and loyal.

And right now, seriously pissed at her.

"So you're doing this for your mother?" he asked.

Isabelle nodded. "My lawyer said that with all the media attention, it's unlikely that your brother will be willing to deal. She'll serve some time."

"Maybe I'd like to see her rot in prison, too," he said.

She felt her hackles rise. Adriana Winthrop had never been anything but kind to him and his mother. She had done *nothing* to hurt them. She'd only been guilty of being married to an overbearing, abusive bastard. And even that wasn't entirely her fault. She had tried to leave and he'd made her live to regret it.

"Your appearance," he said. "Is it supposed to make me feel sorry for you?"

She resisted the urge to look down at the outdated blouse and ill-fitting slacks she had rummaged from the bag of clothes her mother had been donating to charity. Obviously he'd expected her to be wearing an outfit more suited to her previous station, but when her possessions had been seized, she kept nothing. For now, this was the best she could do.

"I don't feel sorry for you, Isabelle. It seems to me you're getting exactly what you deserve."

That was one thing they could agree on.

She could see that coming here had been a waste of time. He wasn't going to help her. He was too bitter.

Oh, well. It had been worth a try.

She rose from the chair, limp with defeat. Her voice trembled as she said, "Well, thank you for seeing me, Mr. Suarez."

"Sit down," he snapped.

"For what? You obviously have no intention of helping me."

"I never said I wouldn't help you."

Something in his eyes softened the slightest bit and hope welled up inside of her. She lowered herself into the chair.

"I'll talk to my brother on your mother's behalf, but I expect something in return."

She had expected as much, but the calculating look he wore sent a cold chill down her spine. "What?"

"You will agree to be my live-in housekeeper for thirty days. You'll cook for me, clean my house, do my laundry. Whatever I ask. At the end of the thirty days, if I'm satisfied with your performance, I'll talk to my brother."

In other words, he would make her work for him the way his mother had worked for her. Clever. Obviously he saw her plea for help as an opportunity to get revenge. What had happened to the sweet and kindhearted boy she used to know? The one who never would have been capable of dreaming up such a devious plan, much less have the gall to implement it. He had changed more than she could ever have guessed, and it stung to know that it was probably her fault. Had she hurt him so much when she left that he'd hardened his heart?

And what of his *offer?* The day her father died she had vowed never to let a man control her again. But this wasn't about her. She was doing this for her mother. She *owed* her. Besides, she had swallowed her pride so many times since the indictment, she was getting used to the bitter taste.

Despite what Emilio believed, she was no longer the

shy, timid girl of her youth. She was strong now. Anything he could dish out, she could take.

"How do I know I can trust you?" she asked. "How do I know that after the thirty days you won't change your mind?"

He leaned forward, eyes flaming with indignation as they locked on hers. "Because I have never been anything but honest with you, Isabelle."

Unlike her, his tone implied. He was right. Even though she'd had a valid reason for breaking her word, but that hardly seemed worth mentioning. Even if she told him the truth she doubted he would believe her. Or care.

He leaned back in his chair. "Take some time to think about it if you'd like."

She didn't need time. She didn't have any to spare. Less than six weeks from now she and her lawyer would meet with the prosecutor, and her lawyer warned her that it didn't look good. For her or her mother.

This wasn't going to be a pleasant thirty days, but at least she knew Emilio wouldn't physically harm her. He may have become cold and callous, but he had never been a violent man. He'd never made her feel anything but safe.

What if he changed? a little voice in her head taunted, but she ignored it. The decision had already been made.

She sat straight, squared her shoulders and told him, "I'll do it."

Isabelle Winthrop was a viper.

A lying, cheating, narcissistic viper.

Yet Emilio couldn't deny that despite the fifteen years that had passed, she was still the most physically beautiful woman he had ever laid eyes on.

But her soul was as black as tar.

She'd had him duped, all those years ago. He thought

she loved him. He had believed, despite the fact that she was a Winthrop and he was the son of a domestic servant, they would be married and live happily ever after. She told him she didn't care about the money or the status. She would be happy so long as they had each other. And he had fallen for it, right up until the minute he read the article in the paper announcing her marriage to finance guru Leonard Betts. A multi*billionaire.*

So much for her not caring about money and status. What other reason would she have to marry a man twenty-five years older?

When all was said and done, his relationship with Isabelle hadn't been a total loss. She had taught Emilio that women were not to be trusted, and he'd learned from her deceit never to put his heart on the line again.

That didn't mean he wasn't ready to dish out a little good old-fashioned revenge.

As for her being a criminal like her husband, he wasn't sure what to believe. According to the law, if she signed it, she was legally responsible. Now that Leonard was dead, someone had to pay.

Guilty or not, as far as Emilio was concerned, she was getting exactly what she deserved. But he was not prepared to be dragged down with her.

"There's just one condition," he told her.

She nervously tucked her pale blond hair behind her ears. Hair that he used to love running his fingers through. It was once shiny and soft and full of body, but now it looked dull and lifeless. "What condition?"

"No one can know about this." If it got out that he was helping her, it could complicate his chances for the CEO position at Western Oil. He was in competition with COO Jordan Everett and his brother, Nathan Everett, Chief Brand Officer. Both were friends and worthy opponents.

But Emilio deserved the position more. He'd earned it through more hard work than either of them could ever imagine with their Harvard educations that Daddy footed the bill for.

Maybe he was a fool to risk everything he'd worked so hard for, but Isabelle was offering an opportunity for revenge that he just couldn't pass up. After his father died, his mother worked her fingers to the bone trying to provide for Emilio and his three brothers. It was years after being fired by the Winthrops when she finally admitted to her children the verbal abuse she'd endured from Isabelle's father. Not to mention occasional improper sexual advances. But the pay was good, so she'd had no choice but to tolerate it. And after he had fired her, accused her of stealing from them, no respectable family would even think of hiring her.

Now Emilio's mother, his entire family, would finally be vindicated.

"Are you sure you don't want to brag to all of your friends?" Isabelle asked him.

"I'm the chief financial officer of this company. It wouldn't bode well for me or Western Oil if people knew I was in business with a woman indicted for financial fraud. If you tell a soul, not only is the deal off, but I will see that you *and* your mother rot in prison for a very long time."

"I can't just disappear for thirty days. My mother will want to know where I am."

"Then tell her you're staying with a friend until you get back on your feet."

"What about the authorities? I'm out on bond. They need to know where I'm staying. I could go back to jail."

"I'll take care of it," he said. He was sure he could work something out with his brother.

She looked wary, like she thought maybe it was a trick, but clearly she had no choice. She needn't have worried though. Unlike her, he honored his word.

"I won't tell anyone," she said.

"Fine." He slid a pad of paper and a pen across the desk to her. "Write down where you're currently staying and I'll have my driver come by to get you tonight."

She leaned forward to jot down the address. He assumed she would be staying with her mother, or in a high-class hotel, but what she wrote down was the name and address for a motel in one of the seedier parts of town. She really must have been in dire straits financially. Or she was pretending to be.

Several million dollars of the money they had stolen had never been recovered. For all he knew, she had it stashed somewhere. Of course, if she had been planning to run, wouldn't she have done it by now? Or was she waiting to cut a deal for her mother, then intending to skip town?

It was something to keep in mind.

"Be ready at seven," he told her. "Your thirty days will start tomorrow. Agreed?"

She nodded, chin held high. She wouldn't look so proud when he put her to work. Isabelle had never lifted a finger to do a thing for herself. He was sorry he wouldn't be home to witness what he was sure would be a domestic disaster.

The thought almost made him smile.

"Do you need a ride back to the hotel?" he asked.

She shook her head. "I borrowed my mother's car."

"That must be a change for you. Having to drive yourself places. It's a wonder you even remember how."

He could tell that she wanted to shoot back a snarky comment, but she kept her mouth shut and her eyes all but dared him to give it his best shot. She was tough, but she had no idea who she was dealing with. He wasn't the naive, trusting man he'd been before.

He stood and she did the same. He reached out to shake on the deal, and she slipped her finely boned hand into his—her breath caught when he enclosed it firmly, *possessively*. Though she tried to hide it, being close to him still did something to her. Which was exactly what he was counting on. Because bringing her into his home as a housekeeper was only a ruse to execute his true plan.

When they were together, Isabelle had insisted they wait until they were married to make love, so he had honored her wishes for a torturous year. Then she left him high and dry. Now it was time for some payback.

He would seduce Isabelle, make her want him, make her *beg* for it, then reject her.

By the time he was through with her, prison would seem like Club Med.

Two

"Is that who I think it was?"

Emilio looked up from his computer to find Adam Blair, the current CEO of Western Oil, standing in his office doorway. He should have known word of his *visitor* would get around fast. Her disguise—if that had been her intention with the ridiculous clothes, the straight, lifeless hair and absence of makeup—not to mention the fake name she had given the guards when she insisted on seeing him, obviously hadn't worked. When he saw her standing there in the lobby, her shoulders squared, head held high, looking too proud for her own good, he should have sent her away, but curiosity had gotten the best of him.

Emilio had warned Adam months ago, just before news of the Ponzi scheme became public, that he had a past connection to Isabelle. But he'd never expected her to turn up at his office. And he sure as hell hadn't considered that she would have the audacity to ask for his help. She was probably accustomed to getting exactly what she wanted.

"That was Isabelle Winthrop-Betts," he told Adam.

"What did she want?"

"My help. She wants her mother's name cleared, and she wants me to talk to my brother on her behalf."

"What about her own name?"

"She more or less admitted her guilt to me. She intends to take full responsibility for everything."

Adam's brows rose. "That's…surprising."

Emilio thought so, too. With a federal prosecutor for a sibling, he had heard of every scheme imaginable from every type of criminal. Freely admitting guilt wasn't usually one of them. Isabelle was clearly up to something. He just hadn't figured out what. He had considered that she and her mother were planning to take the unrecovered money and disappear, but why bother exonerating her first? Maybe he could gain her trust, encourage her to tell him her plans, then report her to the authorities.

"So, will you help her?" Adam asked.

"I told her I would talk to Alejandro." Which he still had to do, and he wasn't looking forward to it.

"Also surprising. The last time we talked about her, you seemed awfully bitter."

Not only was Adam a colleague, he was one of Emilio's closest friends. Still, he doubted Adam would even begin to understand his lust for revenge. He wasn't that kind of man. He'd never been betrayed the way Emilio had. Emilio would keep that part of his plan to himself. Besides, Adam would no doubt be opposed to anything that might bring more negative press to Western Oil.

What he didn't know wouldn't hurt him.

"Call me sentimental," Emilio said.

Adam laughed. "Sorry, but that's the last thing I would

ever call you. Sentimental isn't a word in your vocabulary, not unless it's regarding your mother. Just tell me you're not planning on doing something stupid."

There were many levels of stupid. Emilio was barely scratching the surface.

"You have nothing to be concerned about," he assured Adam. "You have my word."

"Good enough for me." Adam's cell buzzed, alerting him that he had a text. As he read it, he smiled. "Katy just got to the house. She's staying in El Paso for a few days, then we're driving back to Peckins together."

Katy was Adam's fiancée. She was also his former sister-in-law and five months pregnant with their first child. Or possibly Katy's dead sister's baby. They weren't sure.

"Have you two set a date yet?" Emilio asked.

"We're leaning toward a small ceremony at her parents' ranch between Christmas and New Year's. I'll let you know as soon as we decide. I'd just like to make it official before the baby is born." Adam looked at his watch. "Well, I have a few things to finish before I leave for the day."

"Send Katy my best."

Adam turned to leave, then paused and turned back. "You're sure you know what you're doing?"

Emilio didn't have to ask what he meant. Adam obviously suspected that there was more to the situation than Emilio was letting on. "I'm sure."

When he was gone, Emilio picked up the phone and dialed his brother's office.

"Hey, big brother," Alejandro answered when his secretary connected them. "Long time no see. The kids miss their favorite uncle."

Emilio hadn't seen his nephews, who were nine, six and two, nearly often enough lately. They were probably the closest thing he would ever have to kids of his own, so he tried to visit on a regular basis. "I know, I'm sorry. Things have been a little crazy here since the refinery accident."

"Any promising developments?"

"At this point, no. It's looking like it may have been sabotage. We're launching an internal investigation. But keep that between us."

"Of course. It's ironic that you called today because I was planning to call you. Alana had a doctor's appointment this morning. She's pregnant again."

Emilio laughed. "Congratulations! I thought you decided to stop at three."

"We did, but she really wanted to try for a girl. I keep telling her that with four boys in my family, we'd have better luck adopting, but she wanted to give it one more try."

Emilio couldn't imagine having one child now much less four. There had been a time when he wanted a family. He and Isabelle had talked about having at least two children. But that was a long time ago. "Are the boys excited?" he asked his brother.

"We haven't told them yet, but I think they'll be thrilled. Alex and Reggie anyway. Chris is a little young to grasp the concept."

"I don't suppose you've heard from Estefan," Emilio asked, referring to their younger brother. Due to drugs, gambling and various other addictions, they usually only heard from him when he needed money or a temporary place to crash. Their mother lived in fear that one day the phone would ring and it would be the coroner's office asking her to come down and identify his body.

"Not a word. I'm not sure if I should feel worried or relieved. I did get an email from Enrique, though. He's in Budapest."

Enrique was the youngest brother and the family nomad. He'd left for a summer backpacking trip through Europe after graduating from college. That was almost three years ago and he hadn't come home yet. Every now and then they would get a postcard or an email, or he would upload photos on the internet of his latest adventures. Occasionally he would pick up the phone and call. He kept promising he'd be home soon, but there was always some new place he wanted to visit. A new cause to devote his life to.

Emilio and Alejandro talked for several minutes about family and work, until Emilio knew he had to quit stalling and get to the point of his call. "I need a favor."

"Anything," Alejandro said.

"Isabelle Winthrop will be checking out of her motel this evening. As far as your office is concerned, she's still staying there."

There was a pause, then Alejandro muttered a curse. "What's going on, Emilio?"

"Not what you think." He told his brother about Isabelle's visit and his "agreement" with her. Leaving out his plan to seduce her, of course. Family man that Alejandro was, he would never understand. He'd never had his heart broken the way Emilio had. Alana had been his high school sweetheart. His first love. Other than a short break they had taken in college to explore other options—which lasted all of two weeks before they could no longer stand to be apart—they had been inseparable.

"Are you completely out of your mind?" Alejandro asked.

"I know what I'm doing."

"If Mama finds out what you're up to, she's going to kill you, then she's going to kill *me* for helping you!"

"I'm doing this for Mama, for *all* of us. For what Isabelle's father did to our family."

"And it has nothing to do with the fact that Isabelle broke your heart?"

A nerve in his jaw ticked. "You said yourself that she's guilty."

"On paper, yes."

"She all but admitted her guilt to me."

"Well, there've been developments in the case."

Emilio frowned. "What kind of developments?"

"You know I can't tell you that. I shouldn't be talking to you about this, period. And I sure as hell shouldn't be helping you. If someone in my office finds out what you're doing—"

"No one will find out."

"My point is, it won't just be your job on the line."

He hadn't wanted to pull out the big guns, but Alejandro was leaving him no choice. "If it weren't for me, little brother, you wouldn't be in that cushy position."

Though Alejandro had planned to wait until his career was established for marriage and kids, Alana had become pregnant with Alex during Alejandro's last year of law school. With a wife and baby to support, he couldn't afford to stay at the top-notch school he'd been attending without Emilio's financial help.

Emilio had never held that over him. Until now.

Alejandro cursed again and Emilio knew he had him. "I hope you know what you're doing."

"I do."

"I'll be honest though, and you did not hear this from me, but with a little more pressure from her lawyer, we would have agreed to a deal on her mother's charge. She would have likely come out of this with probation."

"Isabelle's lawyer told her you wouldn't deal."

"It's called playing hardball, big brother. And maybe her lawyer isn't giving her the best advice."

"What do you mean?"

"I'm not at liberty to say."

"Is he a hack or something?"

"Not at all. He was Betts's lawyer. Clifton Stone. A real shark. And he's representing her *pro bono*."

"Why?"

"She's broke. All assets were frozen when she and Betts were arrested, and everything they owned was auctioned off for restitution."

"Everything?"

"Yeah. It was weird that she didn't fight for anything. No clothes or jewelry. She just gave it all up."

"I thought there was several million unrecovered."

"If she's got money stashed somewhere, she's not touching it."

That could have simply meant that the minute her mother's name was cleared, she would disappear. Why pay for a top-notch defense when she wouldn't be sticking around to hear the verdict? The crappy motel and the outdated clothes could have all been another part of the ruse.

"So why is her lawyer giving her bad advice?"

"That's a good question."

One he obviously had no intention of answering. Not that it mattered to Emilio either way.

"Are you sure this is about revenge?" Alejandro asked.

"What else would it be?"

"All these years there hasn't been anyone special in your life. What if deep down you still have feelings for her? Maybe you still love her."

"Impossible." His heart had been broken beyond repair, and had since hardened into an empty shell. He had no love left to give.

* * *

Emilio had a beautiful house. But Isabelle wouldn't have expected any less. The sprawling stucco estate was located in one of El Paso's most prestigious communities. She knew this for a fact because, until she married Lenny, she used to live in the very same area. Her parents' home had been less than two blocks away. Though she was willing to bet from the facade that this was even larger and more lavish. It was exactly the sort of place Emilio used to talk about owning someday. He'd always set his sights high, and it looked as though he'd gotten everything he ever wanted.

She was happy for him, because he deserved it. Deep down she wished she could have been part of his life, wished she still could be, but it was too late now. Clearly the damage she had done was irreparable. Some people weren't meant to have it all, and a long time ago she had come to terms with the fact that she was one of those people.

Not that she was feeling sorry for herself. In fact, she considered herself very lucky. The fifteen years she had been married to Lenny, she'd had a pretty good life. She had never wanted for a thing. Except a man who loved and desired her, but Lenny had loved her in his own way. If nothing else, she had been safe.

Until the indictment, anyway.

But she would have years in prison to contemplate her mistakes and think about what might have been. All that mattered now was clearing her mother's name.

The limo stopped out front and the driver opened the door for her. The temperature had dipped into the low fifties with the setting sun and she shivered under her light sweater. She was going to have to think about getting herself some warmer clothes and a winter jacket.

It was dark out, but the house and grounds were well lit. Still, she felt uneasy as the driver pulled her bag from the back. He set it on the Spanish tile drive, then with a tip of his hat he climbed back into the limo. As he drove off, Isabelle took a deep breath, grabbed her bag and walked to the porch, a two-story high structure bracketed by a pair of massive white columns and showcased with etched glass double doors. Above the door was an enormous, round leaded window that she imagined let in amazing morning light.

Since Emilio knew what time she was arriving, she'd half expected him to be waiting there to greet her, but there was no sign of him so she walked up the steps and rang the bell. A minute passed, then another, but no one came to the door. She wondered if maybe the bell was broken, and knocked instead. Several more minutes passed, and she began to think he might not be home. Was he held up at the office? And what was she supposed to do? Sit there and wait?

She had a sudden sinking feeling. What if this was some sort of trick? Some sick revenge. What if he'd never planned to let her in? Hell, maybe this wasn't even his house.

No, he wouldn't do that. He may have been angry with her, he may have even hated her, but he could never be that cruel. When they were together he had been the kindest, gentlest man she had ever known.

She reached up to ring the bell one last time when behind her someone said, "I'm not home."

Her heart slammed against her rib cage and she spun around to find Emilio looking up at her from the driveway. He wore a nylon jacket and jogging pants, his forehead was dotted with perspiration and he was out of breath.

Still a jogger. Back in college, he'd been diligent about

keeping in shape. He'd even convinced her to go to the gym with him a few times, but to the annoyance of her friends, her naturally slim build never necessitated regular exercise.

He stepped up to the porch and stopped so close to her that she could practically feel the heat radiating off his body. He smelled of a tantalizing combination of aftershave, evening air and red-blooded man. She was torn between the desire to lean close and breathe him in, or run like hell. Instead she stood her ground, met his penetrating gaze. He'd always been tall, but now he seemed to tower over her with the same long, lean build as in his youth. The years had been good to him.

He looked at her luggage, then her. "Where's the rest?"

"This is all I brought."

One dark brow rose. A move so familiar, she felt a jab of nostalgia, a longing for the way things used to be. One he clearly did not share.

"You travel light," he said.

Pretty much everything she owned was in that one piece of luggage. A few of her mother's fashion rejects and the rest she'd purchased at the thrift store. When the feds had seized their home, she hadn't tried or even wanted to keep any of the possessions. She couldn't stand the thought of wearing clothes that she knew had been purchased with stolen money.

The clothes, the state of the art electronic equipment, the fine jewelry and priceless art had all been auctioned off, and other than her coffee/espresso machine, she didn't miss any of it.

Leaving the bag right where it was—she hadn't really expected him to carry it for her—Emilio turned and punched in a code on the pad beside the door. She heard a click as the lock disengaged, and as he opened the door the lights automatically switched on.

She picked up her bag and followed him inside, nearly gasping at the magnificence of the interior. The two-story foyer opened up into a grand front room with a curved, dual marble stairway. In the center hung an ornately fashioned wrought iron chandelier that matched the banister. The walls were painted a tasteful cream color, with boldly colored accents.

"It's lovely," she said.

"I'll show you to your quarters, then give you a tour. My housekeeper left a list of your daily duties and sample menus for you to follow."

"You didn't fire her, I hope."

He shot her a stern look. "Of course not. I gave her a month paid vacation."

That was generous of him. He could obviously afford it. She was thankful the woman had left instructions. What Isabelle knew about cooking and cleaning could be listed on an index card with lines to spare, but she was determined to learn. How hard could it be?

Emilio led her through an enormous kitchen with polished mahogany cabinets, marble countertops and top-of-the-line steel appliances, past a small bathroom and laundry room to the maid's quarters in the back.

So, this was where she would spend the next thirty days. It was barely large enough to hold a single bed, a small wood desk and padded folding chair, and a tall, narrow chest of drawers. The walls were white and completely bare but for the small crucifix hanging above the bed. It wasn't luxurious by any stretch of the imagination, but it was clean and safe, which was more than she could say for her motel. Checking out of that hellhole, knowing she would no longer wake in the middle of the night to the sound of roaches and rodents scratching in the walls, and God only knows what sort of illegal activity just outside her door, had in itself almost been worth a month of humiliation.

She set her bag on the faded blue bedspread. "Where is your housekeeper staying while I'm here?" she asked. She hoped not in the house. The idea of someone watching over her shoulder made her uneasy. This would be humiliating enough without an audience.

"She's not a live-in. I prefer my privacy."

"Yet, you're letting *me* stay," she said.

Up went the brow again. "I could move you into the pool house if you'd prefer. Although you may find the lack of heat less than hospitable."

She was going to have to curb the snippy comments. At this point it probably wouldn't take much for him to back out of their deal.

He nodded toward the chest. "You'll find your uniform in the top drawer."

Uniform? He never said anything about her wearing a uniform. For one horrifying instant she wondered if he would seize the opportunity to inflict even more humiliation by making her wear a revealing French maid's outfit. Or something even worse.

She pulled the drawer open, relieved to find a plain, drab gray, white collared dress. The same kind his mother wore when she worked for Isabelle's parents. She almost asked how he knew what size to get, but upon close inspection realized that the garment would be too big.

She slid the drawer closed and turned to face Emilio. He stood just inside the doorway, arms folded, expression dark—an overwhelming presence in the modest space. And he was blocking the door.

She felt a quick jab of alarm.

She was cornered. In a bedroom no less. What if his

intentions were less than noble? What if he'd brought her here so he could take what she'd denied him fifteen years ago?

Of course he wouldn't. Any man who would wait a year to be with a woman knew a thing or two about self-control. Besides, why would he want to have sex with someone he clearly hated? He wasn't that sort of man. At least, he never used to be.

He must have sensed her apprehension. That damned brow lifted again and he asked, with a look of amusement, "Do I frighten you, Izzie?"

Three

Izzie. Emilio was the only one who ever called her that. Hearing it again, after so many years, made Isabelle long to recapture the happiness of those days. The sense of hopefulness. The feeling that as long as they had each other, they could overcome any obstacles.

How wrong she had been. She'd discovered that there were some obstacles she would never overcome. At least, not until it was too late.

She squared her shoulders and told Emilio, "You don't scare me."

He stepped closer. "Are you sure? For a second there, I could swear you looked nervous."

She resisted the urge to take a step back. But not from fear. She just didn't appreciate him violating her personal space. She didn't like the way it made her feel. Out of control. Defenseless. His presence still did something to her after all this time. He would never know how hard it had been to tell him no back then, to wait. So many times she had come *this close* to giving in. If he had pushed a little harder, she probably would have. But he had been too much of a gentleman. A genuinely good guy. He had respected her.

Not anymore.

"I know you," she said. "You're harmless."

He moved even closer, so she had to crane her neck to look into his eyes. "Maybe I've changed."

Unlikely. And she refused to back down, to let him intimidate her.

She folded her arms and glared up at him, and after a few seconds more he backed away, then he turned and walked out. She assumed she was meant to follow him. A proper host would have given her time to unpack and freshen up. He might have offered her something to drink. But he wasn't her host. He was her employer. Or more appropriately, her warden. This was just a prison of a different kind. A prison of hurt and regret.

On the kitchen counter lay the duty list he'd mentioned. He handed it to her and when she saw that it was *eight* pages single-spaced she nearly swallowed her own tongue. Her shock must have shown, because that damned brow quirked up and Emilio asked, "Problem?"

She swallowed hard and shook her head. "None at all."

She flipped through it, seeing that it was efficiently organized by room and listed which chores should be performed on which day. Some things, like vacuuming the guest rooms and polishing the chrome in the corresponding bathrooms, were done on a weekly basis, alternating one of the five spare bedrooms every day. Other duties such as dusting the marble in the entryway and polishing the kitchen counters was a daily task. That didn't even include the cooking.

It was difficult to believe that one person could accomplish this much in one day. From the looks of it, she would be working from dawn to dusk without a break.

"I'm putting a few final touches on the menus, but you'll have them first thing tomorrow," Emilio said. "I'm assuming you can cook."

Not if it meant doing much more than heating a frozen dinner in the microwave or boiling water on a hot plate. "I'll manage."

"Of course you'll be responsible for all the shopping as well. You'll have a car at your disposal. And you're welcome to eat whatever you desire." He gave her a quick once-over, not bothering to hide his distaste. "Although from the looks of you, I'm guessing you don't eat much."

Eating required money and that was in short supply these days. She refused to sponge off her mother, whose financial situation was only slightly less grave, and no one was interested in hiring a thief six weeks from a twenty-to-life visit to the slammer. Besides, Isabelle had been such a nervous wreck lately, every time she tried to eat she would get a huge lump in her throat, through which food simply refused to pass.

She shrugged. "Like they say in Hollywood, there's no such thing as too thin."

"I see you still have the same irrational hang-ups about your body," he snapped back, his contempt so thick she could have choked on it. "I remember that you would only undress in the dark and hide under the covers when I turned the light on."

Her only hang-up had been with letting Emilio see the scars and bruises. He would have wanted an explanation, and she knew that if she'd told him the truth, something bad would happen. She'd done it to protect him and he was throwing it back in her face.

If this was a preview of what she should expect from the next thirty days, it would be a long month. But she could take it. And the less she said, the better.

The fact that she remained silent, that she didn't rise to her own defense, seemed to puzzle him. She waited for his next attack, but instead he gestured her out of the kitchen. "The living room is this way."

If he had more barbs to throw, he was saving them for another time.

She could hardly wait.

Though Emilio's hospitality left a lot to be desired, his home had all the comforts a person could possibly need. Six bedrooms and eight baths, a state of the art media room and a fitness/game room complete with autographed sports memorabilia. He had a penchant for Mexican pottery and an art collection so vast he could open a gallery. The house was furnished and decorated with a lively, southwestern flair.

It was as close to perfect as a home could be, the apotheosis of his ambitions, yet for some reason it seemed…empty. Perfect to the point of feeling almost unoccupied. Or maybe it simply lacked a woman's touch.

When they got to the master suite he stopped outside the door. "This room is off-limits. The same goes for my office downstairs."

Fine with her. That much less work as far as she was concerned. Besides, his bedroom was the last place she wanted to be spending any time.

He ended the tour there, and they walked back down to the kitchen. "Be sure you study that list, as I expect you to adhere to those exact specifications."

Her work would be exemplary. Now that she'd had a taste of how bitter he was, it was essential that she not give him a single reason to find fault with her performance. Too much was at stake. "If there's nothing more, I'll go to my room now," she said.

"No need to rush off." He peeled off his jacket and tossed it over the back of a kitchen chair. Underneath he wore a form-fitting muscle shirt that accentuated every plane of lean muscle in his chest and abs, and she was far from immune to the physical draw of an attractive man. Especially one she had never completely fallen out of love with. Meaning the less time she spent with him, the better.

He grabbed a bottled water from the fridge, but didn't offer her one. "It's early. Stick around for a while."

"I'm tired," she told him. "And I need to study that list."

"But we haven't had a chance to catch up." He propped himself against the counter, as though he was settling in for a friendly chat. "What have you been up to the past fifteen years? Besides defrauding the better part of Texas high society."

She bit the inside of her cheek.

"You know what I find ironic? I'll bet if your parents had to guess who they thought was more likely to go to federal prison, you or me, they would have chosen the son of Cuban immigrants over their precious daughter."

Apparently his idea of catching up would consist of thinly veiled insults and jabs at her character. *Swell*.

"No opinion?" he asked, clearly hoping she would retaliate, but she refused to be baited. Others had said much worse and she'd managed to ignore them, too. Reporters and law officials, although the worst of it had come from people who had supposedly been her friends. But she wouldn't begrudge a single one of them their very strong opinions. Even if the only thing she was truly guilty of was stupidity.

"It's just as well," Emilio said. "I have work to catch up on."

Struggling to keep her face devoid of emotion so he wouldn't see how relieved she was, she grabbed the list and walked to her quarters, ultra-aware of his gaze boring into her back. Once inside she closed the door and leaned against it. She hadn't been lying, she was truly exhausted. She couldn't recall the last time she'd had a decent night's sleep.

She gazed longingly at the bed, but it was still early, and she had to at least make an effort to familiarize herself with her duties before she succumbed to exhaustion.

She hung her sweater on the back of the folding chair and sat down, setting the list in front of her on the desk.

According to the housekeeper's schedule, Emilio's car picked him up at seven-thirty sharp, so Isabelle had to be up no later than six-thirty to fix his coffee and make his breakfast. If she was in bed by ten, she would get a solid eight and a half hours' sleep. About double what she'd been getting at the motel if she counted all the times she was jolted awake by strange noises. The idea of feeling safe and secure while she slept was an enticing one, as was the anticipation of eating something other than ramen noodles for breakfast, lunch and dinner.

If she could manage to avoid Emilio, staying here might not be so bad after all.

Usually Emilio slept like a baby, but knowing he wasn't alone in the house had him tossing and turning most of the night.

It had been odd, after so many years apart, to see Isabelle standing on his front porch waiting for him. After she married Betts, Emilio had intended never to cross paths with her again. He'd declined invitations to functions that he knew she would be attending and chose his friends and acquaintances with the utmost care.

He had done everything in his power to avoid her, yet here she was, sleeping in his servants' quarters. Maybe the pool house would have been a better alternative.

He stared through the dark at the ceiling, recalling their exchange of words earlier. Isabelle had changed. She used to be so subdued and timid. She would have recoiled from his angry words and cowered in the face of his resentment, and she never would have dished out any caustic comments of her own. A life of crime must have hardened her.

But what had Alejandro said? She was guilty on paper, but there had been new developments. Could she be innocent?

That didn't change what she had done to him, and what her father had done to Emilio's family. She could have implored him to keep his mother on as an employee, or to at least give her a positive recommendation. She hadn't even tried.

In a way, he wished he had never met her. But according to her, it was destiny. She used to say she knew from the first moment she laid eyes on him that they were meant to be with one another, that fate had drawn them together. Although technically he had known her for years before he'd ever really noticed her. His mother drove them to school in the mornings, he and his brothers to public school and Izzie to the private girls' school down the road, and other than an occasional "hi," she barely spoke to him. To him, she had never been more than the daughter of his mother's employer, a girl too conceited to give him the time of day. Only later had she admitted that she'd had such a crush on him that she'd been too tongue-tied to speak.

During his junior year of high school he'd gotten his own car and rarely saw her after that. Then, when he was in college, she had shown up out of the blue at the house he'd rented on campus for the summer session. She had just graduated from high school and planned to attend classes there in the fall. She asked if he would show her around campus.

Though it seemed an odd request considering they had barely ever spoken, he felt obligated, since her parents paid his mother's salary. They spent the afternoon together, walking and chatting, and in those few hours he began to see a side of her that he hadn't known existed. She was intelligent and witty, but with a childlike innocence he found compelling. He realized that what he had once mistaken for conceit and entitlement was really shyness and self-doubt. He found that he could open up to her, that despite their vast social differences, she understood him. He liked her, and there was no doubt she had romantic feelings toward him, but she was young and naive and he knew her parents would never approve of their daughter dating the son of the hired help. He decided that they could be friends, but nothing more.

Then she kissed him.

He had walked her back to her car and they were saying goodbye. Without warning she threw her arms around his neck and pressed her lips to his. He was stunned—and aroused—and though he knew he should stop her, the scent of her skin and the taste of her lips were irresistible. They stood there in the dark kissing for a long time, until she said she had to get home. But by then it was too late. He was hooked.

He spent every minute he wasn't at work or in class that summer with her, and when they were apart it was torture. They were only dating two weeks when he told her he loved her, and after a month he knew he wanted to marry her, but he waited until their six month anniversary to ask her formally.

They figured that if they both saved money until the

end of the school year they would have enough to get a small place together, then they would elope. He warned her it would be tight for a while, maybe even years, until he established his career. She swore it didn't matter as long as they were together.

But in the end it *had* mattered.

Emilio let out an exasperated sigh and looked at the clock. Two-thirty. If he lay here rehashing his mistakes he was never going to get to sleep. These were issues he'd resolved a long time ago. Or so he'd thought.

Maybe bringing Isabelle into his home had been a bad idea. Was revenge really worth a month of sleepless nights? He just had to remind himself how well he would sleep when his family was vindicated.

Emilio eventually drifted off to sleep, then roused again at four-fifteen wide-awake. After an unsuccessful half hour of trying to fall back to sleep, he got out of bed and went down to his office. He worked for a while, then spent an hour in the fitness room before going upstairs to get ready for work. He came back down at seven, expecting his coffee and breakfast to be waiting for him, but the kitchen was dark.

He shook his head, disappointed, but not surprised. His new housekeeper was not off to a good start. Her first day on the job could very well be her last.

He walked back to her quarters and raised his hand to knock, then noticed the door wasn't latched. With his foot he gave it a gentle shove and it creaked open. He expected to find Isabelle curled up in bed. Instead she sat slumped over at the desk, head resting on her arms, sound asleep. She was still wearing the clothes from last night, and on the desk, under her arms, lay the list of her duties. Her bag sat open but unpacked on the bed, and the covers hadn't been disturbed.

She must have dozed off shortly after going to her room, and she must have been pretty exhausted to sleep in such an awkward position all night.

He sighed and shook his head. At least one of them had gotten a good night's rest.

A part of him wanted to be angry with her, wanted to send her packing for neglecting her duties, but he had the feeling this had been an unintentional oversight. He would give her the benefit of the doubt. Just this once. But he wouldn't deny himself the pleasure of giving her a hard time about it.

Four

"Isabelle!"

Isabelle shot up with such force she nearly flung the chair over, blinking furiously, trying to get her bearings. She saw Emilio standing in the doorway and her eyes went wide. "Wh-what time is it?"

"Three minutes after seven." He folded his arms, kept his mouth in a grim line. "Were you expecting breakfast in bed?"

Her skin paled. "I was going to set the alarm on my phone. I must have fallen asleep before I had the chance."

"And you consider that a valid excuse for neglecting your duties?"

"No, you're right. I screwed up." She squared her shoulders and rose stiffly from the chair. "I'll pack my things and be out of here before you leave from work."

For a second he thought she was playing the sympathy

card, but she wore a look of resigned hopelessness that said she seriously expected him to terminate their agreement.

He probably should have, but if he let her go now he would be denying himself the pleasure of breaking her. Lucky for her, he was feeling generous this morning. "If you leave, who will make my coffee?"

She gazed up at him with hope in her eyes. "Does that mean you're giving me a second chance?"

"Don't let it happen again. Next time I won't be so forgiving."

"I won't, I promise." She looked over at the dresser. "My uniform—"

"Coffee first."

"What about breakfast?"

"No time. I only have twenty-five minutes until the company car is here to pick me up."

"Sorry." She edged past him through the door and scurried to the kitchen.

He went to his office to put the necessary paperwork in his briefcase, and when he walked back into the kitchen several minutes later the coffee was brewed. Isabelle wasn't there, so he grabbed a travel mug and filled it himself. He took a sip, surprised to realize that it was actually good. A little stronger than his housekeeper, Mrs. Medina, usually made it, but he liked it.

Isabelle emerged from her room a minute later wearing her uniform. He looked her up and down and frowned. The oversize garment hung on her, accentuating her skeletal physique. "It's too big."

She shrugged. "It's okay."

It was an old uniform a former employee had left so he hadn't really expected it to fit. "You'll need a new one."

"It's only for thirty days. It's fine."

"It is not *fine*. It looks terrible. Tell me what size you wear and I'll have a new one sent to the house."

She chewed her lip, avoiding his gaze.

"Are you going to tell me, or should I guess?"

"I'm not exactly sure. I've lost weight recently."

"So tell me your weight and height and they can send over the appropriate size."

"I'm five foot four."

"And…?"

She looked at the floor.

"Your weight, Isabelle?"

She shrugged.

"You don't know how much you weigh?"

"I don't own a scale."

He sighed. Why did she have to make everything so difficult?

"Fitness room," he said, gesturing to the doorway. "I have a scale in there."

She reluctantly followed him and was even less enthusiastic about getting on the digital scale. As she stepped on she averted her eyes.

The number that popped up was nothing short of disturbing. "Considering your height, you have to be at least fifteen or twenty pounds underweight."

Isabelle glanced at the display, and if her grimace was any indication, she was equally unsettled by the number. Not the reaction he would have expected from someone with a "there's no such thing as too thin" dictum.

"Am I correct in assuming this weight loss wasn't intentional?" he asked.

She nodded.

It hadn't occurred to him before, but what if there was something wrong with her? "Are you ill?"

She stepped down off the scale. "It's been a stressful couple of months."

"That's no excuse to neglect your health. While you're here I expect you to eat three meals a day, and I intend to make you climb on that scale daily until you've gained at least fifteen pounds."

Her eyes rounded with surprise.

"Is that a problem?" he asked.

For an instant she looked as though she would argue, then she pulled her lip between her teeth and shook her head.

"Good." He looked at his watch. "I have to go. I'll be home at six-thirty. I expect dinner to be ready no later than seven."

"Yes, sir."

There was a note of ambivalence in her tone, but he let it slide. The subject of her weight was clearly a touchy one. A fact he planned to exploit. And he had the distinct feeling there was more to the story than she would admit. Just one more piece to this puzzle of a woman who he thought he knew, but wasn't at all what he had expected.

Though Isabelle wasn't sure what her father had paid Emilio's mother, she was positive it wasn't close to enough.

She never imagined taking care of a house could be so exhausting. The dusting alone had taken nearly three hours, and she'd spent another two and a half on the windows and mirrors on the first floor. Both tasks had required more bending and stretching than any yoga class she'd ever attended, and she'd climbed the stairs so many times her legs felt limp.

Worse than the physical exhaustion was how inept she was at using the most basic of household appliances. It had taken her ten minutes to find the "on" switch on the vacuum, and one frayed corner on the upstairs runner to learn that the carpet setting didn't work well for fringed rugs. They got sucked up into the spinny thing inside and ripped off. She just hoped that Emilio didn't notice. She would have to figure out some way to pay to get it fixed. And soon.

Probably her most puzzling dilemma was the cupboard full of solutions, waxes and paraphernalia she was supposed to use in her duties. Never had she imagined there were so many different types of cleaning products. She spent an hour reading the labels, trying to determine which suited her various tasks, which put her even further behind in her duties.

Her new uniforms arrived at three-thirty by messenger. Emilio had ordered four in two different sizes, probably to accommodate the weight he was expecting her to gain. The smallest size fit perfectly and was far less unflattering than the oversize version. In fact, it fit better and looked nicer than most of the street clothes she currently owned. Too bad it didn't contain magic powers that made her at least a little less inept at her duties.

When she heard Emilio come through the front door at six-thirty, she hadn't even started on the upstairs guest room yet. She steeled herself for his latest round of insults and jabs and as he stepped into the kitchen, travel cup in one hand, his briefcase in the other, her heart sailed up into her throat. He looked exhausted and rumpled in a sexy way.

He set his cup in the sink. Though she was probably inviting trouble, she asked, "How was work?"

"Long, and unproductive," he said, loosening his tie. "How was your day?"

A civilized response? Whoa. She hadn't expected that. "It was…good."

"I see you haven't burned the house down. That's promising."

So much for being civil.

"I'm going to go change," he said. "I trust dinner will be ready on time."

"Of course." At least she hoped so. It had taken her a bit longer to assemble the chicken dish than she'd anticipated, so to save cooking time, she'd raised the oven heat by one hundred degrees.

He gave her a dismissive nod, then left the room. She heard the heavy thud of his footsteps as he climbed the stairs. With any luck he wouldn't look down.

A minute passed, and she began to think that she was safe, then he thundered from the upstairs hallway, "Isabelle!"

Shoot.

It was still possible it wasn't the rug he was upset about. Maybe he'd checked the guest room and saw that she hadn't cleaned it yet. She walked to the stairs, climbing them slowly, her hopes plummeting when she reached the top and saw him standing with his arms folded, lips thinned, looking at the corner of the runner.

"Is there something you need to tell me?" he asked.

It figured that he would ignore all the things she had done right and focus in on the one thing she had done wrong. "The vacuum ate your rug."

"It *ate* it?"

"I had it on the wrong setting. I take full responsibility." As if it could somehow *not* be her fault.

"Why didn't you mention this when I asked how your day went?"

"I forgot?"

One dark brow rose. "Is that a question?"

She took a deep breath and blew it out. "Okay, I was hoping you wouldn't notice."

"I notice *everything*."

Apparently. "I'll pay for the damage."

"How?"

Good question. "I'll figure something out."

She expected him to push the issue, but he didn't.

"Is there anything else you've neglected to mention?"

Nothing she hadn't managed to fix, unless she counted the plastic container she'd melted in the microwave, but he would never notice that.

She shook her head.

Emilio studied her, as if he were sizing her up, and she felt herself withering under his scrutiny.

"That's better," he said.

She blinked. "Better?"

"The uniform. It actually fits."

Did he just compliment her? Albeit in a backhanded, slightly rude way. But it was a start.

"You ate today?" he asked.

"Twice." For breakfast she'd made herself fried eggs swimming in butter with rye toast slathered in jam and for lunch she'd heated a can of clam chowder. It had been heavenly.

He looked down at the rug again. "This will have to be rebound."

"I'll take care of it first thing tomorrow."

"Let me know how much it will be and I'll write a check."

"I'll pay you back a soon as I can." She wondered what the hourly wage was to make license plates.

"Yes, you will." He turned and walked into his bedroom, shutting the door.

Isabelle blew out a relieved breath. That hadn't gone

nearly as bad as she'd expected. With any hope, dinner would be a smashing success and he would be so pleased he would forget all about the rug.

Though she had the sneaking suspicion that if it was the most amazing meal he'd ever tasted, he would complain on principle.

Dinner was a culinary catastrophe.

She served him overcooked, leathery chicken in lumpy white sauce with a side of scorched rice pilaf and a bowl of wilted salad swimming in dressing. He wouldn't feed it to his dog—if he had one. But what had Emilio expected from someone who had probably never cooked a meal in her entire life?

Isabelle hadn't stuck around to witness the aftermath. She'd fixed his plate, then vanished. He'd come downstairs to find it sitting on the dining room table accompanied by a highball glass *full* of scotch. Maybe she thought that if she got him good and toasted, he wouldn't notice the disastrous meal.

He carried his plate to the kitchen and dumped the contents in the trash, then fixed himself a peanut butter and jelly sandwich and ate standing at the kitchen sink. Which he noted was a disaster area. Considering all the dirty pots and pans and dishes, it looked as though she'd prepared a ten course meal. He hoped she planned to come out of hiding and clean it up.

As he was walking to his office, drink in hand, he heard the hum of the vacuum upstairs. Why the hell was she cleaning at seven-thirty in the evening?

He climbed the stairs and followed the sound to the first guest bedroom. Her back was to him as she vacuumed around the queen-size bed. He leaned in the doorway and watched her. The new uniform was a major improvement, but she still looked painfully thin. She had always been finely boned and willowy, but now she looked downright scrawny.

But still beautiful. He used to love watching her, even if she was doing nothing more than sitting on his bed doing her class work. He never got tired of looking at her. Even now she possessed a poise and grace that was almost hypnotizing.

She turned to do the opposite side of the bed and when she saw him standing there she jolted with alarm. She hit the Off switch.

"Surprised to see me?" he asked.

She looked exhausted. "Did you need something?"

"I just thought you'd like to know that it didn't work."

She frowned. "What didn't work?"

"Your attempt to poison me."

He could see that he'd hurt her feelings, but she lifted her chin in defiance and said, "Well, you can't blame a girl for trying. Besides, now that I think about it, smothering you in your sleep will be so much more fun."

He nearly cracked a smile. "Is that why you're trying to incapacitate me with excessive amounts of scotch?"

She shrugged. "It's always easier when they don't fight back."

She'd always had a wry sense of humor. He just hadn't expected her to exercise it. Unless she wasn't joking. It might not be a bad idea to lock his bedroom door. Just in case.

"Why are you up here cleaning?" he asked.

She looked at him funny, as though she thought it was a trick question. "Because that's what you brought me here to do?"

"What I mean is, shouldn't you be finished for the day?"

"Maybe I should be, but I'm not."

It probably wasn't helping that he'd instructed Mrs. Medina to toss in a few extra tasks on top of her regular duties, though he hadn't anticipated it taking Isabelle quite this long. He'd just wanted to keep her busy during the day. Apparently it had worked. A little *too* well.

"I have work to do and the noise is distracting," he told her.

She had this look, like she wanted to say something snotty or sarcastic, but she restrained herself. "I'll try to keep the noise down."

"See that you do. And I hope you're planning to clean the kitchen. It's a mess."

He could tell she was exasperated but struggling to suppress it. "It's on my list."

He wondered what it would take to make her explode. How far he would have to push. In all the time they were together, he'd never once seen her lose her temper. Whenever they came close to having a disagreement she would just…shut down. He'd always wondered what it would be like to get her good and riled up.

It was an intriguing idea, but tonight he just didn't have the energy.

He turned to leave and she said, "Emilio?"

He looked back.

"I'm really sorry about dinner."

This was his chance to twist the knife, to put her in her place, but she looked so damned humble he didn't have the heart. She really was trying, holding up her end of the bargain. And he…well, hell, he was obviously going soft or something. He'd lost his killer instinct.

"Maybe tomorrow you could try something a little less complicated," he said.

"I will."

As he walked away the vacuum switched back on.

Despite a few screwups, her first day had been less of a disaster than he'd anticipated.

Emilio settled at his desk and booted his computer, and after a few minutes the vacuum went silent. About forty-five minutes later he heard her banging around in the kitchen. That continued for a good hour, then there was silence.

At eleven he shut down his computer, turned off the lights in his office and walked to the kitchen. It was back to its previous, clean state, and his travel cup was washed and sitting beside the coffeemaker. He dumped what was left of his drink down the drain, set his glass in the sink and was about to head upstairs when he noticed she'd left the laundry room light on. He walked back to switch it off and saw that Isabelle's door was open a crack and the desk lamp was on.

Maybe he should remind her to set her alarm, so he didn't have to get breakfast in the coffee shop at work again tomorrow.

He knocked lightly on her door. When she didn't answer, he eased it open. Isabelle was lying face down, spread-eagle on her bed, still dressed in her uniform, sound asleep. She hadn't even taken off her shoes. She must have dropped down and gone out like a light. At least this time she'd made it to the bed. And on the bright side, she seemed in no condition to be smothering him in his sleep.

The hem of her uniform had pulled up, giving him a nice view of the backs of her thighs. They were smooth and creamy and he couldn't help but imagine how it would feel to touch her. To lay a hand on her thigh and slide it upward, under her dress.

The sudden flash of heat in his blood, the intense pull of arousal in his groin, caught him off guard.

Despite all that had happened, he still desired her.

Maybe his body remembered what his brain had struggled to suppress. How good they had been together.

Though they had never made love, they had touched each other intimately, given each other pleasure. Isabelle hadn't done much more than kiss a boy before they began dating. She had been the most inexperienced eighteen-year-old he'd ever met, but eager to learn, and more than willing to experiment, so long as they didn't go all the way. He had respected her decision to wait until marriage to make love and admired her principles, so he hadn't pushed. Besides, it hadn't stopped them from finding other ways to satisfy their sexual urges.

One thing he never understood though was why she had been so shy about letting him see her body. Despite what he had told her yesterday, he'd never believed it had anything to do with vanity. Quite the opposite. For reasons he'd never been able to understand, she'd had a dismally low opinion of herself.

After she left him, he began to wonder if it had all been an act to manipulate him. Maybe she hadn't been so innocent after all. To this day he wasn't sure, and he would probably never know the truth. He was long past caring either way.

He shut off the light and stepped out of her room, closing the door behind him. The lack of sleep was catching up to him. He was exhausted. What he needed was a good night's rest.

Everything would be clearer in the morning.

Five

Isabelle hated lying. Especially to her mother, but in this case she didn't have much choice. There was no way she could admit the truth.

They sat at the small kitchen table in her mother's apartment, having tea. Isabelle had been avoiding her calls for three days now, since she moved into Emilio's house, but in her mother's last message her voice had been laced with concern.

"I went by the motel but they told me you checked out. Where are you, Isabelle?"

Isabelle had no choice but to stop by her mother's apartment on her way home from the grocery store Thursday morning. Besides, she'd picked up a few things for her.

"So, your new job is a live-in position?" her mother asked.

"Room and board," Isabelle told her. "And she lets me use her car for running errands."

"What a perfect position for you." She rubbed Isabelle's arm affectionately. "You've always loved helping people."

"She still gets around well for her age, but her memory isn't great. Her kids are afraid she'll leave the stove on and burn the house down. Plus she can't drive anymore. She needs me to take her to doctor appointments."

"Well, I think it's wonderful that you're moving on with your life. I know the last few months have been difficult for you."

"They haven't been easy for you, either." And all because of Isabelle's stupidity. Not that her mother ever blamed her. She'd been duped by Lenny, too, and held him one hundred percent responsible.

"It's really not so bad. I've made a few new friends in the building and I like my job at the boutique."

Though her mother would never admit it, it had to be humiliating selling designer fashions to women she used to socialize with. But considering she had never worked a day in her life, not to mention the indictment, she had been lucky to find a job at all. Even if her salary was barely enough to get by on. It pained Isabelle that her mother had to leave the luxury of her condo to live in this dumpy little apartment. She'd endured so much pain and heartache in her life, she deserved better than this.

"This woman you work for…what did you say her name is?" her mother asked.

She hadn't. That was one part of the lie she'd forgotten about. "Mrs. Smith," she said, cringing at her lack of originality. "Mary Smith."

Why hadn't she gone with something really unique, like Jane Doe?

"Where does Mrs. Smith live?"

"Not too far from our old house."

Her brow crinkled. "Hmm, the name isn't familiar. I thought I knew everyone in that area."

"She's a very nice woman. I think you would like her."

"I'd like to meet her. Maybe I'll come by for a visit."

Crap. Wouldn't she be shocked to learn that Mrs. Smith was actually Mr. Suarez.

"I'll talk to her children and see if it's okay," Isabelle told her. She would just have to stall for the next month.

"Have you been keeping up with the news about Western Oil?" her mother asked, and Isabelle's heart stalled. Did she suspect something? Why would she bring Emilio up out of the blue like that?

"Not really," she lied. "I don't watch television."

"They showed a clip of Emilio and his partners at a press conference on the news the other day. He looks good. He's obviously done well for himself."

"I guess he has."

"Maybe you should…talk to him."

"Why?"

"I thought that maybe he would talk to his brother on your behalf."

"He wouldn't. And it wouldn't matter if he did. I'm going to prison. Nothing is going to stop that now."

"You don't know that."

"Yes, I do."

She shook her head. "Lenny would never let that happen. He may have been a thief, but he loved you."

"Lenny is dead." Even if he had intended to absolve her of guilt, he couldn't do it from the grave. It was too late.

"Something will come up. Some new evidence. Everything will be okay."

She looked so sad. Isabelle wished she could tell her

mother the truth, so at least she wouldn't have to worry about her own freedom. But she'd promised Emilio.

Isabelle glanced at her watch. "I really have to get back to work."

"Of course. Thank you for the groceries. You didn't have to do that."

"My living expenses are practically nonexistent now, and as you said, I like helping people."

She walked Isabelle to the door.

"That's a nice car," she said, gesturing to the black Saab parked in the lot.

It was, and it stuck out like a sore thumb amidst the vehicles beside it. "I'll drop by again as soon as I can."

Her mother hugged her hard and said, "I'm very proud of you, sweetheart."

The weight of Isabelle's guilt was suffocating. But she hugged her back and said, "Thanks, Mom."

Her mother waved as she drove away, and Isabelle felt a deep sense of sadness. Hardly a week passed when they didn't speak on the phone, or drop by for visits. They were all the other had anymore. What would her mother do when Isabelle went to prison? She would be all alone. And she was fooling herself if she really believed Isabelle could avoid prison. It was inevitable. Even if Emilio wanted to help her—which he obviously didn't—there was nothing he could do. According to her lawyer, the evidence against her was overwhelming.

Isabelle couldn't worry herself with that right now. If she did the dread and the fear would overwhelm her. She had a household to run. Which was going more smoothly than she had anticipated. Her latest attempts in the kitchen must not have been too awful, either, because Emilio hadn't accused her of trying to poison him since Monday, though he'd found fault with practically everything else she did.

Okay, maybe not *everything*. But when it came to his home, he was a perfectionist. Everything had its place, and God help her if she moved something, or put it away in the wrong spot. Yesterday she'd set the milk on the refrigerator shelf instead of the door and he'd blown a gasket. And yeah, a couple of times she had moved things deliberately, just for the satisfaction of annoying him. He did make it awfully easy.

Other than a few minor snafus, the housekeeping itself was getting much easier. She had settled into a routine, and some of her chores were taking half the time they had when she started. Yesterday she'd even had time to sit down with a cup of tea, put her feet up and read the paper for twenty minutes.

In fact, it was becoming almost *too* easy. And she couldn't help but wonder if the other shoe was about to drop.

Emilio stood by the window in Adam's office, listening to his colleagues discuss the accident at the refinery. OSHA had released its official report and Western Oil was being cited for negligence. According to the investigation, the explosion was triggered by a faulty gauge. Which everyone in the room knew was impossible.

That section had just come back online after several days of mandatory safety checks and equipment upgrades. It had been inspected and reinspected. It wasn't negligence, or an accident. Someone *wanted* that equipment to fail.

The question was why?

"This is ridiculous," Jordan said, slapping the report down on Adam's desk. "Those are good men. They would never let something like this happen."

"Someone is responsible," Nathan said from his seat opposite Adam's desk, which earned him a sharp look from his brother.

Somber, Adam said, "I know you trust and respect every man there, Jordan, but I think we have to come to terms with the fact that it was sabotage."

Thankfully the explosion had occurred while that section was in maintenance mode, and less than half the men who usually worked that shift were on the line. Only a dozen were hurt. But one injured man was too many as far as Emilio was concerned. Between lawsuits and OSHA fines, financially they would take a hit. Even worse was the mark on their good name. Until now they'd had a flawless safety record. Cassandra Benson, Western Oil's public relations director, had been working feverishly to put a positive spin on the situation. But their direct competitor, Birch Energy, owned by Walter Birch, had already taken advantage of the situation. Within days of the incident they released a flood of television ads, and though they didn't directly target Western Oil, the implication was clear— Birch was safe and valued their employees. Western Oil was a death trap.

Western Oil was firing back with ads boasting their innovative techniques and new alternative, environmentally friendly practices.

"I don't suppose you'll tell me how the investigation is going," Jordan said.

Adam and Nathan exchanged a look. When they agreed to launch a private investigation, it was decided that Jordan wouldn't be involved. As Chief Operations Officer he was the one closest to the workers in the refinery. They trusted him, so he needed a certain degree of deniability. A fact Jordan was clearly not happy about.

They had promised to keep him in the loop, but

privately Adam had confided in Emilio that he worried Jordan wouldn't be impartial. That he might ignore key evidence out of loyalty to the workers.

Jordan would be downright furious to know that two of the new men hired to take the place of injured workers were in reality undercover investigators. But the real thorn in Jordan's side was that Nathan was placed in charge of the investigation. That, on top of the competition for the CEO position, had thrust their occasional sibling rivalry into overdrive. Which didn't bode well for either of them. And though Emilio considered both men his friends, there had been tension since Adam announced his intention to retire.

"All I can say is that it's going slowly," Nathan told Jordan. "How is morale?"

"Tom Butler, my foreman, says the men are nervous. They know the line was thoroughly checked before the accident. Rumor is someone in the refinery is to blame for the explosion. They're not sure who to trust."

"A little suspicion could work to our advantage," Nathan said. "If the men are paying attention to one another, another act of sabotage won't be so easy."

Jordan glared at his older sibling. "Yeah, genius. Or the men will be so busy watching their coworkers they won't be paying attention to their own duties and it could cause an accident. A real one this time."

Emilio stifled a smile. Normally Jordan was the most even-tempered of the four, but this situation was turning him into a bona fide hothead.

"Does anyone have anything *constructive* to add?" Adam asked, looking over at Emilio.

"Yeah, Emilio," Jordan said. "You've been awfully quiet. What's your take on this?"

Emilio turned from the window. "You feel betrayed,

Jordan. I get that. But we *will* get to the bottom of this. It's just going to take some time."

After several more minutes of heated debate between Nathan and Jordan that ultimately got them nowhere, Adam ended the meeting and Emilio headed out for the day. He let himself in the house at six-thirty, expecting to find Izzie in the kitchen making what he hoped would be an edible meal. She'd taken his advice to heart and was trying out simpler recipes. The last two nights, dinner hadn't been gourmet by any stretch of the imagination. To call it appetizing had been an even wider stretch, but he'd choked it down.

Tonight he found two pots boiling over on the stove— one with spaghetti sauce and the other noodles—and a cutting board with partially chopped vegetables on the counter. Izzie was nowhere to be found. Perhaps she didn't grasp the concept that food could not cook itself. It required supervision.

Grumbling to himself, he jerked the burner knobs into the Off position, noting the sauce splattered all over the stove. Shedding his suit jacket, he checked her room and the laundry room, but she wasn't there, either. Then he heard a sound from upstairs and headed up.

As soon as he reached the top and saw that his bedroom door was open, his hackles rose. She knew damned well his room was off-limits.

He charged toward the door, just as she emerged. Her eyes flew open wide when she saw him. He started to ask her what the hell she thought she was doing, when he noticed the blood-soaked paper towel she was holding on her left hand.

"I'm sorry," she said. "I didn't mean to invade your privacy. I was looking for a first-aid kit. I thought it might be in your bathroom."

"What happened?"

"I slipped with the knife. It's not a big deal. I just need a bandage."

A cut that bled enough to soak through a paper towel would require more than a bandage. He reached for her hand. "Let me see."

She pulled out of his reach. "I told you, it's not a big deal. It's a small cut."

"Then it won't hurt to let me look at it." Before she could move away again, he grabbed her arm.

He lifted away the paper towels and blood oozed from a wound in the fleshy part between the second and third knuckle of her index finger. He wiped it away to get a better look. The cut may have been small, but it was deep.

So much for a relaxing night at home. He sighed and said, "Get your jacket. I'll drive you to the E.R."

She jerked her hand free. "No! I just need a bandage."

"A bandage is not going to stop the bleeding. You need stitches."

"I'll butterfly it."

"Even if that did work, you still should see a doctor. You could get an infection."

She shook her head. "I'll wash it out and use antibiotic ointment. It'll be fine."

He didn't get why she was making such a big deal about this. "This is ridiculous. I'm taking you to the hospital."

"*No,* you're not."

"Izzie, for God sakes, you need to see a doctor."

"I can't."

"Why?"

"Because I have no way to pay for it, okay? I don't have health insurance and I don't have money."

The rush of color to her cheeks, the way she lowered her eyes, said that admitting it to him mortified her.

He assumed she had money stashed somewhere for emergencies, but maybe that wasn't the case. Was she really that destitute?

"Since it was a work-related accident, I'll pay for it," he said.

"I'm not asking for a handout."

"You didn't ask, I offered. You hurt yourself in my home. I consider it my responsibility."

She shook her head. "No."

"Isabelle—"

"I am not going to the doctor. I just need a first-aid kit."

"Obstinado," he muttered, shaking his head. The woman completely baffled him. Why wouldn't she just accept his help? She'd had no problem sponging off her rich husband for all those years. Emilio would have expected her to jump at his offer. Had she suddenly grown a conscience? A sense of pride?

Well, he wasn't going to sit and argue while she bled all over the place. He finally threw up his hands in defeat. "Fine! But I'm wrapping it for you."

For a second he thought she might argue about that too, but she seemed to sense that his patience was wearing thin. "Fine," she replied, then grumbled under her breath, "and you call *me* stubborn."

Six

Isabelle followed Emilio through his bedroom to the bathroom and waited while he grabbed the first-aid kit from the cabinet under the sink. He pulled out the necessary supplies, then gestured her over to the sink and turned on the cold water.

"This is probably going to hurt," he told her, but as he took her hand and placed it under the flow, she didn't even flinch. He gently soaped up the area around the cut with his thumb to clean it, then grabbed a bottle of hydrogen peroxide. Holding her hand over the sink, he poured it on the wound. As it foamed up, her only reaction was a soft intake of breath, even though he knew it had to sting like hell.

He grabbed a clean towel from the cabinet and gently blotted her hand dry. It was starting to clot, so there was hope that a butterfly would be enough to stop any further bleeding if he wrapped it firmly enough. Although he still thought stitches were warranted. Without them it could leave a nasty scar.

He sat on the edge of the counter and pulled her closer, so she was standing between his knees. She didn't fight him, but it was obvious, by the tension in her stance as he spread ointment on the cut, that she was uncomfortable being close to him.

"Something wrong?" he asked, glancing up at her. "You seem…tense."

She avoided his gaze. "I'm fine."

If she were fine, why the nervous waver in her voice? "Maybe you don't like being so close to me." He lifted his eyes to hers, running his thumb across her wrist. The slight widening of her eyes, when she was trying hard not to react, made him smile. "Or maybe you do."

"I definitely don't."

Her wildly beating heart and the blush of her cheeks said otherwise. There was a physical reaction for him, as well. A pull of desire deep inside of him. Despite everything she had done, she was still a beautiful, desirable woman. And he was a man who hadn't been with a woman in several months. He just hadn't had the time for all the baggage that went along with it.

"Are you almost finished?" Isabelle asked.

"Almost." Emilio took his time, applying the butterfly then smoothing a second, larger bandage over the top to hold it in place.

"That should do it," he said, but when she tried to pull her hand free, he held on. "How about a kiss, to make it feel better?"

Her eyes widened slightly and she gave another tug. "That's really not necessary."

"I think it is." And perhaps she did, too, because she didn't try to pull away as he lifted her hand to his mouth and pressed his lips to her palm. He felt her shiver, felt her skin go hot. He kissed her palm again, then the inside of her wrist, breathing warm air against her skin. "You like that."

"Not at all."

"Your body says otherwise."

"Well, obviously it's confused."

That made him smile. "You still want me. Admit it."

"You're delusional," she said, but there was a hitch in her voice, a quiver that belied her arousal. She was hot for him.

This was going to be too easy.

Izzie gently pulled from his grasp. "I have to finish dinner."

She turned, but before she could walk away he slipped his arms around her waist and pulled her close to him. She gasped as her back pressed against his chest, her behind tucked snugly against his groin. When she felt the ridge of his erection, she froze.

He leaned close, whispered in her ear, "What's your hurry, Isabelle?"

All she had to do was tell him to stop and he would have without question, but she didn't. She stood there, unmoving, as if she were unsure of what to do. He knew in that instant she was as good as his. But not until she was begging for it. He wanted total submission. The same unconditional and unwavering devotion he had shown her fifteen years ago.

He nuzzled her neck and her head tipped to the side. He couldn't see her face, but he sensed that her eyes were closed.

"You smell delicious, Isabelle." He caught her earlobe between his teeth and she sucked in a breath. "Good enough to eat."

"We can't do this," she said, her voice uneven, her breathing shallow.

He brushed his lips against her neck. "Are you asking me to stop?"

She didn't answer.

He slid his hands up, over her rib cage, using his thumbs to caress the undersides of her breasts. They were as full and supple as they had been fifteen years ago. He wanted to unbutton her dress and slip his hands inside, touch her bare skin. Taste her.

But all in good time.

"My bed is just a few steps away," he whispered in her ear, wondering just how far she was willing to let this go. He didn't have to wait long to find out.

"Stop."

He dropped his hands and she whirled away from him, her eyes wide. "Why did you do that? You don't even like me."

A grin curled his mouth. "Because you wanted me to."

"I most certainly did not."

"We both know that isn't true, Isabelle." He pushed off the edge of the counter and rose to his feet. He could see that she wanted to run but she stood her ground. "You like it when I touch you. I know what makes you feel good."

"I'm not stupid. You don't really want me."

"I would say that all evidence points to the contrary."

Her gaze darted to his crotch, then quickly away. "I have to go finish dinner."

"Don't bother. I had a late lunch. Save the sauce for later."

"Fine."

"But that doesn't mean you should skip dinner. I want to see another pound on the scale in the morning." She had only gained two so far this week, though she swore she'd been eating three meals a day. "And take something for your hand. It's going to hurt like hell."

"I will," she said, but his concern clearly confused her.

And it was a sensation she would be experiencing a lot from now on, he thought with a smile.

Isabelle headed downstairs on unsteady legs, willing her heart to slow its frantic pace, her hands to stop trembling.

What the *hell* had she been thinking? Why had she let Emilio touch her that way? Why had she let him touch her at all? She had been perfectly capable of bandaging her own finger. She should have insisted he let her do it herself. But she foolishly believed he was doing it because he cared about her, cared that she was hurt.

When would she learn?

He didn't care about her. Not at all. He was just trying to confuse her. This was just some twisted plot for revenge.

And could she blame him? Didn't she deserve anything he could dish out? Put in his position, after the way she'd hurt him, would she have done things any differently?

She'd brought this on herself. That's what her father used to tell her, how he justified his actions. She'd spent years convincing herself that it wasn't her fault, that he was the one with the problem. What if she was wrong? What if she really had deserved it back then, and she was getting exactly what she deserved now? Maybe this was her penance for betraying Emilio.

She heard him come downstairs and braced herself for another confrontation, but he went straight to his office and shut the door.

Limp with relief, she cleaned up the mess from the unfinished meal then fixed herself a sandwich with the leftover roast beef from the night before, but she only managed to choke down a bite or two. She covered what was left with plastic wrap and put it in the fridge—if there was one thing she had learned lately, it was to not waste food—then locked herself in her room. It was still early, but she was exhausted so she changed into her pajamas and curled up in bed. Her finger had begun to throb, but it didn't come close to the ache in her heart. Maybe coming here had been a mistake. In fifteen years she hadn't figured out how to stop loving Emilio.

Maybe she never would.

"How's the finger?" Emilio asked Isabelle the next evening as he ate his spaghetti. He usually sat in the dining room, but tonight he'd insisted on sitting at the kitchen table. If that wasn't awkward enough, he kept *watching* her.

At least he hadn't complained about dinner, despite the fact that the noodles were slightly overdone and the garlic bread was a little singed around the edges. He seemed to recognize that she was trying. Or maybe he thought if he complained she might make good on her threat and smother him in his sleep.

"It's fine," she said. It still throbbed, but the ibuprofen tablets she'd been gobbling like candy all day had at least taken the sharp edge off the pain.

"We'll need to redress it."

We? As if she would let him anywhere near her after last night.

"I'll do it later," she said.

He got up to carry his plate to the sink, where she just happened to be standing, loading the dishwasher. She couldn't move away without looking like she was running from him, and she didn't want him to know he was making her nervous. He already held most of the cards in this game he'd started. And she had little doubt that it was a game.

The key was not letting him know that he was getting to her, that she even cared what he thought.

He put his plate and fork in the dishwasher. "I should check it for signs of infection."

He reached for her arm but she moved out of his grasp. "I can do it myself."

"Suit yourself," he said, wearing a cocky grin as he turned to wash his hands.

Ugh! The man was insufferable. Yet the desire to lean into him, to wrap her arms around him and breathe in his scent, to lay her cheek against his back and listen to the steady thump of his heart beating, was as strong now as it had been all those years ago. She'd spent more than half her life fantasizing about him, wishing with all her heart that they could be together, and for one perfect year he had been hers.

But she had made her choice, one that up until a few days ago, she'd learned to accept. Now her doubts had begun to resurface and she found herself rehashing the same old *what ifs*. What if she had been stronger? What if she stood up to her father instead of caving to his threats?

What if she'd at least had the courage to tell Emilio goodbye?

She had tried. She went to see him, to tell him that she had decided to marry Lenny. She knew he would never understand why, and probably never forgive her, but she owed him an explanation. Even if she could never tell him the truth.

But the instant she'd seen his face, how happy he was to see her, she'd lost her nerve and, because she couldn't bear to see him hurting, she pretended everything was okay. She hadn't stopped him when he started kissing her, when he took her hand and led her to his room. And because she couldn't bear going the rest of her life never knowing what it would be like to make love to him, she'd had every intention of giving herself to him that night.

Emilio had been the one to put on the brakes, to say not yet. He had been concerned that she would regret giving in so close to their wedding day. She hadn't had the heart, or the courage, to tell him that day would never come.

Would things have been different if she had at least told him she was leaving? For all she knew, they might have been worse. He might have talked her into telling him the truth, and that would have been a disaster.

She never expected him to forgive her—she hadn't even forgiven herself yet—but she had hoped that he would have moved on by now. It broke her heart to know how deeply she had hurt him. That after all this time he was *still* hurting. If he wasn't why would he be so hell-bent on hurting her back?

Maybe she should give him what he wanted, allow him his vengeance if that was what it would take to reconcile the past. Maybe she owed it to him—and to herself. Maybe then she could stop feeling so guilty.

After last night she could only assume he planned to use sex to get his revenge. If she slept with him, would he feel vindicated? And was she prepared to compromise her principles by having sex with a man who clearly hated her? Or did the fact that she still loved him make it okay?

Before she could consider the consequences of her actions, she stuck her hand out.

"Here," she said. "Maybe you should check it. Just in case."

He looked at her hand, then lifted his eyes to her face. There was a hint of amusement in their smoky depths. "I'm sure you can manage on your own."

Huh?

He dried his hands, then walked out of the kitchen.

She followed him. "What do you want from me, Emilio?"

He stopped just outside his office door and turned to her. "Want?"

He knew exactly what she meant. "I know I hurt you, and I'm *sorry*. Just tell me what you want me to do and I'll do it."

His stormy gaze leveled on her and suddenly she felt naked. How did he manage to do that with just a look? How did he make her feel so stripped bare?

He took a step toward her and her heart went crazy in her chest. She tried to be brave, to stand her ground, but as he moved closer, she found herself taking one step back, then another, until she hit the wall. Maybe offering herself up as the sacrificial lamb hadn't been such a hot idea, after all. Maybe she should have worked up to this just a little slower instead of jumping right into the deep end of the pool. But it was too late now.

In the past he had always been so sweet and tender, so patient with her. Now he wore a look that said he was about to eat her alive. It both terrified and thrilled her, because despite the years that had passed, deep down she still felt like the same naive, inexperienced girl. Way out of her league, yet eager to learn. And in all these years the gap seemed to widen exponentially.

Emilio braced a hand on one side of her head, leaning in, the faint whisper of his scent filling her senses—familiar, but different somehow. If she were braver she would have touched him. She *wanted* to. Instead she stood frozen, waiting for him to make the first move, wondering how far he would take this, and if she would let him. If she *should*.

Emilio dipped his head and nuzzled her cheek, his breath warm against her skin, then his lips brushed the column of her throat and Isabelle's knees went weak.

Thank goodness she had the wall to hold her steady. One kiss and she was toast. And it wasn't even a *real* kiss.

His other hand settled on the curve of her waist, the heat of his palm scorching her skin through the fabric of her uniform. She wanted to reach up and tunnel her fingers through the softness of his hair, slide her arms around his neck, pull him down and press her mouth to his. The anticipation of his lips touching hers had her trembling from the inside out.

He nipped the lobe of her ear, slid his hand upward and as his thumb grazed the underside of her breast she had to fight not to moan. Her nipples tingled and hardened. Breath quickened. She wanted to take his hand and guide it over her breast, but she kept her own hands fisted at her sides, afraid that any move she made might be the wrong one.

His lips brushed the side of her neck, her chin. This was so wrong, but she couldn't pull away. Couldn't stop him. She didn't *want* him to stop.

His lips brushed her cheek, the corner of her mouth, then finally her lips. So sweet and tender, and when his tongue skimmed hers she went limp with desire. In that instant she stopped caring that he was using her, that he didn't even like her, that to him this was just some stupid game of revenge. She didn't even care that he would probably take her fragile heart and rip it all to pieces. She was going to take what she wanted, what she needed, what she'd spent the last fifteen years *aching* for.

One minute her arms were at her sides and the next they were around his neck, fingers tunneling through his hair, and something inside Emilio seemed to snap. He shoved her backward and she gasped as he crushed her against the wall with the weight of his body. The kiss went from sweet and tender to deep and punishing so fast it stole her breath.

He cupped her behind, arched against her, and she could feel the hard length of his erection against her stomach. If not for the skirt of her dress, she would have wound her legs around his hips and ground into him. She wanted him to take her right there, in the hallway.

But as abruptly as it had begun, it was over. Emilio let go of her and backed away, leaving her stunned and confused and aching for more.

"Good night, Isabelle," he said, his voice so icy and devoid of emotion that she went cold all over. He stepped into his office and shut the door behind him and she heard the lock click into place. She had to fight not to hurl herself at it, to keep from pounding with her fists and demand he finish what he started.

She had never been so aroused, or so humiliated, in her life. She wasn't sure what sort of game he was playing, but as she sank back against the wall, struggling to make sense of what had just happened, she had the sinking feeling that it was far from over.

Damn.

Emilio closed and locked his office door and leaned against it, fighting to catch his breath, to make sense of what had just happened.

What had gone wrong?

Things had been progressing as planned. He had been in complete control. He'd had Isabelle right where he wanted her. Then everything went to hell. Their lips touched and his head started to spin, then she wrapped her arms around his neck, rubbed against him and he'd just…*lost* it.

He'd been seconds from ripping open that god-awful uniform and putting his hands on her. He had been this-close to shoving up the skirt of her dress, ripping off her panties and taking her right there in the hallway, up against the wall. He wanted her as much now as he had fifteen years ago. And putting on the brakes, denying himself the pleasure of everything she offered, had been just as damned hard.

That hadn't been part of the plan.

On the bright side, making Isabelle bend to his will, making her beg for it, was clearly not going to be a problem.

He crossed the room to the wet bar and splashed cold water on his face. This had just been a fluke. A knee-jerk reaction to the last vestiges of a long dormant sexual attraction. It was physical and nothing more. So from now on, losing control wasn't going to be an issue.

Seven

Isabelle stood at the stove fixing breakfast the next morning, reliving the nightmarish events of last night. How could she have been so stupid? So naive?

Just tell me what you want and I'll do it.

Well, she'd gotten her answer. He hadn't come right out and said it, but the implications of his actions had been crystal clear. He wanted to make her want him, get her all hot and bothered, then reject her. Simple yet effective.

Very effective.

As much as she hated it, as miserable and small as he'd made her feel, didn't she deserve this? Hadn't she more or less done the same thing to him fifteen years ago? Could she really fault him for wanting revenge?

She had gotten herself into this mess, she'd asked for his help, now she had to live with the consequences. She could try to resist him, try to pretend she didn't melt when he touched her, but she had always been a terrible liar. And honestly, she didn't have the energy to fight him.

The worst, most humiliating part was knowing that if she told him no, if she asked him to stop, he would. He would never force himself on her. He'd made that clear the other night. The problem was, she didn't *want* to tell him no.

Unlike Emilio, she couldn't switch it off and on. Her only defense was to avoid him as often as possible. And when she couldn't? Well, she would try her hardest to not make a total fool of herself again. She would try to be strong.

She would hold up her end of the bargain, and hopefully everyone would get exactly what they wanted. She just wished she didn't feel so darned edgy and out of sorts, and she knew he was going to sense it the second he saw her.

According to Mrs. Medina's "list," Emilio didn't leave for work until nine-thirty on Saturdays, so Isabelle didn't have to see him until nine when he came down for breakfast. If she timed it just right, she could feed him right when he walked into the kitchen, then hide until his ride got there.

Of course he chose that morning to come down fifteen minutes early. She was at the stove, trying not to incinerate a pan of hash brown potatoes, when he walked into the room.

"Good morning," he said, the rumble of his voice tweaking her already frayed nerves.

She took a deep breath and told herself, *You can do this.* Pasting on what she hoped was a nothing-you-do-can-hurt-me face, she turned…and whatever she had been about to say died the minute she laid eyes on him.

He wasn't wearing a suit. Or a tie. Or a shirt. Or even shoes. All he wore was a pair of black silk pajama bottoms slung low on his hips. That was it. His hair was mussed from sleep and dark stubble shadowed his jaw.

Oh boy.

Most men declined with age. They developed excess flab or a paunch or even unattractive back hair, but not Emilio. His chest was lean and well-defined, his shoulders and back smooth and tanned and he had a set of six-pack abs to die for. He was everything he had been fifteen years ago, only better.

A lot better.

Terrific.

She realized she was staring and averted her eyes. Was it her fault she hadn't seen a mostly naked man in a really long time? At least, not one who looked as good as he did.

Lenny had had the paunch, and the flab, and the back hair. Not that their relationship had ever been about sex.

Ever the dutiful housekeeper, she said, "Sit down, I'll get you coffee." Mostly she just wanted to keep him out of her half of the kitchen.

He took a seat on one of the stools at the island. She grabbed a mug from the cupboard, filled it and set it in front of him.

"Thanks."

Their eyes met and his flashed with some unidentifiable emotion. Amusement maybe? She couldn't be sure, and frankly she didn't want to know.

Make breakfast, run and hide.

She busied herself with cutting up the vegetables that would go in the omelet she planned to make, taking great care not to slice or sever any appendages. Although it was tough to keep her eyes on what she was doing when Emilio was directly in her line of vision, barely an arm's reach away, looking hotter than the Texas sun.

And he was *watching* her.

She would gather everything up and move across to the opposite counter, where her back would be to him instead, but she doubted his probing stare would be any less irritating. She diced the green onions, his gaze boring into her as he casually sipped his coffee.

"Don't you have to get ready for work?" she asked.

"You trying to get rid of me, Isabelle?"

Well, *duh*. "Just curious."

"I'm working from home today."

She suppressed a groan. Fantastic. An entire day with Emilio in the house. With any luck, he would lock himself in his office and wouldn't emerge until dinnertime. But somehow she doubted she would be so lucky. She also doubted it was a coincidence that he chose this particular day to work at home. She was sure that every move he made was calculated.

She chopped the red peppers, trying to ignore the weight of his steely gray stare.

"I want you to clean my bedroom today," he said, reaching across to the cutting board to snatch a cube of pepper.

Of course he did. "I thought it was off-limits."

"It is. Until I say it isn't."

She stopped chopping and shot him a glance.

He shrugged. "My house, my rules."

Another calculated move on his part. He was just full of surprises today. He was manipulating her and he was good at it. He knew she had absolutely no recourse.

He sipped his coffee, watching her slice the mini bella mushrooms. But he wasn't just watching. He was *studying* her. She failed to understand what was so riveting about seeing someone chop food. Which meant he was just doing it to make her uncomfortable, and it was working.

When she couldn't take it any longer, she said in her most patient tone, "Would you please stop that?"

"Stop what?"

"Watching me. It's making me nervous."

"I'm just curious to see what you're going to cut this time. The way you hold that knife, my money is on the tip of your thumb. Although I'm sure if we keep it on ice, there's a good chance they can reattach it."

She stopped cutting and glared at him.

He grinned, and for a second he looked just like the Emilio from fifteen years ago. He used to smile all the time back then. A sexy, slightly lopsided grin that never failed to make her go all gooey inside. And still did.

She preferred him when he was cranky and brooding. She had a defense for that. When he did things like smile and tease her, it was too easy to forget that it was all an act. That he was only doing it to manipulate her.

Although she hoped someday he would show her a smile that he actually meant.

"Despite what you think, I'm not totally inept," she said.

"No?"

"No."

"So the pan on the stove is supposed to be smoking like that?"

At first she thought he was just saying it to irritate her, then she remembered that she'd been frying potatoes. She spun around and saw that there actually was black smoke billowing from the pan.

"Damn it!" She darted to the stove, twisted off the flame, grabbed the handle and jerked the pan off the burner. But she jerked too hard and oil sloshed over the side. She tried to jump out of the way, but she wasn't fast enough and molten hot oil splashed down the skirt of her dress, soaking through the fabric to the top of her thigh.

She gasped at the quick and sharp sting. She barely had time to process what had happened, to react, when she felt Emilio's hands on her waist.

He lifted her off her feet and deposited her on the edge of the counter next to the sink. And he wasn't smiling anymore. "Did you burn yourself?"

"A—a little, I think."

He eased the skirt of her uniform up her thighs. So far up that she was sure he could see the crotch of her bargain bin panties, but protesting seemed silly at this point since he obviously wasn't doing it to get fresh with her. And she knew there was something seriously wrong with her when all she could think was *thank God I shaved my legs this morning.*

The middle of her right thigh had a splotchy red spot the size of a saucer and it burned like the devil.

Emilio grabbed a dish towel from the counter and soaked it with cool water, then he wrung it out and laid it against her burn. She sucked in a breath as the cold cloth hit her hot skin.

"Are you okay?" he asked, his eyes dark with concern. "Do you feel light-headed or dizzy?"

She shook her head. What she felt was mortified.

Not totally inept, huh?

She couldn't even manage fried potatoes without causing a disaster. Although, this was partially his fault. If he'd worn a damn shirt, and if he hadn't been *looking* at her, she wouldn't have been so distracted.

Emilio got a fresh towel from the drawer and made an ice pack large enough to cover the burn, while she sat there feeling like a complete idiot.

"I guess I was wrong," she said.

He lifted the towel to inspect her leg and it immediately began to sting. "About what?"

"I am inept."

"It was an accident."

Huh?

He wasn't going to rub this in her face, try to make her feel like an even bigger idiot? He wasn't going to make fun of her and call her incompetent?

Was this another trick?

"It's red, but it doesn't look like it's blistering. I think your uniform absorbed most of the heat." He laid the ice pack very gently on the burned area. The sting immediately subsided. He looked up at her. "Better?"

She nodded. With her sitting on the counter they were almost eye to eye and, for the first time that morning, she really *saw* him.

Though he looked pretty much the same as he had fifteen years ago, there were subtle signs of age. The hint of crow's-feet branded the corners of his eyes, and there were a few flecks of gray in the stubble on his chin. The line of his jaw seemed less rigid than it used to be, and the lines in his forehead had deepened.

He looked tired. Maybe what had happened at the refinery, compounded by his deal with her, was stressing him out. Maybe he hadn't been sleeping well.

Despite it all, to her he was the same Emilio. At least, her heart thought so. That was probably why it was hurting so much.

But if Emilio really hated her, would it matter that she'd hurt herself? Would he have been so quick to jump in and take care of her? Would he be standing here now holding the ice pack on her leg when she could just as easily do it herself?

He may have been hardened by life, but maybe the sweet, tender man she had fallen in love with was still in there somewhere. Maybe he would be willing to forgive her someday. Or maybe she was fooling herself.

Maybe you should tell him the truth.

At this point it would be a relief to have it all out in the open. But even if she tried, she doubted he would believe her.

"You're watching me," he said, and she realized that he'd caught her red-handed. Oh well, after last night he had to know she still had feelings for him. That she still longed for his touch.

She averted her eyes anyway. "Sorry."

"Did you know that you cursed? When you saw the pan was smoking."

Had she? It was all a bit of a blur. "I don't recall."

"You said 'damn it.' I've never heard you swear before."

She shrugged. "Maybe I didn't have anything to swear about back then."

It wasn't true. She'd had plenty to swear about. But she had been so terrified of slipping up in front of her father, it was safer to not swear at all. He expected her to be the proper Texas debutant. His perfect princess. Though she somehow always managed to fall short.

She still didn't swear very often. Old habits, she supposed. But sometimes a cuss or two would slip out.

He lifted the ice pack and looked at her leg again. "It's not blistered, so it's not that bad of a burn. How does it feel?"

"A little worse than a sunburn."

"Some aloe and a couple of ibuprofen should take care of the pain." He set the pack back on her leg. "Hold this while I go get it."

She was about to tell him that she could do it herself, but she sort of liked being pampered. He would go back to hating her soon, and lusting for revenge. She figured she might as well enjoy it while she could.

Isabelle heard his footsteps going up the stairs, then coming back down and he reappeared with a bottle of aloe and a couple of pain tablets. He got a glass down from the cupboard and filled it with water from the dispenser on the fridge. He gave her that and the tablets and she dutifully swallowed them. She assumed he would hand over the bottle of aloe so she could go in her room and apply it herself. Instead he squirted a glob in his palm and dropped the ice pack into the sink.

There was nothing overtly sexual about his actions as he spread the aloe across her burn, but her body couldn't make the distinction. She felt every touch like a lover's caress. And she wanted him. So badly.

So much for trying to resist him. He wasn't even trying to seduce her and she wanted to climb all over him.

"Why are you being so nice to me?" she asked.

He braced his hands on the edge of the counter on either side of her thighs and looked up at her. "Truthfully, Izzie, I don't know."

It was the probably the most honest thing he had said to her, and before she could even think about what she was doing, she reached up and touched his cheek. It was warm and rough.

His eyes turned stormy.

She knew this was a bad idea, that she was setting herself up to be hurt, but she couldn't stop. She wanted to touch him. She didn't care that it was all an illusion. It felt real to her, and wasn't that all that mattered? And who knows, maybe this time he wouldn't push her away.

She stroked his rough cheek, ran her thumb across his full lower lip. He breathed in deep and closed his eyes. He was holding back, gripping the edge of the countertop so hard his knuckles were white.

She knew she was playing with fire and she didn't care. This time she *wanted* to get burned.

Eight

Isabelle leaned forward and pressed a kiss to Emilio's cheek. The unique scent of his skin, the rasp of his beard stubble, was familiar and comfortable and exciting all at once. Which was probably why her heart was beating so hard and her hands were trembling. The idea that he might push her away now was terrifying, but she wanted this more than she'd ever wanted anything in her life.

She kissed the corner of his mouth, then his lips and he lost it. He wrapped his hands around her hips and tugged her to the edge of the countertop, kissing her hard. Her breasts crushed against his chest, legs went around his waist. This would be no slow, sensual tease like last night.

She had always fantasized about their first time being sweet and tender, and preferably in a bed. There would be candles and champagne and soft music playing. Now none of that seemed to matter. She wanted him with a desperation she'd never felt before. She wanted him to rip off her panties and take her right there in the kitchen, before he changed his mind.

She tunneled her fingers through his hair, fed off his mouth, his stubble rough against her chin. He slid his hands up her sides to her breasts, cupping them in his palms, capturing the tips between his fingers and pinching. She gasped and tightened her legs around him, praying silently, *Please don't stop.*

He tugged at the top button on her uniform, and when it didn't immediately come loose he ripped it open instead. The dress was ruined, anyway, so what difference did it make? And it thrilled her to know that he couldn't wait to get his hands on her.

He peeled the dress off her shoulders and down her arms, pinning them to her sides, ravaging her with kisses and bites—her shoulders and her throat and the tops of her breasts. Then he yanked down one of her bra cups, took her nipple into his mouth, sucking hard, and she almost died it felt so good.

Please, *please* don't stop.

She felt his hand on her thigh, held her breath as it moved slowly upward, the tips of his fingers brushing against the crotch of her panties…

And the doorbell rang.

Emilio cursed. She groaned. Not now, not when they were *so* close.

"Ignore it," she said.

He cursed again, dropping his head to her shoulder, breathing hard. "I can't. A courier from work is dropping off documents. I need them." He glanced at the clock on the oven display. "Although he wasn't supposed to be here until *noon.*"

This was so not fair.

He backed away and she had no choice but to drop her legs from around his waist.

This was *so* not fair.

"You're going to have to get it," he said.

"Me?" Her uniform was in shambles. Ripped and stained and rumpled.

"Consider the alternative," he said, gesturing to the tent in the front of his pajama pants.

Good point.

He lifted her off the counter and set her on her feet. She wrestled her dress back up over her shoulders and tugged the skirt down over her thighs as she hurried to the door. With the button gone she would have to hold her uniform together, or give the delivery guy a special tip for his trouble.

She started to turn and Emilio caught her by the arm.

"Don't think for a second that I'm finished with you."

Oh boy. The heat in his eyes, the sizzle in his voice made her heart skip a beat. Was he going to finish what he started this time? No, what *she* had started.

The idea of what was to come made her knees weak.

The doorbell rang again and he set her loose. "Go."

She dashed through the house to the foyer, catching a glimpse of herself in the full-length mirror by the door. She cringed at her rumpled appearance, convinced that the delivery person would know immediately that she and Emilio had been fooling around. Well, so what if he did? As long as he didn't recognize her, who cared?

Holding the collar of her dress closed, she yanked the door open, expecting the person on the other side to be wearing a delivery uniform. But the man standing on Emilio's porch was dressed in faded jeans, cowboy boots and a trendy black leather jacket. His dark hair was shoulder length and slicked back from his face, and there was something vaguely familiar about him.

He blatantly took in Isabelle's wrinkled and stained uniform, the razor burn on her chin and throat, her mussed hair. One brow tipped up in a move that was eerily familiar, and he asked with blatant amusement, "Rough morning, huh?"

Emilio cursed silently when he recognized the voice of the man on the other side of the door. After three months without so much as a phone call, why did his brother have to pick now to show his face again?

Talk about a mood killer.

He just hoped like hell that Estefan didn't recognize Isabelle, or this could get ugly.

Emilio rounded the corner to the foyer and pushed his way past Isabelle, who didn't seem to know what to say.

"I've got this," he said, and noted with amusement that as she stepped back from the door, she shot a worried glance at his crotch.

"I'll go change," she said, heading for the kitchen.

"Hey, bro," Estefan said, oozing charm. "Long time no see."

He looked good, and though he didn't appear to be under the influence, he was a master at hiding his addictions. Estefan was a handsome, charming guy, which was why people caved to his requests after he let them down time and time again. But not Emilio. He'd learned his lesson.

"What do you want, Estefan?"

"You're not going to invite me inside?"

With Isabelle there? Not a chance. If he had the slightest clue what Emilio was doing, he would exploit the situation to his own benefit.

"I don't even know where you've been for the past three months. Mama has been worried sick about you."

"Not in jail, if that's what you're thinking."

No, because if he'd been arrested, Alejandro would have heard about it. But there were worse things than incarceration.

"I know you probably won't believe this, but I'm clean and sober. I have been for months."

He was right, Emilio didn't believe it. Not for a second. And even if he was, on the rare occasions he'd actually stuck with a rehab program long enough to get clean, it hadn't taken him long to fall back into his old habits.

"What do you want, Estefan?"

"Do I need a reason to see my big brother?"

Maybe not, but he always had one. Usually he needed money, or a place to crash. Occasionally both. He'd even asked to borrow Emilio's car a couple of times, because his own cars had a habit of being repossessed or totaled in accidents that were never Estefan's fault.

He wanted something. He always did.

"Unless you tell me why you're here, I'm closing the door."

The smile slipped from Estefan's face when he realized charm wasn't going to work this time. "I just want to talk to you."

"We have nothing to talk about."

"Come on, Emilio. I'm your baby brother."

"Tell me where you've been."

"Los Angeles, mostly. I was working on a business deal."

A shady one, he was sure. Most of Estefan's "business" deals involved stolen property or drugs, or any number of scams. The fact that he was a small-time criminal with a federal prosecutor for a brother was the only thing that had kept him from doing hard time.

"You're really not going to let me in?" he asked, looking wounded.

"I think I already made that clear."

"You know, I never took you for the type to do the hired help. But I also never expected to see Isabelle Winthrop working for you. Unless the maid's uniform is just some kinky game you play."

Emilio cursed under his breath.

"Did you think I wouldn't recognize her?"

He had hoped, but he should have known better.

"I don't suppose Mama knows what you're doing."

He recognized a threat when he heard one. He held the door open. "Five minutes."

With an arrogant smile, Estefan strolled in.

"Wait here," Emilio said, then walked to the kitchen. Isabelle had changed into a clean uniform and was straightening up the mess from breakfast. She'd fixed her hair and the beard burns had begun to fade.

He should have waited until he shaved to kiss her, but then, he hadn't been expecting her to make the first move. And he hadn't meant to reciprocate. So much for regaining his control. If Estefan hadn't shown up, Emilio had no doubt they would be in his bed right now. Which would have been a huge mistake.

This wasn't working out at all as he'd planned. He wasn't sure if it was his fault, or hers. All he knew was that it had to stop.

She tensed when he entered the room, looking past him to the doorway. He turned to see that his brother had followed him. Figures. Why would he expect Estefan to do anything he asked?

"It's okay," Emilio told Isabelle. "We're going to my

office to talk. I just wanted to tell you to forget about breakfast."

She nodded, then squared her shoulders and met Estefan's gaze. "Mr. Suarez."

"Ms. Winthrop," he said, the words dripping with disdain. "Shouldn't you be in prison?"

The old Isabelle would have withered from his challenge, but this Isabelle held her head high. "Five more weeks. Thanks for asking. Can I offer you something to drink?"

"He's not staying," Emilio said, gesturing Estefan to follow him. "Let's get this over with."

When they were in his office with the door closed, Estefan said, "Isabelle Winthrop, huh? I had no idea you were that hard up."

"Not that it's any of your business, but I'm not sleeping with her." Not yet, anyway. And he was beginning to think making her work as his housekeeper might have to be the extent of his revenge. There were consequences to getting close to her that he had never anticipated.

"So, what is she doing here?"

"She works for me."

"Why would you hire someone like her? After what her family did to our mother. After what she did to you."

"That's my business."

A slow smile crossed his face. "Ah, I get it. Make her work for you, the way our mother worked for her. Nice."

"I'm glad you approve."

"What does she get out of it?"

"She wants Alejandro to cut a deal for her mother, so she won't go to prison."

"So, Alejandro knows what you're doing?"

Emilio took a seat behind his desk, to keep the balance

of power clear. "Let's talk about you, Estefan. What do *you* want?"

"You assume I'm here because I want something from you?"

Emilio shot him a look, putting a chink in the arrogant facade. Estefan crossed the room to look out the window. He didn't even have the guts to look Emilio in the face. "I want you to hear me out before you say anything."

Emilio folded his arms across his chest. *Here we go.*

"There are these people, and I owe them money."

Emilio opened his mouth to say he wouldn't give him a penny, but Estefan raised a hand to stop him. "I'm not asking you for a handout. That's not why I'm here. I have the money to pay them. It's just not accessible at the moment."

"Why?"

"Someone is holding it for me."

"Who?"

"A business associate. He has to liquidate a few assets to pay me, and that's going to take several days. But these men are impatient. I just need a place to hang out until I get the funds. Somewhere they won't find me. It would only be for a few days. Thanksgiving at the latest."

Which was *five* days away. Emilio didn't want his brother around for five minutes, much less the better part of a week.

"Suppose they come looking for you here?" Emilio asked.

"Even if they did, this place is a fortress." He crossed the room, braced his hands on Emilio's desk, a desperation in his eyes that he didn't often let show. "You have to help me, Emilio. I've been trying so hard to set my life straight. After I pay this debt I'm in the clear. I have a friend in rodeo promotions who is willing to give me a job. I could start over, do things right this time."

He wanted to believe his brother, but he'd heard the same story too many times before.

Estefan must have sensed that Emilio was about to say no because he added, "I could go to Mama, and you know she would let me stay, but these are not the kind of people you want anywhere near your mother. There's no telling what they might do."

Leaving Emilio no choice but to let him stay. And Estefan knew it. Emilio should have guessed he would resort to emotional blackmail to get his way. He also suspected that if he refused, it was likely everyone would find out that Isabelle was in his home.

He rose from his chair. "Five days. If you haven't settled your debt by then, you're on your own."

Estefan embraced him. "Thank you, Emilio."

"Just so we're clear, while you're staying in my house there will be no drinking or drugs."

"I don't do that anymore. I'm clean."

"And you won't tell anyone that Isabelle is here."

"Not a soul. You have my word."

"And you will *not* give her a hard time."

Estefan raised a brow.

"My house, my rules."

He shrugged. "Whatever you say."

"I'll have Isabelle get a room ready for you."

"I have a few things to take care of. But I'll be back later tonight. Probably late."

"I'll be in bed by midnight, so if you're not back by then, you're in the pool house for the night."

"If you give me the alarm code—"

Emilio shot him a *not-in-this-lifetime* look.

He shrugged again. "I'll be back by midnight, then."

Estefan left and Emilio went to find Isabelle. She was kneeling on the kitchen floor, cleaning up the oil that spilled by the stove. Only then did he remember that she'd burned her leg, and wondered if it still hurt.

Maybe he should have considered that before he put the moves on her. Of course, he hadn't started it this time, had he? Seducing her had been the last thing on his mind.

Okay, maybe not the *last* thing…

She saw him standing there and shot to her feet. "I'm so sorry. If I had known it was him at the door—"

"I told you to answer it, Isabelle. It's not your fault."

"He won't tell anyone, will he?"

"He promised not to. He's going to be staying here for a few days. Possibly until Thanksgiving."

"Oh."

"It won't change anything. Except maybe you'll be feeding one more person."

"There are always leftovers, anyway."

"What he said to you, it was uncalled for. It won't happen again. I told him that he's not allowed to give you a hard time."

"Because you're the only one allowed to make disparaging comments?"

Something like that. Although now when he thought about saying something rude, it just made him feel like a jerk. He kept thinking about what Alejandro said, about the new developments. That she might be innocent. And even if she was involved somehow, was he so beyond reproach that he felt he had the right to judge her?

That didn't change what she had done to him, and what her father did to his family. For that she was getting exactly what she deserved.

"I'm sorry I ruined breakfast," she said. "I guess hash browns are a little out of my league."

Or maybe it was the result of him distracting her. He never would have done it if he had known she would get hurt. "So you'll make easier things from now on."

"I don't think frying potatoes would be considered complicated. I think I'm just hopeless when it comes to cooking. But thanks for taking care of me. It's been a really long time since someone has done something nice for me. Someone besides my mom, anyway."

"Your husband didn't do nice things for you?" He didn't mean to ask the question. He didn't give a flying fig what her husband did or didn't do. It just sort of popped out.

"Lenny took very good care of me," she said, an undercurrent of bitterness in her voice. "I didn't want for a single thing when I was married to him."

But she wasn't happy, her tone said.

Well, she had made her own bed. Emilio would have given her anything, *done* anything to make her happy. But that hadn't been enough for her.

Her loss.

She pulled off her gloves, wincing a bit when it jostled her bandaged finger.

"It still hurts?" he asked, and she shrugged. "Any signs of infection?"

"It's fine."

That was her standard answer. It could be black with gangrene and she would probably say it was fine. "When was the last time you changed the dressing?"

"Last night…I think."

From the condition of the bandage he would guess it was closer to the night before last. Clearly she wasn't taking care of it. He didn't want to be responsible if it got infected.

He held out his hand. "Let's see it."

She didn't even bother arguing, she just held her hand out to him. He peeled the bandage off. The cut itself had closed, but the area around it was inflamed. There's no way she could not have known it was infected. "Damn, Isabelle, are you *trying* to lose a finger?"

"I've been busy."

"Too busy to take care of yourself?" He dropped her hand. "You still have the antibiotic ointment?"

She nodded.

"Use it. I want you to put a fresh dressing on it three times a day until the infection is cleared up."

"I will. I promise."

"I need you to get one of the guest rooms ready. Preferably the one farthest from mine. Estefan will be back later tonight."

"So, he's not here?"

"He just left."

She was watching him expectantly. He wasn't sure why, but then he remembered what he'd told her when the doorbell rang, that he wasn't finished with her.

"About what happened earlier. I think it would be best if we keep things professional from now on."

"Oh," she said, her eyes filled with confusion. And rejection. He shouldn't have felt like a heel, but he did. Isn't this what he'd wanted? To get her all worked up, then reject her? Well, the plan had worked brilliantly. Even better than he'd anticipated. What he hadn't counted on was how much he would want her, too.

"Well, I had better get the room ready," she said. She paused, as though she was waiting for him to say something, and when he didn't, she walked away, leaving him feeling like the world's biggest jerk.

The last few weeks had been stressful to say the least. He would be relieved when Isabelle was gone, and the investigation at the refinery came to a close, and he was securely in the position of CEO. Life would be perfect.

So why did he have the sneaking suspicion it wouldn't be so simple?

Nine

So much for hoping Emilio might forgive her, that he still wanted her. He wanted to keep their relationship *professional*. And they had come so close this afternoon. If it hadn't been for Estefan showing up…

Oh, well. Easy come, easy go.

Clearly he didn't want Estefan knowing he was involved with someone like her. It was bad enough she was living in his house. And could she blame him for feeling that way? Aside from the fact that her father had ruined their mother's reputation, Isabelle was a criminal.

Alleged criminal, she reminded herself.

Unfortunately, now Emilio seemed to be shutting her out completely. He hadn't come out of his office all day, or said more than a word or two to her. No insults or wry observations. He'd even eaten his dinner at his desk. Just when she'd gotten used to him sitting in the kitchen making fun of her.

Isabelle loaded the last of the dinner dishes in the dishwasher and set it to run. It was only eight and all her work for the day was finished, but the idea of sitting around feeling sorry for herself on a Saturday night was depressing beyond words. Maybe it was time she paid her mom another visit. They could watch a movie or play a game of Scrabble. She could use a little cheering up, and she knew that no matter what, her mother was there for her.

If Emilio would let her go. The only way she could get there, short of making her mother come get her, or taking a cab, was to use his car. She could lie and say she was going grocery shopping, but when she came home empty-handed he would definitely be suspicious. And would he really buy her going shopping on a Saturday night? Besides, she didn't like lying.

She could just sneak out without telling him, and deal with the consequences when she got back.

Yeah, that was probably the way to go.

She changed out of her uniform, grabbed her purse and sweater and when she walked back into the kitchen for the car keys Emilio was there, getting an apple from the fridge. He looked surprised to see her in her street clothes.

Well, shoot. So much for sneaking out.

"Going somewhere?" he asked.

"I finished all my work so I thought I would go see my mother. I won't be late."

"Did Estefan get back yet?"

"Not yet."

"You're taking the Saab?"

She nodded, bracing for an argument.

"Well, then, drive safe."

Drive safe? That was *it*? Wasn't he going to give her a hard time about going out? Or say something about her taking his car for personal use? Instead he walked out of the kitchen and a few seconds later she heard his office door close.

Puzzled, she headed out to the garage, wondering what had gotten into him. Not that she liked it when he acted like an overbearing jerk. But this was just too weird.

The drive to her mother's apartment was only fifteen minutes. Her car was in the lot, and the light was on in her living room. Isabelle parked and walked to the door. She heard laughter from inside and figured that her mother was watching television. She knocked, and a few seconds later the door opened.

"Isabelle!" her mom said, clearly surprised to see her. "What are you doing here?"

"Mrs. Smith didn't need me for the night and I was bored. I thought we could watch a movie or something."

Normally her mother would invite her right in, but she stood blocking the doorway. She looked nervous. "Oh, well…now isn't a good time."

Isabelle frowned. "Is something wrong?"

"No, nothing." She glanced over her shoulder. "It's just…I have company."

Company? Though Isabelle hadn't noticed at first, her mother looked awfully well put together for a quiet night at home. Her hair was swept up and she wore a skirt and blouse that Isabelle had never seen before. She looked beautiful. But for whom?

"Adriana, who is it?" a voice asked. A *male* voice.

Her mother had a *man* over?

As far as Isabelle knew, she hadn't dated anyone since her husband died three years ago. She had serious trust issues. And who wouldn't after thirty-five years with a bastard like Isabelle's father?

But was he a boyfriend? A casual acquaintance?

Her mother blushed, and she stepped back from the door. "Come in."

Isabelle stepped into the apartment and knew immediately that this was no "friendly" social call. There were lit candles on the coffee table and an open bottle of wine with two glasses. The good crystal, Isabelle noted.

"Isabelle, this is Ben McPherson. Ben, this is my daughter."

Isabelle wasn't sure what she expected, but it sure wasn't the man who stood to greet her.

"Isabelle!" he said, reaching out to shake her hand, pumping it enthusiastically. "Good to finally meet you!"

He was big and boisterous with longish salt-and-pepper hair, dressed in jeans and a Hawaiian shirt. He looked like an ex-hippie, with a big question mark on the *ex,* and seemed to exude happiness and good nature from every pore. He was also the polar opposite of Isabelle's father.

And though she had known him a total of five seconds, Isabelle couldn't help but like him.

"Ben owns the coffee shop next to the boutique where I work," her mother said.

"Would you like to join us?" Ben asked. "We were just getting ready to pop in a movie."

The fact that she almost accepted his offer was a testament to how low her life had sunk. The last thing her mother needed was Isabelle crashing her dates. Being the third wheel was even worse than being alone.

"Maybe some other time."

"Are you sure you can't stay for a quick glass of wine?"

"Not while I'm driving. But it was very nice meeting you, Ben."

"You, too, Isabelle."

"I'll walk you to your car," her mother said, and she told Ben, "I'll be right back."

Isabelle followed her mother out the door, shutting it behind them.

"Are you upset?" her mother asked, looking worried.

"About what?"

"That I have a man friend."

"Of course not! Why would I be upset? I want you to be happy. Ben seems very nice."

A shy smile tilted her lips. "He is. I get coffee in his shop before work. He's asked me out half a dozen times, and I finally said yes."

"So you like him?"

"He still makes me a little nervous, but he's such a nice man. He knows all about the indictment, but he doesn't care."

"He sounds like a keeper." She nudged her mom and asked, "Is he a good kisser?"

"Isabelle!" she said, looking scandalized. "I haven't kissed anyone but your father since I was sixteen. To be honest, the idea is a little scary."

They got to the car and Isabelle turned to face her. "Are you physically attracted to him?"

She smiled shyly and nodded. "I think I just need to take things slow."

"And he understands that?"

"We've talked. About your father, and the way things used to be. He's such a good listener."

"How many times have you seen him?"

"This is our third date."

She'd seen him *three* times and hadn't said anything? Isabelle thought they told each other everything.

And who was she to talk when she'd told her mother she worked for the fictional Mrs. Smith?

"You're upset," her mother said, looking crestfallen.

"No, just a little surprised."

"I wanted to tell you, I was just…embarrassed, I guess. If that makes any sense. I keep thinking that he's going to figure out that I'm not such a great catch, and every date we go on will be our last."

She could thank Isabelle's dad for that. He'd put those ideas into her head.

"He's lucky to have you and I'm sure he knows it."

"He does seem to like me. He's already talking about what we'll do next weekend."

"Well, then, I'd better let you get back inside." She gave her mother a hug. "Have fun, but not *too* much fun. Although after three dates, I would seriously consider letting him kiss you."

Her mother smiled. "I will."

"I'll see you Thursday, then. Is there anything you need me to bring?"

"Oh, I was thinking…well, the thing is, my oven here isn't very reliable, and…actually, Ben invited me to Thanksgiving dinner with him and a few of his friends. I thought you could come along."

That would be beyond awkward, especially when his friends found out who she was. But she could see that her mother really wanted to go, and she wouldn't out of guilt if Isabelle didn't come up with a viable excuse.

"Mrs. Smith's family asked me to have dinner with them," she lied. "They've been so kind to me, the truth is I felt bad telling them no. So if you want to eat with Ben and his friends, that's fine."

"Are you sure? We always spend Thanksgiving together."

Not after this year, unless her mother wanted to eat at the women's correctional facility. It was good that she was making new friends, getting on with her life. To fill the void when Isabelle was gone.

She forced a smile. "I'm sure."

She gave her one last hug, then got in the car. Her mother waved as she drove off. It seemed as if she was finally getting on with her life. Isabelle wanted her to be happy, so why did she feel like dropping her head on the steering wheel and sobbing?

Probably because, for a long, long time, Isabelle and her mom had no one but each other. They were a team.

Her mother had someone else now. And who did Isabelle have? Pretty much no one.

But she was not going to feel sorry for herself, damn it. What would be the point of creating new relationships now anyway, when in five weeks she would be going to prison?

She didn't feel like going back to Emilio's yet, so instead she drove around for a while. When she reached the edge of town, she was tempted to just keep going. To drive far from here, away from her life. A place where no one knew her and she could start over.

But running away never solved anything.

It was nearly eleven when she steered the car back to Emilio's house. She parked in the garage next to his black Ferrari and headed inside, dropping her purse and sweater in her room before she walked out to the kitchen to make herself a cup of tea. She put the kettle on to boil and fished around the cupboard above the coffeemaker on her tiptoes for a box of tea bags.

"Need help?"

She felt someone lean in beside her. She looked up, expecting to find Emilio, but it was Estefan standing there.

She jerked away, feeling…violated. He was charming, and attractive—although not even close to as good-looking as Emilio—but something about him always gave her the creeps. Even when they were younger, when his mother would drive them to school, Isabelle didn't like the way he would look at her. Even though he was a few years younger, he made her nervous.

He still did. She had to dig extra deep to maintain her show-no-fear attitude.

Estefan flashed her an oily smile and held out the box of tea bags. She took it from him. "Thank you."

"No problem." He leaned against the counter and folded his arms. *Watching* her.

"Did Emilio show you to your room?" she asked, mainly because she didn't know what else to say.

"Yep. It's great place, isn't it?" He looked around the kitchen. "My brother did pretty well for himself."

"He has."

"Probably makes you regret screwing him over."

So much for Estefan not giving her a hard time. She should have anticipated this.

"It looks like you've got a pretty sweet deal going here," Estefan said.

She wondered how much Emilio had told him. From the tone of their conversation at the front door—yes, she'd eavesdropped for a minute or two—Emilio hadn't been happy to see his brother. Would he confide in someone he didn't trust? And what difference did it make?

"You get to live in his house, drive his cars, eat his food. It begs the question, what is he getting in return?"

Housekeeping and cooking. But clearly that wasn't what he meant. He seemed certain there was more to it than that. Why didn't he just come right out and call her a whore?

The kettle started to boil so she walked around the island to the stove to fix her tea. Emilio had belittled and insulted her, but that had been different somehow. Less... sinister and vindictive. She just hoped that if she didn't give him the satisfaction of a reaction, Estefan would get bored and leave her alone.

No such luck.

He stepped up behind her. So close she could almost feel his body heat. The cloying scent of his aftershave turned her stomach.

"My brother is too much of a nice guy to realize he's being used."

She had the feeling that the only one using Emilio was Estefan, but she kept her mouth shut. And as much as she would like to tell Emilio how Estefan was treating her, she would never put herself in the middle of their relationship. She would only be around a few weeks. Emilio and Estefan would be brothers for life.

She turned to walk back to her room, but Estefan was blocking her way. "Excuse me."

"You didn't say *please*."

She met his steely gaze with one of her own, and after several seconds he let her through. She forced herself to walk slowly to her room. The door didn't have a lock, so she shoved the folding chair under the doorknob—just in case. She didn't really think Estefan would get physical with her, especially with his brother in the house. But better safe than sorry.

Life at Emilio's hadn't exactly been a picnic, but it hadn't been terrible, either, and she'd always felt safe. She had the feeling that with Estefan around, those days were over.

Ten

Though he wouldn't have believed it possible, Emilio was starting to think maybe his brother really had changed this time. Good to his word, he hadn't asked Emilio for a penny. Not even gas money. He'd spent no late nights out partying and, as far as Emilio could tell, had remained sober for the three days he'd been staying there. The animosity that had been a constant thread in their relationship for as many years as Emilio could remember was gradually dissolving.

When they were growing up, Estefan had always been jealous of Emilio, coveting whatever he had. The cool after-school jobs, the stellar grades and college scholarships. He just hadn't wanted the hard work that afforded Emilio those luxuries. But now it seemed that Estefan finally got it; he'd figured out what he needed to do, and he was making a valiant effort to change.

At least, Emilio hoped so.

Though things at Western Oil were still in upheaval, and

he had work he could be doing, Emilio had spent the last couple of evenings in the media room watching ESPN with his brother. He felt as if, for the first time in their lives, he and Estefan were bonding. Acting like real brothers. Besides, spending time with him was helping Emilio keep his mind off Isabelle.

Since he told her that he wanted to keep things professional, he hadn't been able to stop thinking about her. The way she tasted when he kissed her, the softness of her skin, the feel of her body pressed against his. She was as responsive to his touch, as hot for him now, as she had been all those years ago. And now that he knew he couldn't have her, he craved her that much more. This time it had nothing to do with revenge or retribution. He just plain wanted her, and he could tell by the way she looked at him, the loneliness and longing in her eyes, that she wanted him, too. And so, apparently, could Estefan.

"She wants you, bro," Estefan said Tuesday evening after dinner, while they were watching a game Emilio had recorded over the weekend.

"Our relationship is professional," he told his brother.

"Why? You could tap that, then kick her to the curb. It would be the ultimate revenge. Use her the way she used you."

Which was exactly what Emilio had planned to do, but for some reason now, it just seemed...sleazy. Maybe he was ready to let go of the past. Maybe all this time he'd just been brooding. He wasn't the only man to ever get his heart broken. Maybe it was time he stopped making excuses, stopped attaching ulterior motives to her decision and face facts. She left him because she'd fallen in love with someone else, and it was time he stopped feeling sorry for himself and got on with his life.

"Honestly, Estefan, I think she's getting what she has

coming to her. She's widowed, broke and a month away from spending the rest of her life in prison. She's about as low as she can possibly sink, yet she's handling it with grace and dignity."

"If I didn't know better, I might think you actually *like* her."

That was part of the problem. Emilio wasn't sure how he felt about her. He didn't hate her, not anymore. But he couldn't see them ever being best pals. Or even close friends. As the saying went, fool me once, shame on you...

Once she was in prison, he doubted he would ever see her again. It wasn't as if he would be going to visit her, or sending care packages.

If she actually went to prison, that is. The new lead his brother had mentioned could prove her innocence. And if it did? Then what?

Then, nothing. Innocent or guilty, sexually compatible or not, there was nothing she could say or do that would make up for the past. Not for him, and not for his family. Even if he wanted to be with her, his family would never accept it. Especially his mother. And they came first, simple as that.

Estefan yawned and stretched. "I have an early start in the morning. I think I'll turn in."

Emilio switched off the television. "Me, too."

"By the way," Estefan said, "I talked to my business associate today. He hit a snag and it's looking like I won't get that money until a few days after Thanksgiving. I know I said I would be out of here—"

"It's okay," Emilio heard himself say. "You can stay a few extra days."

"You're sure?"

"I'm sure."

"Thanks, bro."

They said good-night and Emilio walked to the kitchen to pour himself a glass of juice to take up to bed with him. By the light of the range hood he got a glass down from the cupboard and the orange juice from the fridge. He emptied the carton, but when he tried to put it in the trash under the sink, the bag was full.

He sighed. Mrs. Medina had specifically instructed Izzie to take the kitchen trash out nightly. He couldn't help but wonder if she'd forgotten on purpose, just to annoy him. If that was the case, he was annoyed.

He considered calling her out to change it, on principle, but it was after eleven and she was usually in bed by now. Instead he pulled the bag out, tied it and put a fresh one in. He carried the full bag to the trash can in the garage, noting on his way the dim sliver of light under Isabelle's door. Her lamp was on. Either she was still awake, or she'd fallen asleep with the light on again.

He dropped the bag in the can, glancing over at the Saab. Was that a *scratch* on the bumper?

He walked over to look, and on closer inspection saw that it was just something stuck to the paint. He rubbed it clean, made a mental note to tell Isabelle to take it to the car wash the next time she was out, then headed back inside. He expected to find the kitchen empty, but Isabelle was standing in front of the open refrigerator door. She was wearing a well worn plaid flannel robe and her hair was wet.

"Midnight snack?" he asked.

She let out a startled squeak and spun around, slamming the door shut. "You scared me half to death!"

He opened his mouth to say something sarcastic when his eyes were drawn to the front of her robe and whatever he'd been about to say melted somewhere into the recesses of his brain. The robe gaped open at the collar, revealing the uppermost swell of her bare left breast. Not a huge deal normally, but in his present state of craving her, he was transfixed.

Look away, he told himself, but his eyes felt glued. All he could think about was what it felt like to cup it in his palm, her soft whimpers as he took her in his mouth and how many years he had wondered what it would be like to make love to her.

Where was his self-control?

Isabelle followed his gaze down to the front of her robe. He expected her to pull the sides together, maybe get embarrassed.

She didn't. She lifted her eyes back to his and just stood there, daring him to make a move.

Nope, not gonna do it.

Then she completely stunned him by tugging the tie loose and letting the robe fall open. It was dark, but he could see that she wasn't wearing anything underneath.

Damn.

You are not going to touch her, he told himself. But Isabelle clearly had other ideas. She walked over to him, took his hand and placed it on her breast.

Damn.

He could have pulled away, could have told her no. He *should* have. Unfortunately his hand seemed to develop a mind of its own. It cupped her breast, his thumb brushing back and forth over her nipple. Isabelle's eyes went dark with arousal.

She reached up and unfastened his belt.

If he was planning to stop her, now would be a good time, but as she undid the clasp on his slacks, he just stood there. She tugged the zipper down, slipped her hand inside…

He sucked in a breath as her hand closed around his

erection, and for the life of him he couldn't recall why he thought this was a bad idea. In fact, it seemed like a damned good idea, and if he was going to be totally honest with himself, it had been an inevitability.

But not here. Not with Estefan in the house. His bedroom wouldn't be a great idea, either.

"Your room," he said, so she took his hand and led him there.

The desk lamp was on, and he half expected her to shut it off, the way she used to. Not only did she leave the light on, but the minute the door was closed, she dropped her robe. Standing there naked, in the soft light… *Damn.* He'd never seen anything so beautiful, and he'd only had to wait fifteen years.

"You have to promise me you won't stop this time," she said, unfastening the buttons on his shirt.

Why stop? If they didn't do this now, it would just happen later. A day, or a week. But it would happen.

He took his wallet from his back pocket, pulled out a condom and handed it to her. "I promise."

Isabelle smiled and pushed his shirt off his shoulders. "You'll never know how many times I thought of you over the years."

Did you think of me when you were with him? He wanted to ask, but what if he didn't like the answer?

She pushed his pants and boxers down and he stepped out of them. "Do you know what I miss more than anything?" she said.

"What do you miss?"

"Lying in bed with you, under the covers, wrapped around each other, kissing and touching. Sometimes we were so close it was like we were one person. Do you remember?"

He did, and he missed it, too, more then she could

imagine. There had been a lot of women since Izzie, some who had lasted weeks, and a few who hung around for months, but he never felt that connection. He'd never developed the closeness with them that he'd felt with her.

She pulled back the covers on the bed and lay down. Emilio slipped in next to her, but when she tried to pull the covers up over them, he stopped her. "No covers this time. I want to look at you."

She reached up to touch his face and he realized that her hands were shaking. Could she possibly be nervous? This woman who, a few minutes ago, seemed to know exactly what she wanted and wasn't the least bit afraid to go after it?

He put his hand over hers, pressing it to his cheek. "You're trembling."

"I've just been waiting for this for a really long time."

"Are you sure you want to do this?"

"Emilio, I have never been more sure of anything in my life." She wound her arms around his neck and pulled him down, wrapped herself around him, kissed him. It was like…coming home. Everything about her was familiar. The feel of her body, the scent of her skin, her soft, breathy whimpers as he touched her.

He felt as if he was twenty-one again, lying in his bed in his rental house on campus, with their entire lives ahead of them. He remembered exactly what to do to make her writhe in ecstasy. Slow and sweet, the way he knew she liked it. He brought her to the edge of bliss and back again, building the anticipation, until she couldn't take it anymore.

"Make love to me, Emilio." She dug her fingers through his hair, kissed him hard. "I can't wait any longer."

He grabbed the condom and she watched with lust-glazed eyes as he rolled it on. The second he was finished she pulled him back down, wrapping her legs around his waist.

He centered himself over her, anticipating the blissful wet heat of that first thrust, but he was barely inside when he met with resistance. She must have been tense from the anticipation of finally making love. He couldn't deny he was a bit anxious himself. He put some weight into it and the barrier gave way. Isabelle gasped, digging her nails into his shoulders and she was *tight*. Tighter than any wife of fifteen years should be.

He eased back, looking down where their bodies were joined, stunned by what he saw. Exactly what he would have expected…if he'd just made love to a virgin.

No way. "Isabelle?"

It was obvious by her expression that she had been hoping he wouldn't figure it out. How was this even possible?

"Don't stop," she pleaded, pulling at his shoulders, trying to get him closer.

Hell no, he wasn't going to stop, but if he had known he could have at least been more gentle.

"I'm going to take it slow," he told her. Which in theory was a great plan, but as she adjusted to the feel of him inside her, she relaxed. Then "slow" didn't seem to be enough for her. She began to writhe beneath him, meeting his downward slide with a thrust of her hips. He was so lost in the feel of her body, the clench of her muscles squeezing him into euphoria, that he was running on pure instinct. When she moaned and bucked against him, her body fisting around him as she climaxed, it did him in. His only clear thought as he groaned out his release was *perfect*. But as he slowly drifted back to earth, reality hit him square between the eyes.

He and Isabelle had finally made love, after all these years, and he was her first. Exactly as it was meant to be.

So why did he feel so damned…guilty?

"You know, I must have imagined what that would be like about a thousand times over the past fifteen years," she said. "But the real thing is way better than the fantasy."

Emilio tipped her face up to his. "Izzie, why didn't you tell me?"

She didn't have to ask what he meant. She lowered her eyes. "I was embarrassed."

"Why?"

"You don't run across many thirty-four-year-old virgins."

"How is this even possible? You're young and beautiful and sexy. Your husband never wanted to…?"

"Can we not talk about it?" She was closing down, shutting him out, but he wanted answers, damn it.

"I want to know how you can be married to a man for fifteen years and never have sex with him."

She sat up and pulled the covers over her. "It's complicated."

"I'm a reasonably intelligent man, Izzie. Try me."

"We…we didn't have that kind of relationship."

"What kind of relationship did you have?"

She drew her knees up and hugged them. "I really don't want to talk about this."

"Did you love him?"

She bit her lip and looked away.

"Isabelle?"

After a long pause she said, "I…respected him."

"Is that your way of saying you were just in it for the money?"

She didn't deny it. She didn't say anything at all.

If she loved Betts, Emilio would understand her leaving

him. It sucked, but he could accept it. Knowing it was only about the money, seeing the truth on her face, knowing that she'd really been that shallow, disturbed him on too many levels to count.

"This was a mistake," he said. He pushed himself up from the bed and grabbed his pants.

"Emilio—"

"No. This never should have happened. I don't know what the hell I was thinking."

She was quiet for several seconds, and he waited to see what she would do. Would she apologize and beg him to stay? Tell him she made a horrible mistake? And would it matter if she did?

"You're right," she finally said, avoiding his gaze. "It was a mistake."

She was agreeing with him, and she was right, so why did he feel like putting his fist through the wall?

He tugged his pants on.

"So, what now?" she asked.

"Meaning what?"

"Are you going to back out on our deal?"

He grabbed his shirt from off the floor. "No, Isabelle, I won't. I keep my word. But I would really appreciate if you would stay out of my way. And I'll stay out of yours."

He was pretty sure he saw tears in her eyes as he jerked the door open and walked out. And just when he thought this night couldn't get any worse, his brother was sitting in the kitchen eating a sandwich and caught him red-handed.

Damn it.

When he saw Emilio his eyes widened, then a wry smile curled his mouth.

Emilio glared at him. "Don't say a word."

Estefan shrugged. "None of my business, bro."

Emilio wished Estefan had walked into the kitchen

before Isabelle started her stripping routine, then none of this would have happened.

But one thing he knew for damned sure, it was not going to happen again.

Eleven

This was for the best.

At least, that was what Isabelle had been trying to tell herself all day. She would rather have Emilio hate her, than fall in love and endure losing her again. That wouldn't be fair. Not to either of them. She was tired of feeling guilty for hurting him. She just wanted it to be over. For good.

She should have left things alone, should never have opened her robe, offered herself to him, but she'd figured for him it was just sex. She never imagined he might still have feelings for her, but he must have, or it wouldn't have matter if she loved Lenny or not.

She ran the vacuum across the carpet in the guest room, cringing at the memory of his stunned expression when he realized she was a virgin. She didn't know he would be able to tell. A testament to how naive and inexperienced she was. But as first times go, she was guessing it had been way above average. Everything she had ever hoped, and she couldn't regret it. She loved Emilio. She'd wanted him to be her first. As far as she was concerned, it was meant to be.

Except for the part where he stormed off mad.

When he'd asked her about Lenny, she had almost told him the truth. It had been sitting there on the tip of her tongue. Now she was relieved she hadn't. It was better that he thought the worst of her.

She turned to do the opposite side of the room, jolting with alarm when she realized Estefan was leaning in the bedroom doorway watching her.

His mere presence in the house put her on edge, but when he watched her—and he did that a lot—it gave her the creeps. When she dusted the living room he would park himself on the couch with a magazine, or if she was fixing dinner he would come in for a snack and sit at one of the island stools. Occasionally he would assault her with verbal barbs, which she generally ignored. But most of the time he just stared at her.

It was beyond unsettling.

Estefan raised the beer he was holding to his lips and took a swallow. Isabelle had distinctly heard him tell Emilio that he was clean and sober, yet the second he rolled out of bed every day, which was usually noon or later, he went straight to the fridge for a cold one.

The breakfast of champions.

It wasn't her place to tattle on Estefan, and even if she told Emilio what he was doing, she doubted he would believe her. It was also the reason she didn't tell him that she'd caught Estefan in his office going through his desk. He claimed he'd been looking for a pen, when she knew for a fact he'd been trying to get into the locked file drawer.

He was definitely up to something.

She turned off the vacuum. She knew she should keep

her mouth shut, but she couldn't help herself. "Would you care for some pretzels to go with that?"

"Funny." His greasy smile made her skin crawl. "Where are the keys for the Ferrari?"

"Why?"

"I need to borrow it."

"I have no idea. Why don't you call Emilio and ask him?"

"I don't want to bother him."

No, he knew his brother would say no, so it was easier to take it without his permission.

"I guess I'll have to take the Saab instead."

"Why don't you take your bike?"

"No gas. Unless you want to loan me twenty bucks. I'm good for it."

She glared at him. Even if she had twenty bucks she wouldn't give it to him. He shouldn't even be driving. He would be endangering not only himself, but everyone else on the road.

He shrugged. "The Saab it is, then."

It wasn't as if she could stop him. Short of calling the police and reporting him, she had no recourse. And in her experience, the police never really helped anyway.

Besides, she had enough to worry about in her own life without sticking her nose into Estefan's business.

"So, this arrangement not working out the way you planned it?" Estefan asked.

She wondered what Emilio had told him, if anything.

"Still a virgin at thirty-four." He shook his head. "Let me guess, was your husband impotent, or did you just freeze him out?"

The humiliation she felt was matched only by her anger at Emilio for telling Estefan her private business. She knew he was mad, but this was uncalled for. Was that his way of getting back at her?

Estefan flashed her that greasy smile again. "If you needed someone to take care of business, all you had to do was ask. I'm twice the man my brother is."

The thought of Estefan coming anywhere near her was nauseating. "Not if you were the last man on earth."

His expression darkened. "We'll see about that," he said, then walked away.

She wasn't sure what he meant by that, but the possibilities made her feel uneasy. He wouldn't have the nerve to try something, would he?

Tomorrow was Thanksgiving and he was supposed to be leaving. She would just have to watch her back until then.

Emilio's Thanksgiving was not going well so far.

He stood in his closet, fresh out of a shower, holding up the shirt Isabelle had just ironed for him, noting the scorch mark on the left sleeve. "This is a three hundred dollar silk shirt, Isabelle."

"I'm sorry," she said, yet she didn't really look sorry.

"I just wanted it lightly pressed. Not burned to a crisp."

"I didn't realize the iron was set so hot. I'll replace it."

"After you pay me back for the rug? And the casserole dish you broke. And the load of whites that you dyed pink. Not to mention the grocery bill that has mysteriously risen by almost twelve percent since you've been here."

"Maybe I could stay an extra week or two and work off what I owe you."

Terrific idea. But she would inevitably break something else and wind up owing him even more. Besides, he didn't want her in his house any longer than necessary. If there was any way he could get his housekeeper back today and let Isabelle go on time served, he would, but he'd promised her a month off.

He balled the shirt up and tossed it in the trash can in the corner. "It would probably be in everyone's best interest if you avoided using the iron."

She nodded.

He turned to grab a different shirt and a pair of slacks. He was about to drop his towel, when he noticed she was still standing there.

He raised a brow. "You want to watch me get dressed?"

"I wasn't sure if you were finished."

"Finished what?"

"Yelling at me."

"I wasn't *yelling.*"

"Okay, disciplining me."

"If I were disciplining you, it would have involved some sort of punishment." Not that he couldn't think of a few. Putting her over his knee was one that came to mind. She could use a sound spanking. But he'd promised himself he was going to stop thinking of her in a sexual way and view her as an employee. Tough when he couldn't seem to stop picturing her naked and writhing beneath him.

"How about…chastising?" she said. "Dressing-down?"

"Exaggerate much? I was *talking* to you."

"If you say so."

Why the sudden attitude? If anyone had the right to be pissed, it was him.

"Is there anything else you need?" she asked.

"Could you tell my brother to be ready in twenty minutes?"

She saluted him and walked out.

He'd like to know what had gotten her panties in such a twist. Maybe she just didn't like the fact that he'd called her out on her marriage being a total sham. That he'd more or less made her admit she married Betts for his money. In which case she was getting exactly what she deserved.

He got dressed, slipped on his cashmere jacket and grabbed his wallet. Estefan was waiting for him in the kitchen. He wore jeans and a button-down shirt that was inappropriately open for a family holiday gathering, and the thick gold chain was downright tacky, but Emilio kept his mouth shut. Estefan was trying. He'd been on his best behavior all week.

Almost *too* good.

"Ready to go?"

"I'll bet you want to let me drive," Estefan said.

Reformed or not, he was not getting behind the wheel of a car that cost Emilio close to half a million dollars. "I'll bet I don't."

Estefan grumbled as they walked out to the garage. Emilio was about to climb in the driver's seat of the Ferrari when he glanced over at the Saab. "Son of a—"

"What's the matter?" Estefan asked.

The rear quarter panel was buckled. For a second he considered that someone had hit it while it was parked, but then he looked closer and noticed the fleck of yellow paint embedded in the black. Not car paint. More like what they used on parking barriers.

He shook his head. "Damn it!"

"Bro, go easy on her. I'm gonna bet she's used to having a driver. It's a wonder she even remembers how to drive."

He walked to the door, yanked it open and yelled, "Isabelle!"

She emerged from her room, looking exasperated. "What did I do this time?"

"Like you don't already know." He gestured her into the garage.

She stepped out. "What?"

"The *car*."

She looked at the Saab. "What about it?

Why was she playing dumb? She knew what she did. "The other side."

She walked around, and as soon as she saw the damage her mouth fell open. "What happened?"

"Are you telling me you don't recall running into something?"

She looked from Emilio, to Estefan, then back to the car. She didn't even have the courtesy to look embarrassed for lying to him. She squared her shoulders and said, "Put it on my tab."

That was it? That was all she had to say? "You might have mentioned this."

"Why? So you could make bad driver jokes about me?"

"What the hell has gotten into you, Isabelle?"

She shrugged. "I guess I'm finally showing my true colors. Living up to your expectations. You should be happy."

She turned and walked back into the house, slamming the door behind her.

"Nice girl," Estefan said.

No, this wasn't like her at all. "Get in the car."

When they were on the road Estefan said, "Dude, she's not worth it."

He knew that, in his head. Logically, they had no future together. The trick was getting the message to his heart. The protective shell he'd built around it was beginning to crumble. He was starting to feel exposed and vulnerable, and he didn't like it.

"Make her leave," Estefan said.

"I can't do that. I gave her my word." Besides, he didn't think she had anywhere else to go.

"Dude, you don't owe her anything."

He'd promised to help her, and in his world, that still meant something. Estefan hadn't kept a promise in his entire life.

They drove the rest of the way to Alejandro's house in silence.

When they stepped through the door, the kids tackled them in the foyer, getting sticky fingerprints all over Emilio's cashmere jacket and slacks, but he didn't care.

"Kids! Give your uncles a break," Alejandro scolded, but he knew they didn't mind.

Chris, the baby, was clinging to Emilio's leg, so he hoisted him up high over his head until he squealed with delight, then gave him a big hug. Reggie, the six-year-old, tugged frantically on his jacket.

"Hey, Uncle Em! Guess what! I'm going to be big brother again!"

"Your dad told me. That's great."

"Jeez, dude," Estefan said with a laugh. "*Four* kids."

Alejandro grinned and shrugged. "Alana wanted to try for a girl. After all these years I still can't tell her no."

"I think she should make a boy," Reggie said. "I don't want a sister."

Emilio laughed and ruffled the boy's hair. "I think she'll get what she gets."

"Hey, Uncle Em, guess who's here!" Alex, the nine-year-old said, hopping excitedly.

"*Alex.*" Alejandro shot his oldest a warning look. "It's supposed to be a surprise."

"Who's here?" Emilio asked him, and from behind him he heard someone say, "Hey, big brother."

He spun around to see his youngest brother, Enrique, standing in the kitchen doorway. He laughed and said, "What the hell are you doing here? I thought you were halfway around the world."

"Mama talked me into it and Alejandro bought my ticket." He hugged Emilio, then Estefan.

"You look great," Estefan told him. "But I'll bet Mama's not very happy about the long hair and goatee."

"She's not," their mama said from the kitchen doorway, hands on her hips, apron tied around her slim waist. She was a youthful fifty-eight, considering the hard life she'd lived. First growing up in the slums of Cuba, then losing her husband so young and raising four boys alone.

"He does look a little scruffy," Alana teased, joining them in the foyer.

"But I finally have all my boys together," their mama said. "And that's all that matters."

Emilio gave his sister-in-law a hug and kiss. "Congratulations, sis."

She grinned. "I'm crazy, right? In this family I'm probably more likely to give birth to conjoined twins than a girl."

Emilio shrugged. "It could happen."

"Why are we all standing around in the foyer?" Alejandro said. "Why don't we move this party to the kitchen?"

For a day that had begun so lousy, it turned out to be the best Thanksgiving in years. The food was fantastic and it was great to have the whole family together again. The best part was that his mama was so excited to have Enrique home, it took her several hours to get around to nagging Emilio about settling down.

"It's not right, you living alone in that big house," she said, as they all sat in the living room, having after dinner drinks. Except Estefan, who was on the floor wrestling with the nephews. He'd been on his best behavior all day.

"I like living alone," Emilio told her. "And if I ever feel the need to have kids, I can just borrow Alejandro's."

"You need to fill it with niños of your own," she said sternly.

"Why don't you nag Enrique about getting married?" Emilio said.

She rubbed her youngest son's arm affectionately. "He's still a baby."

Emilio laughed. "So what does that make me? An old man?"

"You are pretty damn old," Enrique said, which got him plenty of laughs.

Chris climbed into Emilio's lap and hugged him, staring up at him with big brown eyes. And Emilio was thinking that maybe having a kid or two wouldn't be so bad, just as Chris threw up all down the front of his shirt.

"Oh, sweetie!" Alana charged over, sweeping him up off Emilio's lap. "Emilio, I'm so sorry!"

"It's okay," Emilio said, using the tissues his brother handed him to clean himself up.

"Honey, take your brother up and get him a clean shirt. You're the same size, right?"

"I'm sure I have something that will work," Alejandro said, and Emilio followed him upstairs to his bedroom.

Alejandro handed him a clean shirt and said, "While I've got you here, there's something I wanted to ask you."

He peeled off his dirty shirt and gave it to his brother. "What's up?"

"How much do you know about Isabelle's father?"

He was having such a good day, he didn't want to ruin it by thinking about Isabelle and her family. "I'm not sure what you mean. Other than the fact that he was a bastard, not too much I guess."

"Did you know he had a serious gambling problem?"

"So he was an even bigger bastard than we thought. So what?"

"He'd also had charges filed against him."

"For what?"

"Domestic abuse."

Emilio frowned. "Are you sure?"

"Positive. And he must have had friends in high places because I had to dig deep."

Emilio shrugged into the shirt and buttoned it. It was slightly large, but at least it didn't smell like puke. "So he was an even *bigger* bastard."

"There's something else." His grim expression said Emilio probably wasn't going to like this. "There were also allegations of child abuse."

Emilio's pulse skipped. Had Izzie been abused? "Allegations? Was there ever any proof?"

"He was never charged. I just thought you would want to know."

"Can you dig deeper?"

"I could, if it were relevant to my case."

"Are you suggesting I should investigate this further?"

Alejandro shrugged. "That would be a conflict of interest. Although I can say that if it were me, I would try to get a hold of medical records."

"Could this exonerate her?"

"I'm not at liberty to say."

"Damn it, Alejandro."

He sighed. "Probably not, but it might be relevant in her defense."

"I thought she was taking a plea."

"She is, on the advice of counsel, and I think we've already established that she may not be getting the best advice."

So in other words, Alejandro wanted him to dig deeper. He couldn't deny that the idea she might have been mistreated was an unsettling one. He could just ask her, but if she hadn't told him by now, what were the odds she would admit it? And if she had been, wouldn't he have noticed? Or maybe it was something that happened when she was younger.

"I'll look into it."

"Let me know what you find."

He followed his brother back downstairs, but he'd lost his holiday spirit. He felt…unsettled. And not just about the possible abuse. It seemed as though quite a few things lately weren't…adding up. Like why her husband kept her in the lap of luxury and expected nothing in return, and Isabelle's sudden change of personality to Miss Snarky.

"You ready to go?" he asked Estefan an hour later.

"I think I'm going to crash here tonight. Get some quality time with the nephews."

He glanced over at Alejandro, who nodded.

His mama protested him leaving so early, so he used exhaustion from work as an excuse. Everyone knew things had been hectic since the explosion.

He said his goodbyes and headed home. When he pulled into the garage just before nine, he was surprised to find the Saab there. He figured Isabelle would have taken it to her mother's. Or maybe she thought he wouldn't want her driving it now.

He crouched down to look at the dent. He didn't doubt that it was caused by backing into something. She probably wasn't paying attention to where she was going. If she had just fessed up when it happened, it wouldn't have been a big deal. Although it wasn't like her to lie. Every time she screwed up, she owned up to it, and she had looked genuinely surprised when he pointed it out.

Curious, he walked around to the driver's side and got in. He stuck the key in and booted the navigation system, going through the history until he found what he was looking for.

Damn it. What the hell had she been thinking?

Shaking his head, he got out and let himself in the house. There was an empty wine bottle on the counter by the sink. Cheap stuff that Isabelle must have picked up at the grocery store.

He checked the dishwasher and found a dirty plate, fork, cup and pan inside. She hadn't gone to her mother's. She'd spent the holiday alone.

Twelve

Isabelle wasn't in her bedroom, so Emilio went looking for her. He found her asleep in the media room, curled up in a chair in her pajamas, another bottle of wine on the table beside her, this one three quarters empty, and beside it the case for the DVD *Steel Magnolias*. The movie whose credits were currently rolling up the screen. There was a tissue box in her lap and a dozen or so balled up on the seat and floor.

Far as he could tell, she'd spent her Thanksgiving watching chick movies, crying and drinking herself into a stupor with cheap wine.

"Isabelle." He jostled her shoulder. "Isabelle, wake up."

Her eyes fluttered open, fuzzy from sleep, and probably intoxication. "You're home."

"I'm home."

She smiled, closed her eyes and promptly fell back to sleep.

He sighed. Short of dumping a bucket of cold water over her head—which he couldn't deny was awfully tempting—he didn't think she would be waking up any time soon. He just wished she would have told him she was spending Thanksgiving alone.

And he would have...what? Invited her to his brother's? Stayed home with her and ignored his family? He wouldn't have done anything different, other than feel guilty all day.

He picked her up out of the chair and hoisted her into his arms. Her eyes fluttered open and her arms went around his neck. "Where are we going?" she asked in a sleepy voice.

"I'm taking you to bed."

"Oh, okay." Her eyes drifted closed again and her head dropped on his shoulder. He started to walk in the direction of her quarters, but the thought of leaving her in there, alone, isolated from the rest of the house in that uncomfortable little bed...he just couldn't do it.

He carried her upstairs instead, to the spare bedroom beside his room. He pulled the covers back and laid her down, unhooking her arms from around his neck. It was dark, but he could see that her eyes were open.

"Where am I?"

"The guest room. I thought you would be more comfortable here."

"I had too much to drink."

"I know."

She curled up on her side, hugging the pillow. "I don't usually drink, but I didn't think it would be so hard."

"What?"

"Being alone today."

Damn. "Why didn't you go to your mother's?"

"She wanted to be with Ben and his friends."

He had no idea who Ben was. Maybe a friend or boyfriend. "You couldn't go with her?"

"She needs to meet people, make new friends, so it won't be as bad when I'm gone."

By gone he assumed she meant in prison. So she'd spent the day alone for her mother's sake. Not the actions of a spoiled, selfish woman.

He thought about the news his brother had sprung on him tonight and wondered if it could be true, if Isabelle had been abused as a child.

He sat on the edge of the bed. "Isabelle, why didn't you tell me the truth about the car?"

"I told you why."

"What I mean is, why didn't you tell me that it wasn't you who caused the damage?"

She blinked. "Of course I did."

More lies. "I looked in the navigation history. Unless you spent the afternoon at a strip joint downtown, it was Estefan who took the car." He touched her cheek. "Why would you take the fall for him?"

Looking guilty, she shrugged. "You're brothers. I didn't want to get between you."

"You're right, we are brothers. So I know exactly what he's capable of." He brushed her hair back, tucked it behind her ear. "Is there anything else? Anything I should know?"

She gnawed her lip.

"Isabelle?"

"He's been drinking."

Emilio cursed. "How much?"

"As soon as he gets up, pretty much until you get home." She took his hand. "I'm sorry, Emilio."

"I'm disappointed, but not surprised. I've been through this too many times with him before."

"But it sucks when people let you down."

She would know.

"I have a confession to make," she said.

"About Estefan?"

She shook her head. "I ruined your shirt on purpose."

Oddly enough, his first reaction was to laugh. "Why?"

"I was mad at you. For telling Estefan that I was a virgin."

What? "I never told him that. I never told him anything about us, other than it was none of his business."

"So how did he know? He made a remark about it yesterday."

"He was in the kitchen when I walked out of your room. Maybe he heard us talking?"

"All the way from the kitchen? We weren't talking *that* loud."

She was right. He would have had to be listening at the door.

She must have reached the same conclusion, because she made a face and said, "Ew."

"He's staying at Alejandro's tonight, and tomorrow he's out of here."

"No offense, but he's always given me the creeps. Even when he was a kid. I didn't like the way he stared at me."

Then she probably wouldn't want to know that Estefan used to have a crush on her. Apparently he thought that someday they would be together, because he had been furious when he found out that Emilio was dating her. He accused Emilio of stealing her from him.

"Emilio?" she said, squeezing his hand.

"Huh?"

"I didn't marry Lenny for his money. That isn't why I left you. You can think whatever horrible things about me that you want, but don't think that. Okay?"

"I don't think you're horrible. I wanted to, but you're making it really hard not to like you."

"Don't. I don't want you to like me."

"Why?"

"Because I'm going to prison and I don't want to hurt you again. It's better if you just keep hating me."

"Do you hate me?"

"No. I *love* you," she said, like that should have been perfectly obvious. "I always have. But we can't be together. It's not fair."

He didn't even know what to say to that. How could he have ever thought she was selfish? The truth is, she hadn't changed at all. She was still the sweet girl he'd been in love with fifteen years ago. And if her leaving him really had nothing to do with Betts's money, why did she do it?

He knew if he asked her, she wouldn't tell him. He could only hope that the medical records would be the final piece to the puzzle. But there was still one thing he'd been wondering about.

"How was it your mother wound up indicted?"

"After my father died, she knew virtually nothing about finances. She didn't even know what she and my father were worth, and it was a lot less than she expected. He was heavily in debt, and nothing was in my mother's name. After the debts were paid, there wasn't much left. Lenny said he could set up a division of the company in her name. He would do the work and she would reap the benefits, only it didn't turn out that way. She's in trouble because of me."

"I fail to see how that's your fault."

"I encouraged her to sign. I trusted Lenny."

"Does she blame you?"

"Of course not. If she knew I was planning to take a plea in exchange for her freedom, she would have a fit. But my lawyer said that was the only way. She's been through enough."

Izzie's mother had always been kind to him and his brothers, and his mother never had a negative thing to say about her. If she wasn't involved, he didn't want to see her go to jail, either, but if Isabelle was innocent she shouldn't be serving herself up as the sacrificial lamb. She should be trying to fight this.

"I'm sleepy," she said, yawning.

After all that wine, who wouldn't be? "And you're probably going to have one hell of a hangover in the morning."

"Probably."

"Scoot over," he said.

"Why?"

He unbuttoned his shirt. "So I can lie down."

"But—"

"Just go to sleep." The one thing they had never done was spend the night together. He figured it was about time.

And drunk or not, he'd be damned if he was going to let her spend the rest of her Thanksgiving alone.

Isabelle woke sometime in the night with her head in a vise, in a strange room, curled up against Emilio's bare chest.

Huh?

Then she remembered that he had carried her to bed, and the conversation they'd had. Though that part was a little fuzzy. She was pretty sure the gist of it was that Emilio wasn't mad at her anymore. Which was the exact opposite of what she had wanted.

She considered getting up and going to her own bed, but she must have fallen asleep before she got the chance. The next time she woke, Emilio was gone, and someone was inside her skull with a jackhammer.

She crawled out of bed and stumbled downstairs to the kitchen. Emilio was sitting at the island dressed for work, eating a bowl of cereal. When he heard her walk in he turned. And winced.

She must have looked as bad as she felt.

"Good morning," he said.

Not. "Shoot me and put me out of my misery."

"How about some coffee and ibuprofen instead?"

Honestly, death sounded better, but she took the tablets he brought to her and choked down a few sips of coffee.

"Why are you up so early?" he asked.

"I'm supposed to be up. It's a work day."

"Not for you it isn't." He took her coffee cup and put it in the sink, then he took her by the shoulders and steered her toward the stairs. "Back to bed."

"But the house—"

"It can wait a day."

He walked her upstairs to the guest room and tucked her back into bed. "Get some sleep, and don't get up until you're feeling better. Promise?"

"Promise."

He kissed her forehead before he left.

She must have conked right out, because when she woke again, sunshine streamed in through the break in the curtains, and when she sat up she felt almost human. She looked over at the clock on the dresser and was stunned to find it was almost noon. After a cup of coffee and a slice of toast and a few more ibuprofen, she was feeling almost like her old self, so she showered, dressed in her uniform and got to work. She wouldn't have time to do all her chores, but she could make a decent dent in them.

She was polishing the marble in the foyer when Estefan came in, looking about as bad as she felt this morning.

"Rough night?" she asked.

He smirked and walked straight to the kitchen. She heard the fridge open and the rattle of a beer bottle as he pulled it out. Figures. The best thing for a hangover was more alcohol, right?

She went back to polishing, but after several minutes she got an eerie feeling and knew he was watching her.

"Is there something you needed?" she asked.

"Have you got eyes in the back of your head or something?"

She turned to him. "Are you here for your things?"

His eyes narrowed. "Why?"

She just assumed Emilio would have called him by now. Guess not.

His eyes narrowed. "What did you tell Emilio?"

She squared her shoulders. "Nothing he didn't already know."

"You told him about the car?"

"I didn't have to. He looked up the history on the GPS. He knows it was you driving."

He cursed under his breath and mumbled, "It's okay. I can fix this."

She knew she should keep her mouth shut, but she couldn't help herself. "He knows about the drinking, too, and the fact that you were listening outside my bedroom door the other night."

He cut his eyes to her, and with a look that was pure venom, tipped his half-finished beer and dumped it onto her newly polished floor.

Nice. Very mature.

He walked up the stairs to his room. Hopefully to pack.

Isabelle cleaned up the beer with paper towels then repolished the floor. She cleaned all the main floor bathrooms next, buffing the chrome fixtures and polishing the marble countertops.

When she was finished she found Estefan in the living room, booted feet up on the glass top coffee table, drinking Don Julio Real Tequila straight from the bottle.

"You're enjoying this, aren't you?" he asked. "That I have to go, and you get to stay. That once again you mean more to him than his own brother."

Once again? What was that supposed to mean?

"You're leaving him no choice, Estefan."

"What the hell do you know? Emilio and I, we're family," he said, pounding his fist to his chest. "He's supposed to stand behind me. This is all your fault."

She knew his type. Everything was always someone else's fault. He never took responsibility for his own actions.

He took another swig from the bottle. "I loved you, you know. I would have done anything to have you. Then Emilio stole you from me."

Stole her?

So in his mind they had been embroiled in some creepy love triangle? Well, that wasn't reality. Even if there had been no Emilio, she never would have been attracted to Estefan.

He shoved himself up from the couch, wavering a second before he caught his balance. "I'm tired of coming in second place. Maybe I should take what's rightfully mine."

Meaning what?

He started to walk toward her with a certain look, and every instinct she had said *run*.

First thing when he got to work, Emilio called the firm Western Oil had hired to investigate the explosion and explained what he needed.

"Medical records are privileged," the investigator told him.

"So you're saying you can't get them?"

"I can, but you can't use the information in court."

"I don't plan to."

"Give me the name."

"Isabelle Winthrop."

There was a pause. "The one indicted for fraud?"

"That's the one." There was another pause, and he heard the sound of typing. "How long will this take?"

"Hold on." There was more typing, then he said, "Let me make a call. I'll get back to you in a couple of hours."

The time passed with no word and Emilio began to get impatient. He ate lunch at his desk, then forced himself to get some work done. By three o'clock, he was past impatient and bordering on pissed. He was reaching for the phone to call the firm back when his secretary buzzed him.

"Mr. Blair would like to see you in his office."

"Tell him I'll be there in a few minutes."

"He said right now."

He blew out a breath. "Fine."

When he got there Adam's secretary was on the phone, but she waved him in.

Adam stood at the window behind his desk, his back to the door.

"You wanted to see me, boss?"

He didn't turn. "Close the door and sit down."

He shut the door and took a seat, even though he preferred to stand, wondering what he could have done to earn such a cool reception. "Something wrong, Adam?"

"You may not know this, but due to the sensitive nature of the information we receive from the investigators in regard to the refinery accident, the mail room has implicit instruction to send any correspondence directly to my office."

Oh hell.

"So," he said, turning and grabbing a thick manila envelope from his desk, "When this arrived with your name on it, it came to me."

Emilio could clearly see that the seal on top had been broken. "You opened it?"

"Yeah, I opened it. Because for all I know you were responsible for the explosion, and you were trying to reroute key information away from the investigation."

The accusation stung, but put in Adam's place, he might have thought the same thing. He never should have used the same agency. He had just assumed they would call him, at which point he would have told them to send the files to his house.

"You want to explain to me why you need medical records for Isabelle Winthrop?"

"Not really."

Adam sighed.

"It's personal."

"How personal?"

"I just…needed to know something."

He handed Emilio the file. "You needed to know if someone was using her as their own personal punching bag?"

Emilio's stomach bottomed out. He hoped that was an exaggeration.

He pulled the file out of the envelope. It was thorough. Everything was there, from the time she was born until her annual physical the previous year. He flipped slowly through the pages, realizing immediately that Adam was not exaggerating, and what he read made him physically ill.

It seemed to start when she was three years old with a dislocated shoulder. Not a common injury for a docile young girl. From there it escalated to several incidences of concussions and cracked ribs, and a head injury so severe it fractured her skull and put her in the hospital for a week. He would venture to guess that there were probably many other injuries that had gone untreated, or tended by a personal physician who was paid handsomely to keep his mouth shut.

He scraped a hand through his hair. Why hadn't anyone connected the dots? Why hadn't someone *helped* her?

What disturbed him the most, what had him on the verge of losing his breakfast, was the hospital record from fifteen years ago. That weekend had been engraved in his memory since he opened the morning paper and saw the feature announcing Isabelle and Betts's wedding. Four days earlier Isabelle had been treated for a concussion and bruised ribs from a "fall" on campus. Emilio had seen her just two days later and he hadn't had a damned clue.

In the year they had been together what else hadn't he seen?

Then he had a thought that had bile rising in his throat. He was pretty sure that last concussion and the bruised ribs were his fault.

"Son of a bitch."

"Emilio," Adam said. "What's going on?"

Emilio had forgotten Adam was standing there.

"My brother thinks she might be innocent." In fact, he was ninety-nine point nine percent sure she was. "She's… she's been staying with me the last couple of weeks."

Adam swore and shook his head. "You said you wouldn't do anything stupid."

"If she's innocent, she needs my help. That's more clear now than ever."

"Just because someone knocked her around, it doesn't mean she's not a criminal."

"If you knew her like I do, you would know she isn't capable of stealing anything."

"Sounds like your mind is already made up."

It was. And he was going to help her. He had to.

"Emilio, if it gets out to the press what you're doing—"

"It's not going to."

"And if it does? Is she worth decimating your career? Your reputation?"

He was stunned to realize that the answer to that question was yes. Because it would only be temporary, then everyone would know she didn't do it. He would spend his last penny to get to the truth if that's what it took.

"If the press gets hold of this, I'll take full responsibility. As far as I'm concerned, Western Oil is free to hang me out to dry."

"Wow. You must really care about this woman."

"I do." But what really mattered was that fifteen years ago he'd failed her. In the worst possible way. He refused to make that mistake again.

Thirteen

Emilio left work early, and when he opened the front door he heard shouting and banging.

What the hell?

He dropped his briefcase by the door, followed the sound and found Estefan outside his office. The door was closed and Estefan was pounding with his fist shouting, "Let me in, you bitch!"

"What the hell is going on?"

Estefan swung around to face him. He was breathing hard, his eyes wild with fury. "Look what she did to me!"

Deep gouges branded his right cheek. Nail marks.

"*Isabelle* did that? What happened?"

"Nothing. She just attacked me."

That didn't sound like her at all. She'd never had a violent bone in her body. "Move out of the way," he said. "I'll talk to her."

He reluctantly stepped back.

"Wait in the living room."

"But—"

"In the living room."

"Fine," he grumbled.

Emilio waited until his brother was gone, then knocked softly. "Isabelle, it's Emilio. Let me in."

There was a pause, then he heard the lock turn. He opened the door and stepped into the room, and Isabelle launched herself into his arms. She clung to him, trembling from the inside out.

"Let me look at you. Are you okay?" He held her at arm's length. Her uniform was ripped open at the collar and she had what looked liked finger impressions on her upper arms.

He didn't have to ask her what happened. It was obvious. "Son of a bitch."

"He said he was going to take what was rightfully his," she said, her voice trembling. "He was drinking again."

Son of a bitch.

"I kind of accidentally told him that you were going to make him leave. He was really mad."

"I'm going to go talk to him. I want you to go upstairs, in my bedroom, shut the door and wait for me there. Understand?"

She nodded.

If this got out of hand he wanted her somewhere safe. He watched as she dashed up the stairs, waited until he heard the bedroom door close, then walked to the living room, where his brother was pacing by the couch. "What the hell did you do, Estefan?"

Outraged, his brother said, "What did *I* do? Look at my face!"

"You forced yourself on her."

"Is that what she told you? She's a liar. Man, she *wanted* it. She's been coming on to me for days. She's a whore."

Teeth gritted, Emilio crossed the room and gave his brother a shove. Estefan staggered backward, grabbing the couch to stop his fall. He righted himself, then listed to one side, before he caught his balance.

He *was* drunk.

"What's the matter with you, Emilio?"

"What's the matter with *me?* You tried to *rape* her!"

Estefan actually laughed. "If you wanted to keep her all to yourself you should have said so."

Emilio swung, connecting solidly with Estefan's jaw. Estefan jerked back and landed on the floor.

"Emilio, what the hell!"

It took every ounce of control Emilio possessed not to beat the hell out of his brother. "You've crossed the line. Get your stuff and get out."

"You would choose that lying bitch over your own flesh and blood?"

"Isabelle has more integrity in the tip of her finger than you've ever had in your entire miserable excuse for a life."

His expression went from one of outrage to pure venom. This was the Estefan that Emilio knew. The one he had hoped he'd seen the last of. "I'll make you regret this."

Regret? He was already full of it. He thought about what might have happened if he hadn't come home early and he felt ill. What if Estefan had gotten into his office? "The only thing I regret is thinking that this time you might have changed."

"She's using you. Just like she did before."

"You know nothing, Estefan."

"I know her daddy wasn't very happy when I told him about your so-called engagement."

"You told him?"

"You should be thanking me. You were too good for her."

"You stupid son of a bitch. You have no clue what you did."

"I saved your ass, that's what I did."

He'd never wanted to hurt someone as much as he wanted to hurt Estefan right now. Instead he took a deep, calming breath and said, "Pack your things, and get out. As far as I'm concerned, we are no longer brothers."

While his brother packed, Emilio stood watch by the door and called him a cab. Estefan was too drunk to drive himself anywhere. Emilio didn't care what happened to him, but he didn't want him hurting someone else.

Estefan protested when Emilio snatched his keys away.

"Call me and tell me where you are, and I'll have your bike delivered to you."

He slurred out a few more threats, then staggered to the cab. Emilio watched it drive away, then he grabbed his case and headed up to his bedroom. Isabelle was sitting on the edge of his bed. She shot to her feet when he stepped in the room.

"He's gone," Emilio said. "And he isn't coming back."

She breathed a sigh of relief.

Emilio dropped his case on the floor by the bed, pulled her into his arms and held her. "I am so sorry. If I even suspected he would pull something like this I never would have let him stay here. And I sure as hell wouldn't have left you alone with him."

"I guess it was a case of unrequited love," she said, her voice still a little wobbly. "Who knew?"

He had, but he never imagined Estefan was capable of rape. He had been raised to respect women. They all had. There was obviously something wrong in Estefan's head.

"When I think what might have happened if I hadn't come home early…" He squeezed her tighter.

"He's going to tell people that I'm staying here, isn't he?"

"You can count on it." Definitely the family. With any luck he wasn't smart enough to go to the press, or they wouldn't listen.

She looked crestfallen. "If I leave today, right now, maybe it won't be so bad. You can deny I was here at all. And I will, too. No one has to know."

She was nearly raped, and she was worried about *him*. It was sickening how he had misjudged her, how he thought she could have anything to do with her husband's crimes. "You're not going anywhere, Izzie."

"But—"

"I don't care if anyone knows you're here."

"Why?"

"Because you're innocent."

"How do you know that?"

He shrugged. "Because I do."

She didn't seem to know what to say.

"There's something we need to talk about, something I need to know."

She frowned, as though she knew she wasn't going to like what was coming next.

"What did your father do when he found out we were eloping?"

"What makes you think he knew?"

"Because Estefan told him."

She sucked in a quiet breath.

"He did it to get back at me. He said he did it to help me, but I know he was just jealous."

"I always wondered how my father found out."

"Is that why he did it?"

"Did what?"

He opened his briefcase, pulled out the file and handed it to her. She started to read the top page and the color leeched from her face. She sank to the edge of the bed.

He sat beside her. "The concussion, the bruised ribs. He did that because of me, didn't he?"

She flipped through the pages, then looked up at him, eyes wide. "Where did you get this?"

"Why didn't you tell me, Izzie? Why didn't you tell me what he did to you?"

She shrugged, setting the file on the bed beside her. "Because that's not the way it works."

"I could have helped you."

She shook her head. "No one could help us."

Us? "Your mother, too?"

"My father was a very angry man. But if there's any justice in this world, I can rest easy knowing he's rotting in hell for what he did to us."

He could barely wrap his head around it. How could he have been so blind? Why didn't he see?

"I know you don't like to talk about it, but I have to know. Why did you do it? Why did you leave me for Betts?"

"It was the only way to keep her safe."

"Your mother?"

She nodded.

"Tell me what happened."

She bit her lip, wringing her hands in her lap.

He took her hand in his and held it. "Please, Isabelle."

"My father found out about us and *punished* me. When he was finished, he told me that if I ever saw you again he was going to disown me. I would be completely cut off. I was so sick of it, I told him I didn't care. I said I didn't want his money, and I didn't care if I ever saw him again.

I said I was going to marry you, and my mother was going to come live with us and nothing he could do would stop me." She took a deep, unsteady breath. "And he said...he said that if I married you, something terrible would happen to my mother. He said she would have an 'accident.'" She looked up at him. "My father did not make idle threats, and the look in his eyes...I knew he would kill her just to spite me. And to prove his point he punished her, too, and it was even worse than what he did to me. She couldn't get out of bed for a week."

Sick bastard. If Isabelle had a concussion and bruised ribs, he couldn't even imagine what he must have put her mother through.

Emilio felt sick to his stomach, sick all the way to his soul. "Did he force you to marry Betts?"

"Not exactly. Usually he was good about hiding the marks, but this time he didn't even try. My parents had been friends with Lenny for years. Long story short, he happened to stop by and saw the condition we were in. He was horrified. He'd suspected that my father was abusive, but he had no idea how bad it was. He wanted to call the police, but my mom begged him not to."

"Why? They could have helped you."

"Because she tried that before. My father was a very powerful man. The charges had a way of disappearing."

Alejandro had said as much.

"Lenny figured if he couldn't help my mother, he could at least get me out of there. He knew my father would agree to a marriage."

"A marriage between his nineteen-year-old daughter and a man in his forties?"

"My father saw it as a business opportunity. He had debts, and Lenny promised to make them go away."

The gambling Alejandro had mentioned. Just when

Emilio didn't think he could feel more disgust, her father sank to a whole new level of vile. "He *sold* you."

She shrugged. "More or less."

"So what was the going rate for a nineteen-year-old virgin?"

She lowered her eyes. "Lenny wouldn't tell me. Hundreds of thousands. Maybe millions. Who knows."

"If you had told me then, I would have taken you away. You and your mother. I would have killed your father if that's what it took to keep you both safe. I would kill him now if he wasn't already dead."

"And that's exactly why I couldn't tell you. If you only knew how many times she tried to leave. But he always found us and brought us back. He would have hurt you if you had tried to help. Look what he did to your mother just to spite me. At least Lenny had been able to take me away from it. And you were safe and free to live your life."

It was hard to fathom that Izzie's husband, a man that Emilio had despised for so many years, had really saved her life.

Only to turn around and ruin it again, he reminded himself.

"The sad fact is, I never should have come to see you that day on campus," Izzie said. "I should have known he would never let it happen, not if there wasn't something in it for him."

"I've never said this about another human being, but I'm glad your father is dead."

Her smile was a sad one. "No more than my mother and I."

"I'm sorry I've been such a jerk."

She shrugged. "I hurt you."

"That doesn't make it right."

She reached up, stroked his cheek. "Emilio, not a day

has gone by when I didn't miss you, and wished it were you I had married. It's going to sound silly, but I never stopped loving you. I still haven't."

A sudden surge of emotion caught him completely by surprise. He slipped his arms around her and pulled her against him, pressed his face against the softness of her hair. He wanted to hold her close and never let go, yet he couldn't help thinking he didn't deserve her love. He'd failed her, and all because he couldn't see past his own wounded pride. He should have trusted her. When he read in the papers that she was marrying Betts, he should have known something was wrong, that she would never willingly betray him.

He had promised to take care of her, to protect her and he'd let her down when she needed him most.

"Isabelle—"

She put her fingers over his lips to shush him. "No more talking."

She slid her arms around his neck and kissed him. And kept kissing him, until the past ceased to matter. All he cared about was being close to her. They would start over today, this very minute, and things would be different this time. He would take care of her and protect her. The way it should have been fifteen years ago.

Though there was no rush, Isabelle seemed in a hurry to get them both naked. She shoved his jacket off his shoulders, then undid the buttons on his shirt and pushed that off, too. Then she unbuttoned her dress and pulled it up over her head. Her bra was next to go, until all that was left was her panties.

She took those off, then pulled back the covers and stretched out on the bed, summoning him with a smile and a crooked finger.

"I like that you're not shy anymore," he said rising to take off his pants.

"There are no bruises or marks to hide now."

He hadn't even considered that. "Is that why you never let me see you undressed?"

"I wanted to, but I knew there would be questions."

"Isabelle."

"No more talking about the past. Let's concentrate on today. On right now. Make love to me, and nothing else will matter."

That was by far the best idea she'd had all day.

Fourteen

Emilio stripped out of his clothes and climbed into bed with Isabelle. Since Tuesday she hadn't stopped thinking about making love to him again. Only this time she wasn't nervous. This time she had nothing to hide. He knew her secrets. She could relax and be herself. Until the weight of everything she had hidden from him was finally gone, she hadn't realized what a heavy load she'd carried. And when Emilio took her in his arms and kissed her, she knew he was back to being the man he used to be. Sweet and tender and thoughtful.

Ironically that wasn't what she wanted now. She was eager to experiment. She wanted it to be crazy and exciting. There were hundreds of different ways to make love and she wanted to try as many as she could before she had to go. She wanted it to be fun.

"Emilio, I'm not going to break."

He gazed down at her, brow furrowed. "I just don't

want to hurt you again. And after what happened to you today…if you want to wait, we can take a few days."

They had so little time left, she didn't want to waste any of it. And she didn't want him to feel as if he had to treat her with kid gloves. "First of all, if you're referring to Tuesday night, you did not hurt me."

Up went the brow.

"Okay, maybe it hurt a little, but only for a minute. And it wasn't a bad hurt, if that makes sense. And after that it was…*amazing*. And as far as what happened today, yeah it scared the hell out of me, but that has nothing to do with us. I know you would never hurt me."

"But I did." He stroked her hair back from her face, touched her cheek. "I've been a total jerk the last couple weeks, and you've done absolutely nothing to deserve it."

"Except the rug, and the casserole dish, and the pink laundry. And of course the scorched shirt."

"That doesn't count. I put you in a position to fail so I could throw it back in your face."

"And I've forgiven you."

He sighed and rolled onto his back. "Maybe that's part of the problem. Maybe I feel like I don't deserve your forgiveness."

She sat up beside him. "In that case, you have to forgive *yourself.* You've got to let it go. Trust me on this one. If I hadn't made peace with my father, and Lenny, I would probably be in a padded room by now."

"How? How do you let it go?"

She shrugged. "You just do."

"I'm just so…*mad.*"

"At yourself?"

"At myself, and at your father. For what he did to you, and everything he stole from us. Everything that we could have been. If it wasn't for him, we would be married, we would probably have kids." He pushed himself up on his elbows. "I'm pissed at Estefan for ratting us out, and Alejandro for prosecuting you when I'm pretty sure he knows damn well that you're innocent. I'm pissed at every person who suspected your father was abusive and did nothing about it. I feel like I'm mad at the whole damned world!"

"So let it out."

"I can't."

"Yes, you can." She reached over and pinched his left nipple. Hard.

"Hey!" He batted her hand away, looking stunned, as if he couldn't believe she would do something like that. Sweet, nonconfrontational Isabelle. "What was that for?"

He was going to have to accept that she had changed. "Did it hurt?"

"Yeah, it hurt."

"Good." She did the same thing to the right side.

"Ow! Stop that!"

She pinched the fleshy skin under his bicep next and he jerked away.

"Izzie, stop it."

She climbed into his lap, straddling his thighs. "Make me."

She moved to pinch him again and his hand shot out to manacle her wrist, and when she tried to use her other hand, he grabbed that wrist, too. She struggled to yank free, but he held on tighter, almost to the point of pain. But that was good, that was what she wanted. She didn't want him to look at her as some frail flower he needed to protect. She wanted him to know how tough she was.

Since her hands were restrained, she leaned in and bit him instead, on his left shoulder. Not hard enough to break the skin, but enough to cause pain.

He jerked away. "Isabelle! What's gotten into you?"

"Are you pissed?"

"Yes, I'm pissed!"

"Good." She leaned in to do it again, but he'd apparently had enough. Finally. He pulled her down on top of him then rolled her onto her back, pinning her wrists over her head.

She'd never thought of herself as the type who would be into anything even remotely kinky, but she was so hot for him, she was afraid she might spontaneously combust. Emilio settled between her thighs, holding her to the mattress with the weight of his body, and it was clear that he liked it, too. A lot.

She hooked her legs around his, arching against him. He groaned and his eyes went dark, breath rasped out. So she did it again, bucking against him.

"Izzie." His voice held a warning, stop or else, but she *wanted* the "or else."

Lifting her head, she scraped her teeth across his nipple. She would keep biting and pinching and bucking until he gave her what she wanted. Only this time he turned the tables on her. He dipped his head and took her nipple in his mouth, sucked hard.

She cried out, pushing against his hands, digging her nails into her palms. *"Yesss."*

"You *like* this," he said.

His eyes said that he'd finally figured it out. He knew what she wanted.

It was about damned time.

She knew Emilio liked to be composed at all times, but she wanted him to lose control, to do something crazy.

He kissed her, like he never had before. A hard, punishing kiss. He started to work his way down, to her neck and her shoulders, kissing and nipping. Then he slipped lower still, letting go of her wrists so he could press her thighs wide. She thought they would make love right away, but clearly he had other ideas.

She held her breath in anticipation, gasping as he took her in his mouth. Oral sex had been a regular routine for them, and it was always good, but never like this. He was *devouring* her. She clawed her nails through his hair, so close to losing it…then he thrust a finger inside of her, then another, then a third, slow and deep, and pleasure seized her like a wild animal.

Emilio rose up and settled between her thighs, thrusting hard inside of her, and the orgasm that had begun to ebb slowly away suddenly picked up momentum again, only this time from somewhere deep inside. Somewhere she'd never felt before. Maybe her soul. It erupted into a sensation so beautiful and perfect, so exactly what she ever hoped it could be, tears welled in her eyes. And she was so utterly lost in her own pleasure she didn't realize he had come, too, until he flopped onto his back beside her.

"Wow," he said, breathing hard.

"So, are you still mad?"

He laughed—a genuine honest to goodness laugh. A sound she hadn't heard out of him in a very long time. "Not at all. In fact, I can't recall the last time I was so relaxed."

She smiled and curled up against his side. "Good."

"I didn't hurt you?"

"Are you kidding? That was *perfect*." And it must have been really good for him, too, because he was still mostly hard. Then she realized something that made her heart drop. "Emilio, you didn't use a condom."

"I know."

She shot up in bed. "You *know?* You did it *deliberately?*"

He didn't even have the decency to look remorseful.

"Not exactly. I realized the minute I was inside of you, but I didn't think you would appreciate me stopping to roll one on."

"Did it occur to you that I could get pregnant?"

"Of course."

"What did you think? That me being pregnant with his brother's baby will stop Alejandro from putting me in prison? They put pregnant women in prison all the time. Are you prepared to raise a baby alone? To be a single dad for the next twenty-to-life? Maybe if I get out early on good behavior I'll see him graduate high school."

"You're not going to prison."

She groaned and dropped her head in her hands. The man was impossible.

"Do you think you could be pregnant?" he asked.

"My period is due soon, so I'd say it's unlikely."

He actually looked disappointed. How had he gone from hating her one day, to wanting to have babies with her the next? This was crazy. Even if she didn't go to prison his family would never accept her.

"Can I ask you a question?" he said.

"Sure."

"Since you've told me everything else, would you explain how you never slept with Lenny? Because I really don't get it. I can't go five minutes without wanting to rip your clothes off."

"He had a heart condition and he was impotent. Ultimately he did screw me, just not in the bedroom."

"After your father died you could have divorced him."

"There didn't seem to be much point. There was only one other man I wanted." She touched his arm. "And I knew he would never take me back, never forgive me."

"I guess you were wrong."

"It would probably be better if you hadn't."

"You're *not* going to prison."

"Yes, I am. Nothing is going to stop that now."

"I just got you back, Izzie. I'm not letting you go again."

But he was going to have to. He couldn't keep her out of prison by sheer will. He was going to have to accept that they were living on borrowed time.

"Things are going to change around here," he said.

"What things?"

"First off, I'm calling my housekeeper back."

"You can't do that. You gave her the month off. It's not fair."

"So I'll hire a temp."

"But I like doing it."

He raised a brow at her.

"I do. And it gives me something to do. A way to pass the time, since I doubt all those charities I used to volunteer for would be interested in my services any longer."

"Are you sure?"

"Positive."

"Okay, but you're not allowed to wear the uniform anymore. And I'm buying you some decent clothes."

"There's no point."

"There sure as hell is. The ones you have are awful."

"And I'll only need them for another few weeks. Getting anything new would be a waste of money."

She could tell he wanted to argue, but he probably figured there was no point. She was not going to budge on this one. Besides, the last thing she wanted was for him to spend money on her. She didn't deserve it.

"You're obviously not staying in the maid's quarters any longer. You're moving in here with me. If you want to."

"Of course I do." It was probably a bad idea. The closer they got, the harder it would be when she had to go, but she had the feeling nothing would prevent that now. They might as well spend all the time they could together.

"You have a say in this, too," he said. "Is there anything you'd like to add? Anything you want?"

There were so many things she wanted. She wanted to marry him, and have babies with him. She wanted to do everything they had talked about before. It's all she had ever wanted. But why dwell on a future that wasn't meant to be?

The phone rang, so she grabbed the cordless off the bedside table and handed it to him. He looked at the display and cursed under his breath. "Well, that didn't take long."

He sat up and hit the talk button. "Hello, Mama."

Isabelle winced. Estefan hadn't wasted any time running to his mother, had he?

He listened for a minute, then said, "Yes, it's true."

She could hear his mother talking. Not what she was saying, but her tone came through perfectly. She was upset.

"I know he was drunk. Are you really surprised?"

More talking from his mother's end, then Emilio interrupted her. "Why don't I come over there right now so we can talk about this?"

She must have agreed, because then he said, "I'll be over as soon as I can."

He hung up and set the phone back on the table. "I guess you got the gist of that."

"Yeah."

"I shouldn't be too long."

"Take your time." He wasn't the only one who needed to talk to their mother. "I was thinking maybe I could go talk to my mother, too. I'd hate for her to hear it from someone besides me."

"I think that's a good idea. I'll pick up Chinese food on my way home."

"Sounds good." Although after dealing with their parents, she wondered if either of them would have much of an appetite.

Fifteen

Emilio parked in the driveway of his mother's condo. The year he'd made his first million he'd bought it for her. He'd wanted to get her something bigger and in a more affluent part of the city, but she had wanted to live here, in what was a primarily Hispanic neighborhood. Not that this place was what anyone would consider shabby. It had been brand-new when he bought it, and he made sure it had every upgrade they offered, and a few he requested special. After sacrificing so much for Emilio and his brothers, she deserved the best of everything.

He walked to the front door and let himself inside. "Mama?"

"In the kitchen," she called back.

He wasn't surprised to find her at the counter, apron on, adding ingredients to a mixing bowl. She always baked when she was upset or angry.

"What are you making?"

"Churros, with extra cinnamon, just the way you like them." She gestured to the kitchen table. "Sit down, I'll get you something to drink."

She pulled a pitcher of iced tea from the fridge and poured him a glass. He would have preferred something stronger, but she never kept alcohol of any kind in the house.

Handing it to him, she went back to the bowl, mixing the contents with a wooden spoon. "I guess you saw your brother's face."

"I saw it."

"He said she attacked him. For no good reason."

"Attempted rape is a pretty good reason."

She cut her eyes to him. "Emilio! Your brother would never do that. He was raised to respect women."

Emphatically as she denied it, something in her eyes said she was afraid it might be true.

"If you had seen Isabelle, the ripped uniform and the bruises on her arms… She was terrified."

She muttered something in Spanish and crossed herself.

"He needs help, Mama."

"I know. He told me that bad people are after him. He asked to stay here. I told him no."

"Good. We can't keep trying to save him. We have to let him hit rock bottom. He has to want to help himself."

"You told him you're no longer brothers. You didn't mean it."

"I did mean it. He hurt the woman I love."

"How can you love her after what she did to you? She left you for that rich man. She only cared about money. That's the only reason she's back now."

"She came to me because she wanted help for her mother, not herself. And she didn't marry Betts for his money. The only reason she left me for him is because her father threatened to hurt her mother."

He waited for the shock, but there was none, confirming what he already suspected. "You knew about the abuse, didn't you? You knew that Isabelle's father was hurting them. You *had* to."

She didn't answer him.

"Mama."

"Of course I knew," she said softly. "The things that man did to them." She closed her eyes and shook her head, as if she were trying to block the mental image. "It made me sick. And poor Mrs. Winthrop. Sometimes he beat her so badly, she would be in bed for days. And Isabelle, she always stayed right by her mother's side. I never speak ill of the dead, but that man did the world a favor when he died."

"You should have told me. I could have helped her."

She shook her head. "No. He would have hurt you, too. I was always afraid that something bad would happen if he found out about you and Isabelle."

"Well, he found out." He almost told her that Estefan was the one who ratted him out, but he didn't want to hurt her any more than necessary.

"You had the potential to go so far, Emilio. I was relieved when she left you."

"Even though you knew how much I loved her?"

"I figured you would get over her eventually."

"But I didn't. As bitter as I was, I never stopped loving her."

Was that guilt in her eyes? "What difference does it make now? Alejandro said she's going to prison."

"Not if I can help it."

She set the spoon down and pushed the bowl aside. "She stole money."

"No, she didn't. She's innocent."

"You know that for a fact?"

"I know it in my heart. In every fiber of my being. She's not a thief."

"Even if that's true, everyone thinks she's guilty."

He shrugged. "I don't care what everyone thinks."

"Emilio—"

"Mama, do you remember what you told me when I asked you why you never remarried? You said Papa was your one true love, and there could be no one else. I finally understand what you meant. I was lucky enough to get Izzie back. I can't lose her again."

"Even if it means ruining everything you've worked so hard for?"

"That's not going to happen. First thing Monday, I'm hiring a new attorney."

"People will find out."

"They probably will."

"And I could argue with you until I'm blue in the face and it won't do any good, will it?"

He shook his head.

She drew in a deep breath, then blew it out. "Then I will pray for you, Emilio. For you and Isabelle."

"Thank you, Mama." At this point, he would take all the help he could get.

Isabelle called her mother Friday, but she was out with Ben. They went to dinner with friends, then they left Saturday morning for an overnight trip to Phoenix to see an old college buddy of Ben's. Isabelle didn't get a chance to talk to her until Monday morning. She took the news much better than Isabelle expected. In fact, she suspected all along that Isabelle had been "bending" the truth.

"Sweetheart," she said, fixing them each a cup of tea

in her tiny kitchenette. "You know I can always tell when you're lying. And, *Mrs. Smith?*"

Isabelle couldn't help but smile. "Not very creative, huh?"

"I thought it was awfully coincidental that you were working in the same neighborhood where Emilio lived. Then I mentioned him and you got very nervous."

"And people think I'm capable of stealing millions of dollars." She sighed. "Not only am I a terrible liar, but I don't even know how to balance a checkbook."

Her mother walked over with their tea and sat down at the table.

"I'm sorry I lied to you, but I promised Emilio I wouldn't tell anyone I was staying there. It was part of our deal."

"Emilio is going to help you, right?"

"He's going to talk to his brother on your behalf. You won't be serving any time."

"But what about you?"

They had been through this so many times. "There isn't anything he can do. You know what Lenny's lawyer said. The evidence against me is indisputable."

"There has to be something Emilio can do. Can't he talk to his brother? Make some sort of deal?"

She was just as bad as Emilio, refusing to accept reality. She wished they would both stop being so stubborn. But she didn't want her mother to worry so she said, "I'll ask him, okay?"

Her mother looked relieved.

"So, tell me about this weekend trip. Did you have fun?"

She lit up like a firefly. "We had a *wonderful* time. Ben has the nicest friends. The only thing that was a little unexpected was that they put us in a bedroom together."

Her brows rose. "Oh really?"

"Nothing happened," she said, then her cheeks turned

red and she added, "Well, nothing much. But he is a very nice kisser."

"Only nice?"

Her smile was shy, with a touch of mischief. "Okay, better than nice."

They talked about her trip with Ben and what they had planned for the coming weekend. He clearly adored her mother, and the feeling was mutual. Isabelle was so happy she had found someone who appreciated her, and made her feel good about herself. At the same time she was a little sad that she wouldn't be around to see their relationship grow. Of course, they could always write letters, and her mother could visit.

Maybe she was a little jealous, too, that she had finally found her heart's desire, and it had to end in only a few weeks. They wouldn't even get to spend Christmas together.

She drove back to Emilio's fighting the urge to feel sorry for herself. When she pulled in the driveway there was an unfamiliar car parked there. A silver Lexus. She considered pulling back out. What if it was someone who shouldn't know she was staying there? But hadn't Emilio said he didn't care who knew?

She pulled the Saab in the garage and let herself in the house. Emilio met her at the door. "There you are. I was about send out a search party."

"I went to see my mother."

"Is everything okay? She wasn't angry?"

"Not at all."

"I need to get you a cell phone, so I can reach you when you're out."

For less than a month? What was the point? "Is there something wrong?"

"Nothing. In fact, I have some good news. Come in the living room, there's someone I want you to meet."

There was a man sitting on the couch, a slew of papers on the table in front of him. When they entered the room, he stood.

"Isabelle, this is David Morrison."

He was around Emilio's age, very attractive and dressed in a sharp, tailored suit. "Ms. Winthrop," he said, shaking her hand. "It's a pleasure to meet you."

"You, too," she said, shooting Emilio a questioning look.

"David is a defense attorney. One of the best. He's going to be taking over your case."

"What?"

"We're firing Clifton Stone."

"But...why?"

"Because he's giving you bad advice," Mr. Morrison said. "I've been going over your case. The evidence against you is flimsy at best. We'll take this to trial if necessary, but honestly, I don't think it will come down to that."

"I was using Lenny's lawyer because he was representing me pro bono. I can't afford a lawyer."

"It's taken care of," Emilio said.

She shook her head. "I can't let you do this."

"The retainer is paid. Nonrefundable. It's done."

"But I can't go to trial. The only way my mother will avoid prison is if I plead out." She turned to her "new" attorney. "Mr. Morrison—"

"Please, call me David."

"David, I really appreciate you coming to see me, but I can't do this."

"Ms. Winthrop, do you want to spend the next twenty years in prison?"

Was this a trick question? Did anyone *want* to go to prison? "Of course not."

"If you stick with your current attorney, that's what will happen. I've seen lawyers reprimanded and in some cases disbarred for giving such blatantly negligent counsel. Either he's completely incompetent, or he has some sort of agenda."

Agenda? How could he possibly benefit from her going to prison? "What about my mother? What happens to her?"

"Alejandro already told me they wouldn't ask for more than probation," Emilio said.

"When did he say that?"

He hesitated, then said, "The day you came to see me in my office."

So all this time she'd been working for him for no reason? She should be furious, but the truth was, it was a million times better here than at that dumpy motel. And if she hadn't come here, Emilio would have gone the rest of his life hating her. Maybe now they even had some sort of future together. Marriage and family, just like they had planned. Hope welled up with such intensity she had to fight it back down. She was afraid to believe it was real.

"You really think you could keep me and my mother out of prison?" she asked David.

"Worst case you may end up with probation. It would go a long way if the last few million of the missing money were to surface."

"If I knew where it was I would have handed it over months ago. I gave them everything else."

"I'm going to do some digging and see what turns up. In the meantime, I need you to sign a notice of change of counsel to make it official."

She signed the document, but only after thoroughly reading it—she had learned her lesson with Lenny—then David packed up his things and left.

"I told you I wouldn't let you go to prison," Emilio said,

sounding smug, fixing himself a sandwich before he went back to work.

"I still don't like that you're paying for it. What if someone finds out?"

"I've already said a dozen times—"

"You don't care who finds out. I know. But I do. Until I know for sure that I'm not going to prison, I don't want anyone to know. Even if that means waiting through a trial."

"I suppose that means we'll have to wait to get married."

Married? She opened her mouth to speak, but nothing came out. She knew he wanted to be with her, but this was the first time he had actually mentioned marriage.

"I was hoping we could start a family right away," he said, putting the turkey and the mayo back in the fridge. "If we haven't already, that is. But we've waited this long. I guess a few more months won't kill me. Just so long as you know that I love you, and no matter what happens, I'm not letting you go again."

He loved her, and wanted to marry her, and have a family with her. She threw her arms around him and hugged him tight. This was more than she ever could have hoped for. "I love you, too, Emilio."

"This is all going to work out," he told her, and she was actually starting to believe it.

"So, do you have to go back to work?" she asked, sliding her hands under his jacket and up his chest.

He grinned down at her. "That depends what you have in mind."

Though they had spent the better part of the weekend making love in bed—and on the bedroom floor and in the shower, and even on the dining room table—she could never get enough of him. "We haven't done it in the kitchen yet."

He lifted her up and set her on the counter, sliding her skirt up her thighs. "Well, that's an oversight we need to take care of immediately."

Sixteen

Isabelle never imagined things could be so wonderful. She and Emilio were going to get married and have a family—even though he hadn't officially asked her yet—and she and her mother weren't going to prison. Her life was as close to perfect as it could be, yet she had this gut feeling that the other shoe was about to drop. That things were a little *too* perfect.

Emilio wasn't helping matters.

He called her from work Thursday morning to warn her that a package would be arriving. But it wasn't one package. It was a couple dozen, all filled with clothes and shoes from department stores and boutiques all over town. It was an entire wardrobe, and it was exactly what she would have picked for herself.

Her first instinct was tell him to send it back, but now that she wasn't going to prison she did need new clothes.

"How did you know what I would like?" she asked Emilio when she called to thank him.

"I had help."

"What kind of help?"

"A personal shopper, so to speak. I swore her to secrecy."

Her? Who would know her exact taste, that Emilio knew to contact? There was really only one person. "My *mother?*"

"I knew you wouldn't get the clothes yourself, and who better to know what you like?"

"I talked to her this morning and she didn't say a word."

"She wanted it to be a surprise. If there's anything that you don't like just put it aside and I'll have it returned."

"It's all perfect."

"There should be something coming later this afternoon, too. A few things I picked out."

Isabelle called her mother to thank her, but she wasn't home so she left a message. After that she waited, very impatiently, until the package with Emilio's purchases arrived later that afternoon. She carried it into the living room where she had been sorting and folding all the other things.

Sitting on the couch, she ripped it open. It was lingerie. The first two items she pulled out were soft silk gowns in pink and white. When she saw what was underneath the gowns she actually blushed. Sexy items of silk and lace that were scandalously revealing. She'd never owned anything so provocative. There had never been any point.

She called Emilio immediately to thank him.

"I wasn't sure if they would be a little too racy," he said.

"No, I love them!"

"You'll have to try them on for me later."

"I might just be wearing one when you walk in the door," she said, and could practically feel his sexy smile right through the phone line.

"In that case I may just have to come home early."

After they hung up Isabelle was gathering all her new clothes to take upstairs when the doorbell rang again.

More new clothes?

She walked to the foyer and pulled the door open, expecting another delivery man, but when she saw who was standing there her heart plummeted. "Mrs. Suarez."

"May I come in?" Emilio's mother asked.

"Of course," she said, stepping aside so she could come inside. "Emilio isn't here."

"I came to talk to you."

The last time she had seen Mrs. Suarez, Isabelle's father had been accusing her of stealing from them. And after threatening to have her arrested, and her younger children taken away by Social Services, he'd fired her.

The phone started to ring. "Let me grab that really fast," Isabelle said, dashing to the living room where she'd left the cordless phone, answering with a breathless, "Hello?"

It was her mother. "Hi honey, I just got your message. I'm so glad you like the clothes. Wasn't that a sweet thing for Emilio to do?"

"Yes, it was. Mom, can I call you back?"

"Is everything okay?"

"Everything is fine." She glanced over and realized Mrs. Suarez had followed her. She was looking at the piles of clothes strewn over the furniture, specifically the lingerie, and she did not look happy.

Oh, hell.

"I'll call you soon." She disconnected and turned to Mrs. Suarez. "Sorry about that."

"How is your mother?"

"Really good." She gestured to the one chair that wasn't piled with clothes. "Please, sit down. Can I get you something to drink?"

His mother sat. "No, thank you."

Isabelle moved some of the clothes from the end of the couch and sat down.

"It looks like you've been shopping." With her son's money her look said. Talk about awkward.

"Actually, Emilio had my mother pick them out and they were delivered a little while ago."

"He's a very generous man." Her tone suggested that generosity was wasted on someone like Isabelle. Or maybe Isabelle was being paranoid. Put in his mother's position, she might not trust her, either.

There was an awkward pause, and Isabelle blurted out, "I'm so sorry for what happened with Estefan."

She looked puzzled. "Why are *you* sorry? Emilio said Estefan forced himself on you. You had every right to defend yourself. I see the bruises are fading."

Isabelle glanced down at her arms. The marks Estefan had left there had faded to a greenish-yellow. "I still feel bad for scratching him."

"Estefan is part of the reason I'm here. I wanted to apologize on his behalf. I felt it was my duty as his mother."

"Is he okay?"

"I don't know. He disappeared again. It could be months before I see him." Isabelle must have looked guilty because Mrs. Suarez added, "This is not your fault."

Logically she knew that, but she felt responsible.

"I also wanted to talk to you about Emilio."

She'd assumed as much.

"He says you're innocent."

"I have a new attorney. He says he thinks I'll be acquitted, or let off with probation."

"And Emilio is paying for this new lawyer?"

"I didn't want him to, but he insisted. And if he hadn't, I would have spent the next twenty years in prison."

"Emilio has done you many favors. Now I want you to do him a favor."

"Of course. Anything."

"Leave."

Leave? She didn't know what to say.

"Only until you are found innocent." Her eyes pleaded with Isabelle. "My son has worked so hard to get where he is, and because he loves you, he would risk throwing it all away. If you love him, you won't allow that to happen."

"And if I'm not acquitted? If I wind up with probation?"

Mrs. Suarez didn't say anything, but it was written all over her face. She wanted Isabelle to leave him for good. And her reasoning was totally logical.

The CFO of a company like Western Oil couldn't be married to a woman out on probation for financial fraud. They would have no choice but to fire him, and he would never find another job like it. At least, not one that would pay him even a fraction of what he was worth. Not to mention that he would lose all his friends.

Because of her, he would be a pariah.

He said he loved her and didn't care what people thought, but with his life in shambles he might feel differently. He would begin to resent her, and they would be right back to where they were before, only this time he would hate her not for leaving, but for staying. She couldn't do that to him.

Just once she had wanted something for herself, she

had wanted to be happy. For the first time in her life she wanted to do something selfish.

But Mrs. Suarez was right. It was time for her to go.

"I had an interesting talk with Cassandra," Adam said from Emilio's office doorway.

He glanced up from his computer screen. He had just a few things he needed to finish up before he went home for the night. "Is there another public relations nightmare on the horizon?"

"You tell me."

"Meaning what?"

He stepped into his office and shut the door. "Cassandra got a call from a reporter asking if it was true that there was a connection between Isabelle Winthrop-Betts and the CFO of Western Oil."

He sighed. *Here we go.*

"What did she tell them?"

"That she knows of no association, then she came and asked me about it. So I'm asking you, what's the status of her case? Someone is digging, and I get the feeling something big is about to break."

"I hired a new attorney. He wants to take it to trial. He thinks he can get an acquittal."

"But it will take some time."

"Probably."

Adam shook his head.

"If you have something to say, just say it, Adam."

"If she goes to trial and the story breaks about the two of you… Emilio, the damage will be done. You'll never make CEO. The board would never allow it. I can't guarantee they won't vote to terminate you immediately."

"Let me ask you something. Suppose Katy was accused

of a crime, and you knew she was innocent. Would you stand behind her, even if it meant making sacrifices?"

Adam took a deep breath and blew it out. "Yes, of course I would."

"Then why is everyone so surprised that I'm standing behind Isabelle? Do I want to be CEO? Do I think I'm the best man for the job? You're damn right I do. But what kind of CEO, what kind of *man* would I be if didn't stand up for the things I believe in? If I abandoned Isabelle when she needs me most?"

"You're right," Adam said. "I admire what you're doing, and I'll back you as long as I can."

"I know you will. And when it comes to the point that you can't help me, don't lose a night's sleep over it. This is my choice."

His secretary buzzed him. "I'm sorry to interrupt, Mr. Suarez, but your brother is on line one. He says it's important."

"Which brother?"

"Alejandro."

"Go ahead and take it," Adam said. "We'll talk later."

Adam left, and Emilio hit the button for line one. "Hey, Alejandro, what's up?"

"Hey, big brother, I was wondering if you're going to be home this evening."

"This was so important you would interrupt a meeting with my boss?"

"Actually, it is. I need to talk to you. In person."

"What time?"

"The earlier the better. Alana doesn't like it when I come home too late."

Emilio thought about Isabelle's promise to model the new lingerie. If he met with Alejandro early, then he and Isabelle would have the rest of the evening.

"Why don't you meet me at my house in an hour?"

"Sounds good. Will Isabelle be there?"

"Of course. Is that a problem?"

"No, I'll see you in an hour."

Seventeen

As his driver took him home, Emilio got to thinking about what Alejandro could possibly need to discuss that was so urgent. It couldn't have anything to do with Isabelle's case, because he wasn't allowed to question her without her lawyer present.

His driver dropped him at the front door and Emilio let himself inside—and nearly tripped over the suitcases sitting there. "What the hell?"

Isabelle appeared at the top of the stairs, and she was clearly surprised to see him. She was dressed in what he was guessing were her new clothes. She looked young and hip and classy. So different from the scrawny, desperate woman who had come to see him in his office.

"You're home early," she said, her tone suggesting that wasn't a good thing.

"Yeah, I'm home." He set his briefcase on the floor next to the open door. "What the hell is going on?"

She walked down the stairs, met him in foyer. "I was going to leave you a note."

"You're going somewhere?"

"I'm moving out."

"Why?"

"Because I have to. I can't let you risk your career for me."

"Isabelle—"

"I'm not talking forever. As soon as I'm acquitted we can be together again. But until then, we can't see each other. Not at all. If your career was ruined because of me, your family would never forgive me, and I would never forgive myself."

"And what if you aren't acquitted? David said you might possibly get probation."

She bit her lip, and he could guess the answer.

"I'm not losing you again, Isabelle."

"Hopefully you won't have to. I'm going to fight it Emilio. I will do anything I have to for an acquittal. But if I don't get it…I'm not sure how, but I'll pay you back for the lawyer's fee."

"I don't give a damn about the lawyer's fees. And I'm not letting you do this."

"You don't have a choice."

He could see by her expression that she meant it. She was really leaving, whether he liked it or not. His heart started to race and suddenly he couldn't pull in enough air. The thought of losing her again filled him with a sense of panic that seemed to well up from the center of his being.

This could not be happening. Not again.

"Knock, knock," someone said, and they both turned to see Alejandro standing on the porch at the open door. He stepped inside, saw the suitcases and asked Isabelle, "Going somewhere?"

"Nowhere out of your jurisdiction, if that's what you're worried about. I'm going to stay at my mother's for a while."

"No, she isn't," Emilio said.

She cut her eyes to him. "*Yes,* I am."

"Can I ask why?" Alejandro said.

"She's worried that her being here is going to damage my career, despite the fact that I keep telling her I don't give a *damn* about my career."

"I think you both need to listen to what I have to say."

"If has to do with my case, I can't talk to you without my lawyer present," Isabelle said.

"Trust me, you're going to want to hear this."

"I won't answer any questions."

"You won't have to." He handed her a white 6x9 envelope Emilio hadn't even noticed he was holding. "Open it."

She did and dropped the contents into her hand, looking confused. "My passport?"

"I don't get it," Emilio said. "Are you suggesting she should leave the country?"

Alejandro laughed. "I thought she might like it back, now that all the charges against her have been formally dropped."

Emilio was certain he misheard him. "Say again?"

"All the charges against Isabelle have been dropped."

Emilio looked over at Isabelle and realized she was practically hyperventilating.

"And my mother?" she asked.

"Your mother, too."

"You're serious?" she said. "This isn't just some twisted joke?"

"It's no joke."

She pressed her hand over her heart and tears welled in her eyes. She turned to Emilio. "Oh, my God, it's over."

He held out his arms and she walked into them, hugging him hard, saying, "I can't believe it's really over."

"What the hell happened?" Emilio asked his brother.

Isabelle turned in his arms and said, "Yeah, what the hell happened?"

Alejandro grinned. "You want the full story, or the condensed version?"

"Maybe we should go for the condensed version," she said. "Since you'll have to explain it all to me again when my head stops spinning."

"It was your husband's lawyer, Clifton Stone. He had the missing money."

"Stone?" Isabelle said, looking genuinely shocked. "I had no idea he was involved. I never even considered it."

"Is that why he wanted her to take a plea?" Emilio asked. "To take the attention off himself?"

"Yeah. Dumb move on his part. It's what made us suspicious in the first place, but we knew he wouldn't cooperate. We had to flush him out. We figured if we were patient he would do something stupid."

"So you knew all along that she was innocent?" Emilio asked.

"If I thought she was guilty do you think I would have dropped you all those bread crumbs, Emilio? I wanted you to get curious, to take matters into your own hands. And it worked. When you hired the new defense attorney, Stone panicked. He was going to run, and he led us right to the money."

"And he told you I wasn't involved?" Isabelle asked.

"He must have been paranoid about being caught because he saved every piece of correspondence between himself and your husband. Phone calls, emails, texts, you name it. He offered them up in exchange for a plea. He said they would exonerate you and your mother."

"And they did?" Emilio asked.

"Oh yeah. They were full of interesting information. If Betts hadn't died, I'm sure Stone would have flipped on him to save his own neck."

"So that's it?" Isabelle asked. "It's done?"

"The case is officially closed."

Emilio shook his brother's hand. "Thank you, Alejandro."

"Yes, thank you," Isabelle said.

"Well, I'm going to get out of here. I get the feeling you two have a lot to talk about." He started out the door, then stopped and turned back. "How about dinner at my place this weekend? Just the four of us. And the kids, of course."

That was an olive branch if Emilio had ever seen one.

"I'd like that," Isabelle said.

"Great. I'll have Alana call you and you can figure out a time." He shot his brother one last grin then left, shutting the door behind him.

Isabelle turned to Emilio and wrapped her arms around him. "I still can't believe it's really over. It feels like a dream."

"Does this mean you'll stay now?"

She looked up at him. "Only if you want me to."

He laughed. "You think? I had only reduced myself to *begging*."

She smiled up at him. "Then yes, I'll stay."

"We need to celebrate. We should open some champagne."

"Definitely."

"Or we could go out and celebrate."

She rose up on her toes to kiss him. "I think I'd rather

stay in tonight. I seem to recall a promise to model some lingerie."

A smile spread across his face. "I think I like the sound of that. But there's something I need to do first. Something I should have done a long time ago."

"What?"

He had hoped to do this in a more romantic setting, but he couldn't imagine a better time than now. "Isabelle, I never thought we would get a second chance together, and I don't want to spend another day without knowing that you'll be mine forever." He dropped down on one knee and took her hand. "Would you marry me?"

Tears welled in her eyes. "Of course I'll marry you."

He rose and pulled the ring box from his jacket pocket. "This is for you."

She opened it, and her look of surprise, followed by genuine confusion, was understandable.

"At this point you're wondering why a man of my means would give you a 1/4 carat diamond ring of questionable quality."

She was too polite to say he was right, but he could see it in her face.

"When I asked you to marry me before, I couldn't afford a ring, and you couldn't wear one anyway, because your father would find out. We decided that we would look for one together the day before we eloped. Remember?"

"I remember."

"Well, I couldn't wait. I saved up for months and bought this for you."

"And you kept it all this time?"

He shrugged. "I just couldn't let it go. I guess maybe deep down I hoped we'd get a second chance. I know it's small, and if you don't want to wear it I completely understand. I thought you might want to turn it into a necklace, or—"

"No." She took the ring from him, tears rolling down her cheeks, and slipped it on her finger. "You could offer me the Hope Diamond and it would never come close to meaning as much to me as this does."

"Are you sure?"

"Absolutely. I'll wear it forever."

He touched her cheek. "I love you, Isabelle."

"I love you so much." She rose up on her toes and kissed him, then she touched his face, as if she couldn't believe it was real. "Is this really happening?"

"Why do you sound so surprised?"

"Because I always thought I wasn't supposed to be this happy, that it just wasn't in the cards for me. That for some reason I didn't deserve it. And suddenly I've got everything I ever hoped for. I keep thinking it has to be a dream."

"It's very real, and you do deserve it." And he planned to spend the rest of his life proving it to her.

* * * * *

Read on for a sneak preview of Carol Marinelli's
PUTTING ALICE BACK TOGETHER!

Hugh hired bikes!

You know that saying: 'It's like riding a bike, you never forget'?

I'd never learnt in the first place.

I never got past training wheels.

'You've got limited upper-body strength?' He stopped and looked at me.

I had been explaining to him as I wobbled along and tried to stay up that I really had no centre of balance. I mean *really* had no centre of balance. And when we decided, fairly quickly, that a bike ride along the Yarra perhaps, after all, wasn't the best activity (he'd kept insisting I'd be fine once I was on, that you never forget), I threw in too my other disability. I told him about my limited upper-body strength, just in case he took me to an indoor rock-climbing centre next. I'd honestly forgotten he was a doctor, and he seemed worried, like I'd had a mini-stroke in the past or had mild cerebral palsy or something.

'God, Alice, I'm sorry—you should have said. What happened?'

And then I had had to tell him that it was a self-diagnosis. 'Well, I could never get up the ropes at the gym at school.' We were pushing our bikes back. 'I can't blow-dry the back of my hair...' He started laughing.

Not like Lisa who was laughing at me—he was just laughing and so was I. We got a full refund because we'd only been on our bikes ten minutes, but I hadn't failed. If anything, we were getting on better.

And better.

We went to St Kilda to the lovely bitty shops and I found these miniature Russian dolls. They were tiny, made of tin or something, the biggest no bigger than my thumbnail. Every time we opened them, there was another tiny one, and then another, all reds and yellows and greens.

They were divine.

We were facing each other, looking down at the palm of my hand, and our heads touched.

If I put my hand up now, I can feel where our heads touched.

I remember that moment.

I remember it a lot.

Our heads connected for a second and it was alchemic; it was as if our minds kissed hello.

I just have to touch my head, just there at the very spot and I can, whenever I want to, relive that moment.

So many times I do.

'Get them.' Hugh said, and I would have, except that little bit of tin cost more than a hundred dollars and, though that usually wouldn't have stopped me, I wasn't about to have my card declined in front of him.

I put them back.

'Nope.' I gave him a smile. 'Gotta stop the impulse

spending.'

We had lunch.

Out on the pavement and I can't remember what we ate, I just remember being happy. Actually, I can remember: I had Caesar salad because it was the lowest carb thing I could find. We drank water and I *do* remember not giving it a thought.

I was just thirsty.

And happy.

He went to the loo and I chatted to a girl at the next table, just chatted away. Hugh was gone for ages and I was glad I hadn't demanded Dan from the universe, because I would have been worried about how long he was taking.

Do I go on about the universe too much? I don't know, but what I do know is that something *was* looking out for me, helping me to be my best, not to **** this up as I usually do. You see, we walked on the beach, we went for another coffee and by that time it was evening and we went home and he gave me a present.

Those Russian dolls.

I held them in my palm, and it was the nicest thing he could have done for me.

They are absolutely my favourite thing and I've just stopped to look at them now. I've just stopped to take them apart and then put them all back together again and I can still feel the wonder I felt on that day.

He was the only man who had bought something for me, I mean something truly special. Something beautiful, something thoughtful, something just for me.

© Carol Marinelli 2012
Available at millsandboon.co.uk

A sneaky peek at next month...

Desire™

PASSIONATE AND DRAMATIC LOVE STORIES

2 stories in each book - only **£5.30!**

My wish list for next month's titles...

In stores from 17th February 2012:

❏ Marriage at the Cowboy's Command – Ann Major

& How to Seduce a Billionaire – Kate Carlisle

❏ Dante's Honour-Bound Husband – Day Leclaire

& A Clandestine Corporate Affair – Michelle Celmer

❏ One Night, Two Heirs – Maureen Child

& The Rebel Tycoon Returns – Katherine Garbera

❏ Wild Western Nights – Sara Orwig

& Her Tycoon to Tame – Emilie Rose

Available at WHSmith, Tesco, Asda, Eason, Amazon and Apple

Just can't wait?

0212/51

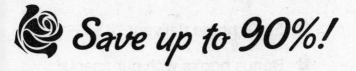

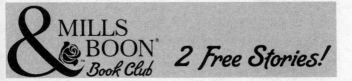

MILLS & BOON®
Book Club
2 Free Stories!

Get your free stories now at
www.millsandboon.co.uk/freebookoffer

Or fill in the form below and post it back to us

THE MILLS & BOON® BOOK CLUB™—HERE'S HOW IT WORKS: Accepting your free stories places you under no obligation to buy anything. You may keep the stories and return the despatch note marked 'Cancel'. If we do not hear from you, about a month later we'll send you 2 Desire™ 2-in-1 books priced at £5.30* each. There is no extra charge for post and packaging. You may cancel at any time, otherwise we will send you 4 stories a month which you may purchase or return to us—the choice is yours. *Terms and prices subject to change without notice. Offer valid in UK only. Applicants must be 18 or over. Offer expires 31st July 2012. **For full terms and conditions, please go to www.millsandboon.co.uk**

Mrs/Miss/Ms/Mr (please circle)
_____

First Name
_____

Surname
_____

Address
_____

_____

Postcode
_____

E-mail
_____

Send this completed page to: Mills & Boon Book Club, Free Book Offer, FREEPOST NAT 10298, Richmond, Surrey, TW9 1BR

Find out more at
www.millsandboon.co.uk/freebookoffer

Visit us Online

0112/D2XEA

Have Your Say

You've just finished your book.
So what did you think?

We'd love to hear your thoughts on our
'Have your say' online panel
www.millsandboon.co.uk/haveyoursay

🌹 Easy to use

🌹 Short questionnaire

🌹 Chance to win Mills & Boon®
   goodies

*Visit us
Online*

Tell us what you thought of this book now at
www.millsandboon.co.uk/haveyoursay

YOUR_SAY

Special Offers

Every month we put together collections and longer reads written by your favourite authors.

Here are some of next month's highlights— and don't miss our fabulous discount online!

On sale
17th February

On sale
17th February

On sale
17th February

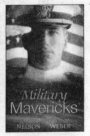

On sale
2nd March

Save 20% on all Special Releases

Find out more at
www.millsandboon.co.uk/specialreleases

Visit us Online

0212/ST/MB363